To Jake,

& God Bless Your Father
for serving.

Go HawkEyes!!

All my best.

Henry "Buzz" Wombles
9/17/2017

UNDER *the* FLAGPOLE

FIRST EDITION

HENRY "BUZZ" WOMBLES

ISBN: 978-1-4834-3421-6 (sc)
ISBN: 978-1-4834-3420-9 (e)

Lulu Publishing Services rev. date: 08/20/2015

To my wife, Jeanne, who has one foot in heaven
for putting up with me all these years.

A special thank you to Lucy Bassett for all her assistance and inspiration that made this book possible.

ONE

··

Hazard, Kentucky
Monday, November 28, 1938

Miles Hudson, age eleven, dreaded going out into the snow. The wind howled all night and created a snowdrift over a foot deep against the house and barn by daybreak. Miles pushed the front door open and stepped out onto the plank porch. He buttoned up his coat, pulled his toboggan down over his ears, hunched his shoulders, and faced the late November cold. Slipping and sliding as he followed the path and crossed the swinging bridge that led to the road out of Jack Lot Hollow, Miles hurried to meet Cecil and Wilbur at their usual spot, the huge, old oak tree by Mr. Herd's springhouse.

Miles heard the hounds baying in the distance as he reached Mr. Herd's house. Mr. Herd must have heard them, too. He was on the porch looking toward the springhouse. Miles stopped, not wanting Mr. Herd to see him. "It's just those boys again," he said to his wife as he went back in, shutting the door behind him.

Miles hurried on knowing that Cecil and Wilbur were already at the springhouse, getting into character for the game. Today Miles was the fox, and Cecil and Wilbur were the hounds. Miles and his friends played this game every morning on their way to school. The hounds always gave the fox a 50-yard head start, waiting until the fox was down the road by the old abandoned coal tipple before they broke into a full run. Then the race was on. The fox was free to hide or run until he was tagged, or until he touched the flagpole in the Browns Fork School Yard.

When Miles reached the oak, Cecil and Wilbur ran in circles around him, jumping and baying like hounds in a chase. Miles grinned and let them wear themselves out a bit before he broke out of the circle and took off for the coal tipple. He ran for over a mile, hiding behind outhouses, bushes, and trees to catch a quick breath. Finally he could see the gray clapboard schoolhouse in the distance. It was his last hiding place - Miller Couch's outhouse. Only a lone holly tree full of berries and an otherwise open field lay between him and the school yard. Miles was now far ahead of the hounds. He moved out into the open when they got closer, making sure they could see him. Miles stood still, letting Cecil and Wilbur close the distance between them. Then he turned and began to run again, full speed for the flagpole.

"You big show-off," Cecil said when he reached the flagpole several steps behind Miles.

"Yeah, you always win." Wilbur was a few steps behind Cecil.

All three boys bent over laughing and trying to catch their breath under the flagpole. Miles recovered first. He idly twirled the end of the flag chain, waiting for Cecil and Wilbur to begin breathing normally again. Finally Cecil spoke. "Miles, did you get all your long-division problems worked for Miss Savage last night?"

"Yeah, but Evaline had to work late, and she was too tired to check them for me." Miles looked up at the flag, the beautiful red, white, and blue against a light blue sky. He wished his sister did not have to work so much. She had to quit school so she could work at Doris Anderson's Country Store. She had to if they were going to eat. Four years earlier, his father, Landon Hudson, and two other coal miners were killed by a slate fall at the Number Seven Mine. Drucella, or Cella, as most people called Miles' mother, kept the house, cooked their meals and took in sewing to help the family get by.

"My Pa checked my long-division problems for me," Cecil said proudly. "He said they were all right, and if Miss Savage finds another excuse to beat the hell out of me, then he's coming to school, and it won't be a pretty sight, either!"

Just then the bell rang, and all the students lined up to go inside. In line for Miss Savage's fifth grade classroom, Miles opened his math book, making sure that his homework was safely tucked inside. He frowned, worried again that some of his long-division problems might not be correct.

As the students entered her classroom, Miss Savage, paddle in hand, checked everyone for cleanliness. She was a strong, big-boned, heavyset woman in her middle forties. The rumor was that she had never been married and wore a wig because she was bald. No one knew for sure since she was not from the mountains. She had come to Hazard from a small college town near Lexington in the area of Kentucky known as the Bluegrass.

Miles, like all the other students in his class, knew what to do for Miss Savage's inspection. When it was his turn, he stood before her with an open mouth and extended hands. She approved his teeth and hands. He then turned his head to one side and then to the other. Miss Savage checked the cleanliness of his ears and neck. He passed inspection.

Miss Savage began, "Jessie, you may take your seat…Nettie, you may take your seat…Cecil, you may take…Cecil, your neck has a ring around it. Your ears look like a rat's nest." Miss Savage moved quickly. "Cecil! Holdout your hands." As soon as Cecil held out his hands, Miss Savage delivered several hard blows with her paddle to Cecil's knuckles. When she had finished, she said, "Now go downstairs and clean up."

As Cecil turned away, Miles saw tears streaming down his face. Miles looked away quickly. Wilbur, who had been watching, took a step forward, opened his mouth and extended his hands. Miss Savage repeated one of her favorite sayings as she inspected Wilbur, "Boys and girls! Why, Cecil thinks he's the President of the United States! Why, Cecil thinks he's Mr. Roosevelt, and he can do as he chooses!" There were other dreaded teachers at the Browns Fork School, but none more dreaded, or more frightening, than Miss Savage.

The inspection was complete and all the other students were seated before Cecil came back into the room. Miss Savage sat at her desk in the back of the room, ready to begin the school day. "Everyone get out your No. 2, pencils," she announced. Miles and Nancy Ann got up immediately and walked to the cloakroom where a pencil sharpener was attached to the inside of the door.

Miss Savage had various duties for certain students to carry out each day, the first being the sharpening of the No. 2, pencils, a duty she had assigned to Miles and Nancy Ann on the first day of school when she had made it plain that she would not tolerate any type of pencil except a No. 2. The lead in a No. 2, pencil was darker than a No. 1, and Miss Savage preferred the No.2 because her eyes were failing, and it was difficult for her to read a student's work if it were written with a No. 1 pencil. She made it clear that anyone caught without a No. 2, would be severely punished.

Miles emptied the pencil shavings from the previous day's sharpening into the waste basket. "Row one," Miss Savage called out. The students in row one stood and marched to the back of the room where Nancy Ann stood by the sharpener. One by one as the students passed Nancy Ann, they handed her their pencils. Nancy Ann checked to make sure each pencil was a No. 2, and then passed it on to Miles to recheck and to sharpen.

Sharpening the pencils of the students sitting in the first three rows went smoothly. Miss Savage called row four and the first student of row four now stood in front of Nancy Ann. Miles reached out to accept the pencil from Nancy Ann, but she had frozen, staring at the pencil she held. When she turned and looked at Miles, she was as pale as if she had seen a ghost. She looked back at Eugene, who was standing in front of her, in horror. She slowly handed Miles the pencil. No one had ever given Nancy Ann and Miles a No. 1, pencil to sharpen. Miles looked at Nancy Ann and then into Eugene's worried eyes. Eugene was his friend. He quickly sharpened the pencil and passed it back to Eugene.

After all the pencils had been sharpened, and everyone had handed in their homework, Miss Savage gave the class the weekly spelling test. Sarah collected the spelling papers and passed them on to Miss Savage. "Class, take out your history books and read *The Settling of Boonesborough,* Chapter Ten, while I grade your spelling tests."

The students read quietly, and Miss Savage worked at her desk, but Miles couldn't concentrate. Eugene had used a No. 1, pencil on that spelling test. If Miss Savage handed back the spelling tests without noticing, everything would be fine. But, all of a sudden, Miss Savage slammed her paddle against her desk so that it sounded like a clap of thunder. A few students jumped, accidentally dropping their history books on the floor. Miles stiffened. He glanced over to Nancy Ann, noticing that she was even paler now than she had been at the pencil sharpener.

"Eugene!" Miss Savage screamed, "Bring your No. 2, pencil up here right now!"

Eugene slowly stood up. "Miss Savage, I don't have one." He spoke quietly. Miles could hear fear in his voice.

"What did you say, Eugene? I didn't hear you."

"I…I don't have one."

"That's what I thought you said. Now get back there and sit in the dunce chair." The dunce chair faced a corner in the back of the room. Miss Savage's face was a mean blood-red, and she stared straight at Miles and Nancy Ann. For the first time in Miles' young life he wished someone were dead. If Miss Savage had a heart attack, and if she didn't die, then maybe, at least, she would never be able to teach again. Now with her largest paddle in hand, and clad in her black dress, she strode down the aisle between Miles' and Nancy Ann's desks like a giant storm cloud moving down a valley, distorting everything it touched. Stopping at Nancy Ann's desk, she said, "Why, Miles thinks he's the President, and Nancy Ann thinks she's Mrs. Roosevelt, and they can do as they please. They don't have to obey the rules."

Miss Savage grabbed Nancy Ann's hand, pulled her out of her seat, and delivered four hard licks to her backside with the paddle. Nancy Ann, a small, frail eleven-year-old, slowly slid back into her seat, put her head on her desk and cried as if her heart were broken.

Miles was not as lucky as Nancy Ann. "Now, Mr. President, it's your turn. Stand up." Miles, more embarrassed than fearful, stood up. Realizing all eyes were on him, he stepped back and bowed to the class as if to say, "So what?"

Infuriated by his act of defiance, Miss Savage jerked Miles by the arm and turned him around. With all her strength she delivered blow after blow to Miles' behind. Facing the corner, Eugene didn't see the blows, but he felt each one. When Miss Savage finished, her face was an unhealthy red and she was gasping for breath. She let go of Miles' arm and made her way back to her desk, holding on to several chairs to keep from falling. As soon as she turned her back, Miles gave the class another bow. No one smiled or acknowledged Miles' performance, but Miles knew he had the admiration of the entire class.

As he sat back down, Miles tried not to show his pain. I'll just be damned if I'll let that old bitch make me cry, he thought, as he bit his lower lip and looked straight ahead. He made a vow this would never happen again. Why hadn't he brought an extra pencil and slipped it into his pocket?

Miss Savage collapsed into her chair. She was too worn out to punish Eugene. She gave him a cold stare. "Eugene, take your seat. Someone lend Eugene a No. 2, pencil. And Eugene, may Heaven help you if you come in here tomorrow without a No. 2, pencil."

The bell finally rang at 3:10, which meant the day was coming to an end. Then, row-by-row everyone filed into the cloakroom to get their coats and to prepare for the last bell.

The snow had stopped falling, and the sun had broken through the gray clouds. Miles, Nancy Ann, Eugene, Cecil, and Wilbur hurried down the stairs, through the hallway, out the entrance doors and onto the school yard. Nancy Ann and her girlfriends turned right and headed to Cedar Street. Miles and his buddies turned left and headed toward town. The mountain air was filling Miles' lungs. He wanted to let loose, put this school day and Miss Savage behind him and get into town. Miles quickened his pace.

"Miles, slow down," Wilbur called out. But Miles walked faster. He didn't even turn around. "Miles! My turn to be the fox tomorrow! Don't forget!"

"I won't!" Miles yelled out as he broke into a full, joyful run.

TWO

The small mountain town of Hazard in the mid-to-late 1930's was a thriving community. The town boasted four hotels, the largest of which was the Palace; two drug stores, Fouts Drug and Rexall Drug; and two picture shows, the Virginia and the Family. Next door to the Virginia Theater was a small confectionary shop, The Sweet Shop, which sold hotdogs for 15 cents and hamburgers for 20 cents. There were several cafes-- The City Lunch, Joe's Café, and Gross's Café--and a few other restaurants. Of the four department stores, Majors attracted the most people, but Al's Department Store drew a fair number in with its huge sign at the entrance: "Al beats the law to the draw." No one seemed to know exactly what that meant, but it sure was catchy. Like other small eastern Kentucky towns in the thirties and forties, Hazard had all the stores it needed to survive. And typical of small town, bible-belt, pre-war America, churches of various denominations were scattered across town.

After school, Miles had about an hour and a half in town each afternoon before it was time to head toward Jack Lot Hollow and meet Evaline at Doris Anderson's store for their walk home. He used the time to try and make some extra money. His first stop was the Farmer Hotel, not as large as the Palace, but the rooms were clean and it was right across the railroad tracks from the train station. When strangers got off the train, they often made it only as far as the Farmer Hotel. If business was good, Mr. Farmer paid Miles to clean. In the lobby, Miles vacuumed the carpets, emptied all the trash and dusted the furniture. Then he cleaned the front windows and the outer glass door which opened to a foyer with a revolving door that opened into the lobby. Miles didn't mind doing any of these menial tasks. And the work was made easier because Miles liked Mr. Farmer.

When Mr. Farmer was low on liquor, he sent Miles to the Broke Spoke Liquor Store for one or more bottles of whisky to replenish his supply. Mr. Farmer often reminded Miles it didn't matter that Miles was a minor because he was only transporting the whisky, and besides that, it wasn't even a sale of whisky in the first place because no actual money ever changed hands. Mr. Farmer was such a good customer that he kept a charge account at the Broke Spoke.

"Hello Mr. Farmer! Looks like you might need some cleaning today."

"I don't know, Miles, not too many guests checked in last night. I can probably take care of everything myself."

Miles knew better. There was nothing Mr. Farmer hated more than cleaning the lobby, and he only did so when Mrs. Farmer put her foot down and forced him. Just then, Mrs. Farmer walked out of the small hotel office.

"Hello, Miles," she said without looking at him. "Well, if you're here to do Oscar's work for him, you're wasting your time. Last night we had five salesmen, two government men and a preacher. Not even enough money to pay the light bill." She turned and looked in her husband's direction. "Oscar, send this boy on his way and get busy. This lobby looks like a cyclone hit it. I'm leaving for the day. Morris will be here to relieve you at eight o'clock. I'll see you when you get home."

Miles was out the door and up the street before Mrs. Farmer could cross the street to her new Buick. He quickly turned his back to the street, and to Mrs. Farmer, and looked in the Sterling Hardware storefront window, pressing his face to the glass and shading his eyes from the glare in order to see better.

The window was decorated for Christmas: baseball gloves, pocket knives, basketballs and a square shiny box that toasted bread. What he admired most, however, was a gleaming Lionel train set with smoke coming out of the engine, which pulled five cars and a red caboose. The train made a circle and then went through a tunnel and out the other side. A clerk saw Miles' face pressed against the window. He walked over to the inside window, pushed a button and blew the train's whistle and then made the train change tracks. Miles watched the train until Mrs. Farmer's Buick was out of sight, then he turned around and went back to the hotel.

When he stepped out of the revolving door and into the lobby, Miles saw that Mr. Farmer had the vacuum and cleaning supplies ready for him. "Lord, Miles, that woman could drive a man as batty as hell if he did everything she told him to do! Now, hurry and get this lobby cleaned up." With a twinkle in his eye, Mr. Farmer smiled and added, "By the way, I'm going to need you to run a little errand for me when you finish cleaning. Hurry up boy! You want to make that extra twenty-five cents today, don't you? Lord, Miles, my throat's as dry as the Sahara Desert."

Miles worked for nearly an hour before getting to his final cleaning chore. He always saved cleaning the grandfather clock for last. He took the key from the top of the clock and unlocked the glass door. Then he slowly reached inside and opened the small can of 3-in-1 oil and put one drop on each of the working parts. Then he wound the clock with the key, just as Oscar had taught him, but always remembering, "Miles, it must be tight, but not too tight." By doing the clock last, Miles could check the time and get ready for his trip to the Broke Spoke. Usually Oscar only paid Miles a quarter for cleaning, but when he made his run to the liquor store, he was paid fifty cents.

As Miles passed the hardware store this time, he glanced at the Lionel Train without stopping. He had only about fifteen minutes for his run to the liquor store. If he were going to make his stop at the Underworld Poolroom, and still be on time to meet Evaline, he had to hurry.

Miles stood outside the Broke Spoke and tried to appear invisible. He looked up and down the street. He didn't want anyone seeing him going inside a liquor store. Convinced no one was watching, he quickly pushed the door open and slipped inside.

Manuel, who was opening boxes and stocking shelves, looked up. "Well, if it isn't Mr. Hudson, Mr. Farmer's partner in crime. C'mon in, Miles. I guess you'll be needing a package today." The two men standing at the counter took a quick look at Miles and went back to their conversation about the Kentucky basketball team.

"Mr. Farmer sent this check to be paid on his account," Miles said, holding out a check.

"Well son, I didn't think he sent it to me for a Christmas present." Manuel laughed, took the check, and looked it up one side and then down the other. Even though Mr. Farmer was a good customer, Manuel took no chances on getting a bad check. Satisfied the check would clear, Manuel took down a bottle of Old Grand Dad and a bottle of Four Roses, put them in a paper sack and handed the sack to Miles. "Now get on out of here before one of Sheriff Sizemore's men sees you in here. I could end up losing my liquor license!"

With the package from the Broke Spoke tucked safely under his arm, Miles returned to the hotel, collected his pay, and made his way to the Underworld Pool Room, not one of Miles' favorite places, but today he had business there.

THREE

A floating cloud of gray cigarette smoke hung from the ceiling of the Underworld Poolroom, a dark, one-room establishment below Watson's Department Store, offering six pool tables, side-by-side, and 15 elevated chairs for people with nothing to do but smoke and watch others play pool. The smoke stung Miles' eyes. A jukebox played a Roy Acuff song, but no one seemed to be listening. It was just smoke, cussing and pool. Everything all the preachers in town were against.

Miles scanned the elevated chairs for the man he had come to meet. He felt guilty as he sat down beside Hart James. Hart was tall and thin, with dark eyes, heavy eyebrows, and a pencil mustache. He wore a starched white shirt, creased dress pants and a well-tailored sport coat. Women found him handsome, but they didn't trust him.

Now, his dark eyes focused intently on the pool game at the front table, as he sized up the players, one of whom just might be his next "pigeon." People who knew Hart, and everyone in Hazard knew him or knew of him, were well aware he was a pool shark. When Hart challenged a new pigeon to a game, the sport coat came off, and Hart carefully folded it and laid it across the back of a chair. Then he rolled his shirt sleeves up to the elbow, he didn't want his cuffs dirtied by dragging them across the table, and leaned into the pool table for some serious playing. At that point, as they say, everything was over but the shouting.

In addition to his pool games, Hart's other enterprises included the poker games he organized in a room at the Palace hotel and his bookie joint which employed three runners. His under-the-table dealings had earned him the appropriate nickname Black Hart. Black Hart had a reputation for welching on his bets. If he won, he was more than eager to collect his money. If he lost, which he rarely did, he told his pigeon that he'd pay him next week, and did his best to avoid any further contact with him.

Black Hart, who had been watching the pool game, turned in his chair to look at his "runner." He looked Miles up and down and took a few seconds to study Miles' face before he spoke. "Well, Miles, how's everything today?" Without giving Miles time to answer, he continued. "You know, I was in Doris Anderson's store today, and that stuck-up sister of yours hardly spoke to me. She sure thinks she's the Queen Bee. I got news for her. She's no better than anyone else in this one-horse coal-mining town, but I'll give her credit for one damned thing. She's about as pretty a thing as you're going to find anywhere."

Miles quickly changed the conversation to business. "Black Hart, you got any errands for me today?"

"No, not really. Business is slow right now. Most all the racetracks are closed for the winter. The only bets I can get right now are when Kentucky plays a game. Why do you think I'm sitting in this hell-forsaken poolroom? For my health? Hell, I have to catch someone from out of town to make a little money on a pool game. Can't get a game with anyone who knows me."

Miles looked up at the clock over the jukebox. It was four-thirty. Evaline would be expecting him at five and he still had the twenty-minute walk to Anderson's store. "It's getting late anyway. I got to go, but can you pay me the seventy-five cents you owe me for last week?"

"Hellfire, boy! You got hearing problems? I just told you how bad business is. I'm barely making enough money to buy a hot dog, and you come in here crying over a lousy seventy-five cents I owe you?"

"But, last week you said …"

"I know what I said!" Black Hart reached into his hip pocket, slipped his billfold out, opened it and closed it immediately, and stuck it back into his hip pocket in one practiced, fluid motion, like a magician doing a trick. "Damn it, boy! You think I can control how people are going to spend their money?" He scowled at Miles.

Miles backed off. The last thing he wanted was to make Black Hart James angry. "I was just asking. I didn't mean to make you mad. Anyway, I got to go. I'm going to be late meeting Evaline."

Black Hart motioned for Miles to stay seated. He seemed to calm a bit. "Miles, just sit tight in the boat. You're going to get your seventy-five cents and a lot more as soon as things pick up." Black Hart reached into his shirt pocket and took out a small, thin box of cigars. He pulled one out, put it to his nose, sniffed it, and bit off the tip which he spit onto the floor. He took a fancy gold lighter from his pocket, lit up and took a couple of puffs. "Hell, I'll need you every evening to run bets as soon as the weather warms up. Now go on and meet your sister. Tell her to get her nose out of the clouds. It might rain and she'll drown."

As Miles walked out the door, Black Hart smiled, pleased with his performance. He turned back to the pool game and decided it was time to take off his sport coat.

When Miles arrived at Doris Anderson's store, Evaline was standing just inside the door with her coat on, and Doris was turning off the lights, preparing to close for the day.

Glad you finally got here, Slow Poke," said Evaline, with a smile. No way she was going to give Miles a hard time because she knew how conscientious he was, and the responsibilities he had assumed at a very early age.

Each lost in their thoughts, not much was said as they made their way home. Just before arriving, Miles said, "It's been a long day, but a good day," and then to himself said, and an even better day if Black Hart had paid me.

FOUR

I t was the first Saturday of December, and at Doris Anderson's Country Store, located at the mouth of Jack Lot Hollow, the screen door, with its faded Kern's Bread sign, had banged constantly as customers came and went. The coal companies had made their payrolls, and the miners were stocking up on flour, corn meal, bacon, lard, canned goods, yards of fabric, cigarettes--all their needs until the next payday came back around in two more weeks. Doris, her husband Jack, and their three employees, Evaline, Betty Jo, and Hernando, were taking care of the customers. Doris ran a tight ship, making all the business decisions for the store. Jack Anderson, her husband, was the store's mild-mannered butcher.

Late in the day, Doris was busily working on an order from the Powell Wholesale Grocery when the truck driver gave her the invoice to sign. "Oh hell!" she said, and she waved to Evaline for help. The fingers of Doris' right hand were curved into that awful claw that signaled an arthritis flare up. Gingerly, Doris placed the fingertips of her right hand on the counter. She placed her left hand on top of the right and pushed gently to flatten and separate the stiffened fingers. Signing the invoice would have to wait a moment.

Across the store, Evaline winced, a sympathetic reaction to the pain she knew gnawed at Doris' joints, especially her fingers, and sometimes brought tears to her eyes. "I'll be right there, Doris."

Mr. Britches, Doris' cat, brushed against Doris' legs. Mr. Britches, like Evaline, seemed to sense when Doris was in pain with

17

her arthritis. If her pain were severe enough to cause her to sit down, he was always ready to jump into her lap and console her. All Doris' regular customers knew Mr. Britches, and there was no doubt that the cat had the run of the place. He knocked over cans and boxes, anything that got in his way, including the Christmas decorations in the window. He slept on the counter whenever he pleased, and never once got a cross word from Doris.

Miles liked coming to this store, and Mr. Britches liked Miles. If Miles sat on a wooden milk crate by the stove eating one of Doris' baloney, tomato, and onion sandwiches, Mr. Britches calmly placed himself directly in front of Miles and watched each and every bite Miles took. By the time Miles got down to the last bite, guilt would completely overtake him, and he would grudgingly hand over the last bite to Mr. Britches. Only then, when he was satisfied he had taken Miles for all he could get, would Mr. Britches jump up on the window display, stretch out by the cereal boxes, and patiently wait for his next victim.

What Miles enjoyed most about Doris Anderson's store was that Evaline worked there. The greeting she never failed to give him when he came into the store was extra special to Miles. Sure enough, when Evaline saw Miles, her face lit up, and she gave him that big smile that made the dimple in her chin more visible, that smile that said Evaline was eager to see her brother.

Evaline was proud of Miles. He had shown great strength and character after their father's death. At only 11-years old, he had accepted responsibility as head of the Hudson family. She had no doubt that someday Miles would accomplish great things.

Miles was also proud of Evaline. He watched as she waited on the man with the tobacco stained goatee at the counter, Billy "Goat" Jones, patiently explaining why he might want to buy the 1-pound bag of sugar rather than the 2.5-pound bag: Not only was it cheaper (three 1-pound bags would, over the course of time, cost less than a 2.5-pound bag), but it would also be easier to carry. Evaline nodded as she helped Billy Goat check the items off his list, and each time she nodded, her dark hair put up in a tight bun gleamed under the light that hung over the counter. Miles knew that each nod meant Evaline was keeping a mental tally of the order total in her head. The bun in her hair certainly made her look a bit older than her sixteen years and more businesslike, but even that tight bun couldn't disguise the fact that Evaline was a beauty. Pretty and smart Miles thought. He wished again that Evaline hadn't dropped out of school. She said her work was to help support the family, but he knew her principal reason was to make certain he stayed in school.

Evaline finished with Billy Goat, her last customer of the day, and reached into the drawer for the charge account book that Doris had provided her. She added another five cents to her total. "Miles get yourself a Milky Way or Baby Ruth. I'll be ready in a few minutes."

It was exactly five minutes to five o'clock. Mr. Britches walked over to his customary spot beside the door. Miles grabbed a Milky Way and joined Mr. Britches. Miles finished his candy bar just as Doris and Evaline emerged from the back room, laughing and chatting; it was one minute to five o'clock. When they reached the door, Doris held up her hand to break off the chat and turned to her husband who was doing the final clean up. Evaline winked at Miles and whispered, "I wonder which meat didn't sell this week."

"Jack," Doris said, exactly on cue, "pick me up two of those pork chops in the far end of the meat cooler and I'll fix them for supper tonight. They've been there for a while." Except for the type of meat that had been in the cooler the longest, the Saturday closing ritual never changed. At exactly five o'clock, the four of them, Doris and Mr. Britches and Evaline and Miles walked out the door and headed to their homes.

Miles skipped ahead of Evaline, jumping over logs, or lagging behind her, picking up rocks and tossing them into the creek, as they made their way home down the country road that led into Jack Lot Hollow. Miles thought about Christmas, only a few weeks away, and about the Lionel Train some other lucky young boy or girl would find under the tree. Although he knew he wouldn't be getting the train, he had no idea what he would be getting. Lost in his thoughts about Christmas, he had lagged behind again. He ran to catch up. "What are you getting me for Christmas, Evaline?" he blurted out as he danced around her.

"Oh, I don't know Miles. I hadn't even thought about anything for you." Evaline paused. "Unless it would be a lump of coal in your stocking, but I don't know if you're worth a lump of coal," she laughed.

Evaline was older than Miles, but not too old to feel the same childlike happiness and anticipation of Christmas, as did Miles. "And by the way, what are you getting me? I know what I want. I want one of those white party dresses like you see in the magazines in Fouts Drug Store. Maybe one like Katherine Hepburn wore in *Stage Door*. Think you can afford one of those, Mr. Big Shot?"

When Miles didn't answer, she feared her kidding had hurt his feelings. After all, she thought, he's only eleven years old. He's only seen ten Christmas trees.

Evaline frowned. She had spoiled the happy Christmas mood. Perhaps she could restore it before she brought up what she really wanted to talk to Miles about. "Miles, Oscar Farmer came in the store the other day. He was telling everyone how much he likes you.

Right in front of everyone he said if he and Clara could have had a son, he would have wanted him to be just like you!"

"Well, maybe **he** would have," Miles grinned, "but I'm not so sure about Clara."

Evaline smiled back at Miles. They were nearing the bend in the road, and soon their house would be in view. It was now or never if she wanted to talk to Miles. "Miles, I don't think it's such a good thing for you to be seen hanging around Black Hart James. You know, he's not exactly one of the pillars of this community." The words came rushing out in a tone Evaline hadn't intended.

Miles stopped in surprise. He didn't like it when Evaline preached at him, and besides, how did Evaline know he was running bets for Black Hart? His face reddened with shame. Evaline waited for his response. "But Evaline, Black Hart says I can make lots of money as soon as the weather warms up. He says …"

Before Miles could continue, Evaline put her hands on his shoulders and shook him, but Miles knew her gesture showed only concern, not anger. "Miles, Black Hart says a lot of things, and from what I understand, they're mostly lies."

"I know, Evaline, but he owes me seventy-five cents."

"Miles, let Black Hart keep the seventy-five cents. He probably never intended to pay it, anyway." She pointed a finger at him, preaching again. "Now, I'm saying it for the last time. You stay away from Black Hart. You listen to me. Do you hear what I'm saying?"

Miles avoided her eyes. He hung his head and watched the scuffed toe of his right brogan scratching in the dirt. "Yeah, I hear," he said. Then he leaned down to tie his shoe lace. "I guess I knew all along he was no good," Miles mumbled, more to his shoe than to Evaline.

As he stood up, Miles picked up a smooth round rock. Now it was his turn to restore the Christmas mood. No more talk about Black Hart. "I bet you I can hit the knothole in that tree up there with this rock." He pointed to a hickory tree thirty-five or forty feet away, but Evaline had already begun walking up the road. Throwing a rock into the knothole on his way home had become a ritual with Miles. Every day he looked for a rock, took his stance and aimed for the knothole. More often than not, his aim was accurate. Today he hit the knothole square on. If Evaline noticed, she didn't say anything. Miles ran to catch up again and walked quietly beside Evaline for several steps. "What would you **really** like for Christmas, Evaline?"

"Oh, I **really** don't know." Her brow wrinkled in thought. Then she smiled, thinking of what she had seen recently in the Star Furniture Company window - a beautifully decorated table with a green tablecloth, red Christmas candles and place settings for six people. "I wish I could buy that table and chairs for Momma for Christmas, but I really don't have the money. What I would really like for myself for Christmas is a restful day with one of Momma's Christmas dinners." She paused, smiled at Miles, and said, "And maybe a movie magazine to curl up with the rest of the day."

If Evaline had a vice, Miles knew, it was the movies. They didn't go very often, but when they did go, many times it was on a Sunday afternoon. Evaline tried to make sure it was a Cary Grant or, even better, a Fred MacMurray movie, because MacMurray reminded Evaline of their late father, Landon.

They crossed the swinging bridge over the creek and followed the path that led up to the front door of their five-room "camp" house, one of many similar houses built in the early 1920's by Jack Lot

Mining, and other mining companies, to rent to their coal miner employees. The areas where the mining company owned houses were located became known as coal camps, and the houses were called "camp houses." Jack Lot Mining, which had been closed five years, had discontinued operations a short time after the big slate fall that killed Landon Hudson and the two other miners.

Landon Hudson and the other two miners had been "pulling pillars," one of the most dangerous of all mining methods, and which involved mining the coal that had been left to keep the roof from caving in while the other coal was being removed by standard mining methods.

Having decided to discontinue pulling pillars following the accident, Jack Lot Mining announced it would be selling the mining equipment and the camp houses. The families living in the camp houses would be given the choice of moving, or buying their homes for five hundred dollars. Rather than move, the majority of families chose to purchase their homes.

Mr. Carpenter, the owner of Jack Lot Mining, made other arrangements for the camp houses occupied by Drucella Hudson and the widows of the other two miners. He had gone to the Courthouse and had deeds prepared, awarding each of the widows, free and clear titles to their houses and lots.

The Hudson house, six rooms with kitchen, dining room, living room and three bed rooms was old and needed paint. The floor squeaked, and when the wind blew during a storm, one could almost swear the old place was groaning from the strain. Drucella had made a few improvements, some of the woodwork had been painted gray and the living room was papered in a pattern of small spring flowers--but Drucella had little spare time and little extra money for decorating. It was just another camp house, the one at the end of

Jack Lot Hollow, but it was home to the Hudsons, and they owned it lock, stock, and barrel.

As Miles and Evaline climbed the hill and stepped onto the porch, Drucella looked up from her sewing machine by the fireplace. She smiled, relieved her children were home. Drucella was a tall mountain woman with dark black hair, high cheekbones and eyes that sparkled when she smiled or lost her temper. She claimed to be one-quarter Cherokee on her father's side.

"Lord a-Mercy, I'm glad you all are home! There's a pot of vegetable soup on the cook stove and a pan of corn bread still warming in the oven. I'm not going to sew another stitch today." Drucella pushed her chair away from the sewing machine, sat up straight and pulled her shoulders back to release the tension of sitting and bending over the sewing machine for so long. Then she rolled her shoulders and stood up. "Miles, after you all eat, go out to the barn and bring in that Christmas tree you cut yesterday. I'll get down the lights, and we'll get it decorated. Why, Christmas is just around the corner."

Miles could smell the rich beef aroma of the soup simmering on the cook stove that sat "catty-corner" by the kitchen window. The fire in the cook stove burned until late in the evening, and the ashes would fall into the drawer in the bottom of the stove. It was Miles' job to check the ashes regularly, and to empty the ash drawer every two to three days. Putting the ashes on the path that ran from the Jack Lot road to the house cut down on the mud from rain and snow that often got on their shoes, and ended up in the house.

Miles also chopped the wood, which was plentiful in the mountain forest just behind the barn, and kept a good supply on hand at all times. Fragrant cedar was the choice wood, but not as available as it once was, as logging companies had cut much of the cedar from the forest. Oak was too hard to chop for everyday, and dogwoods, which sprang up everywhere, didn't yield much wood. Most often, Miles cut a poplar to drag down the mountain to the chopping block out beside the barn.

In addition to the cookstove, the kitchen contained a cook table covered with shiny red oilcloth, a storage cabinet and a sink. The Hudsons were one of the first mining families to have water indoors. Their water came mostly from an underground-fed spring located about 300-feet or so from the house. A cistern was located under the house, and before Landon's accident, he had dug a ditch and laid pipe from the spring to the cistern. He had also installed another pipe at the corner of the house which funneled water into the cistern. A small sink and a bright red pump were located in the kitchen directly above the cistern. Miles could remember how excited everyone was when Landon pumped the handle up and down, and the first water came pouring into the sink.

Miles and Evaline poured soup into the bowls Drucella had left for them on the cook table beside the stove and headed into the dining room. There was nothing fancy or elaborate about the dining room. Under one of the windows was a small cabinet with shelves and two doors, and a pie safe, which Drucella used for cooling her freshly baked apple and peach pies. Each door of the pie safe consisted of a wooden frame with cloth stretched from top to bottom. When the doors were closed, heat could escape from the pies, and yet the pies were kept safe from flies. Against one dining room wall sat a small antique desk where Miles did his homework and entertained himself by writing short stories. In the corner was their most prized possession: a large Kelvinator refrigerator where they kept ice water, milk, butter, eggs and occasionally, bacon. A round oak table stood in the middle of the floor with four straight-back chairs around it.

Drucella joined them at the table, bringing in the plate of still warm corn bread.

Miles took his normal seat, looking out the window. Darkness was beginning to fall, but Miles could still make out the silhouette of the barn behind the house. Beyond the barn lay the pasture where Drucella kept her chickens and Brownie, a friendly Jersey cow with large brown eyes. Everyone in the mountains knew that Jersey cows' milk made the best butter. Brownie was almost like family. Without Brownie, there would be no milk or butter, and of course, little or no fertilizer for Cella's vegetable garden.

Miles gulped down his soup and took an extra piece of cornbread. He was eager to bring in the Christmas tree and get it decorated. Drucella and Evaline's conversation about the sewing Drucella had started today didn't interest him too much anyway. He was just about ready to ask to be excused when Drucella changed the subject.

"Oh, by the way, Evaline, Charlie Wills brought us a pickup load of cedar wood to burn over the holidays. He said it just wasn't Christmas if you didn't have cedar wood burning in the fireplace. Gives off a nice Christmas smell. I invited him to come by tonight and drink some apple cider and help decorate the tree."

Miles hoped that Evaline would be happy to have company. He liked Charlie. But Evaline never looked up, and Drucella kept talking. "I hope you don't mind." She was fishing for a pleasant response. "Why, he seemed real pleased to be invited."

"Momma, why did you do that?" Evaline looked up and glared at her mother. She felt warm all over, but hoped her face wasn't betraying her. She tried to shrug it off. "You know I can't stand Charlie Wills," she said, combing her fingertips through the hair at the nape of her neck. "He makes me as nervous as a cat. He comes in the store, buys a Coke and candy bar, and sits by the stove and watches me like a hawk."

"Don't talk like that, Evaline. Charlie's a good boy. Anna Mae and Everett have raised that boy up right. Never heard of him getting in the first bit of trouble. Now, you be good to Charlie and don't say anything to make him fret."

"Okay, Momma, but I hope he doesn't stay long."

An hour later, the tree stood inside the living room filling the corner window, and cedar wood burned in the fireplace. Evaline, in a new sweater she had knitted from yarn that matched her brilliant eyes, sat in the rocking chair crossing and uncrossing her legs, trying to strike just the right pose that would say she had no interest in Charlie Wills. Miles sat in a cane-bottom chair by the window, pulling the curtains back so he could look toward the road for the lights of Charlie's pickup.

"Get away from that window," Evaline whispered when she saw the lights through the window. "You want him to think we never had a drop of company before? And Miles, let him knock three or four times before you open the door."

Miles wrinkled his forehead. "You sure you don't like Charlie just a little bit?"

"Oh, hush! Go to the door and remember what I told you."

After the third knock, Miles opened the door. "Hello, Charlie, come on in."

Charlie took off his toboggan and stuffed it in his coat pocket as he stepped inside. Surprised to see the tree already brought in and standing in the corner, he turned to Miles with raised eyebrows.

"Yeah, I got the tree up already. How do you like it? I had to go all the way to the top of the mountain to get this good one. Why, I was right in sight of Silver-Eyed Jane's house before I found it!"

Charlie smiled. Miles had a right to be proud. He had picked a good tree. "Well, Miles, I like that tree fine, but let me warn you about Silver-Eyed Jane. Some people say she's a devil, a witch." He winked in Evaline's direction wanting to pull her into the story he was about to weave for Miles, but she had stood up and was headed toward the tree. He turned back to Miles.

"Why," said Charlie, "she can put a spell on you, and it'll be years before your bad luck runs out. She became angry with Sheriff Sizemore when she heard he'd said she should be run out of town for selling moonshine to Billy Goat Stacy. Billy Goat was one of her best customers, and Sheriff Sizemore had caught him with Jane's moonshine and threatened to lock him up and throw away the key if he ever bought moonshine in Hazard again. When Jane found out that Sheriff Sizemore had threatened Billy Goat, Jane put a spell on the Sheriff, and a day later he broke out with the hives, and nearly scratched himself to death! Worst sight you ever saw. The Sheriff ended up buying every bottle of Calamine Lotion in town."

Evaline stood by the Christmas tree looking bored. "Well, Charlie Wills, did you come here to talk about Silver-Eyed Jane, or to help decorate our tree?"

While Evaline and Drucella sorted through the box of ornaments, Charlie and Miles wrapped the tree with lights, large pointed bulbs of red, green, white, blue and orange. Charlie could reach the top of the tree without any trouble. He was over six-feet-tall, and his long arms reached well below his pockets. His neck was long and thin. When he got excited and talked fast, his Adam's apple jumped up and down like a frog. His face was round and his ears stuck out. Charlie didn't look anything like Cary Grant or Fred MacMurray, but he always had a big smile for everyone, and he could turn a small story into a great adventure. Everyone liked Charlie. Some of the younger boys in the hollow called him Ichabod Crane, but not to his face.

With the lights on the tree, and the icicles hanging down, Miles smiled, ready to plug in the lights. "Everyone ready?"

"No, not yet," Drucella said, looking a little sad. "We have one more thing to put on the tree." Miles and Evaline looked at each other, ashamed that they had forgotten. No one spoke. Drucella walked into her bedroom and opened the trunk at the foot of her bed. She reached under several quilts, down to the bottom, unearthing a beautiful, carved wooden angel with golden hair and pink cheeks.

Drucella returned to the living room and handed the angel to Charlie. "Mr. Wills, it would give me great pleasure and be my honor to see you put my husband Landon's angel on our tree. I remember that he carved that angel out of a piece of pine."

"Mrs. Hudson, it would be my honor."

With the angel secured to the top of the tree, Miles plugged in the lights. The tree had few decorations, but it was beautifully shaped. The reflected lights sparkled off the icicles and white cotton balls hung from the pine branches like snowflakes. It was breathtaking.

In the glow of the tree, Charlie edged closer to Evaline. "Beautiful sweater. Is that new?" he asked.

"No, silly. I started knitting it a month ago."

Drucella had taken dried peaches from the cellar and made fried peach pies to go with the apple cider she had made some time ago. She and Evaline served everyone in the living room. When they were finished, Charlie, supposedly one of the best harmonica players in the county, took his harmonica from his pocket and played *Silent Night*.

Having music in the house was a rarity. The Hudsons didn't have a radio. With the coals glowing brightly in the fireplace and the soft music filling the house, a warm feeling welled up inside Miles.

Charlie held the harmonica close to his mouth as the last notes drifted away. He lowered the instrument slowly, enjoying the quiet peace of the moment and trying to think of something clever to say to Evaline.

"Charlie could you teach me to play the harmonica?" Miles spoke first.

"No sweat," Charlie replied. "I can have you playing "Little Brown Jug" before you know it."

"Can you play 'Little Brown Jug' Charlie?"

"Sure. That's one of my favorites."

Charlie Wills, who had recently turned 19, wasn't the best-looking guy in the mountains, but there was nothing dumb about him. What better excuse to come by and see Evaline than to teach Miles to play the harmonica?

FIVE

The following Monday morning, Miles was up early, He poured himself a cup of strong, black coffee from the metal pot Drucella always kept steaming on the stove. She would never be accused of having the bad manners not to offer her company a cup of coffee as soon as they entered the Hudson home. The two strips of bacon, left warming on a plate on the stove, Miles crumbled into the last of a pot of oatmeal and took his breakfast into the dining room.

"I would bet anything that you are the only person in Kentucky who mixes bacon in oatmeal," laughed Evaline as she poked her head in to say good-bye before leaving for work.

Miles finished breakfast quickly, eager to meet Wilbur and Cecil by the oak tree. This morning, Wilbur was the fox and Miles and Cecil, the hounds. The excitement of the holidays and the last day of school before Christmas had filled the three of them with energy. Within sight of the schoolhouse, only 100 yards from the flagpole, Wilbur urged his legs to pump faster. His heart raced from the effort and from the thought that he would, for once, win the game. But then Miles appeared out of nowhere, running at full speed, looking more like a fox than a hound. Wilbur gave it everything he had, but it was not enough. Miles easily passed Wilbur, tagging him on the back as he raced by. Only Miles had never lost a game while he was the fox.

Now under the flagpole and out of breath Wilbur claimed foul. "Miles, that's not fair! You and Cecil didn't give me enough of a head start. I had hardly made it to the coal tipple before you started the chase. It's not fair that you win all the time, Miles!"

Miles laughed and wondered if he had never been caught because of his Cherokee blood. Drucella had told him stories, passed down from her grandfather, about what good runners the Indians were and how they loved games of strength and speed.

"Miles, I believe you could outrun anyone in the Browns Fork grade school or maybe even the entire Hazard High School," said Cecil. He poked Wilbur playfully in the ribs and the two of them laughed with Miles. Their friend Miles was simply the fastest runner and there was no need to be mad about that.

When the laughter stopped, Cecil became serious. "Last night I told my Pa about Miss Savage hitting my knuckles with her paddle."

"What did he say?" Wilbur asked as he stole an anxious look at Miles.

"Well, that's what got me worried. He didn't say anything. He just got out of his chair by the fireplace, didn't say a word. He opened the door and walked outside. Why, he looked like he could kill someone. He stayed outside in the cold for over an hour. Didn't even have a coat on! I was really scared."

The three of them stood silently in their tight, little circle beneath the flagpole thinking about Cecil's Pa, Bo Collins. Cecil might have reason to be scared. Bo was a hard-working coal miner who worked in the dark, damp mine each day, his shift beginning just before daylight, and ending after sunset. He worked six days a week, seeing daylight only on Sunday, the only day the Old Kentuck Coal Company didn't work. Bo didn't talk much, but when he did, it was always short and to the point. Everyone knew Bo was a fair and honest man who did and meant what he said. He wouldn't provoke a fight, but he would fight for what he thought was right.

Cecil looked up to face Wilbur and Miles. "You don't think he'd …" He stopped mid-sentence when he saw Wilbur's face suddenly tighten. Cecil turned to face the school yard. His face paled and his left knee trembled. It was Bo, moving across the school yard like a very angry, dangerous mountain cat, not fast or slow, but keeping a steady pace toward the flagpole and Cecil. His shoulders were wide, his hips slim. His arms were big and strong from years of digging and loading coal. From this distance, his eyes looked hollow, set back in his wrinkled face.

Miles could see Bo had come straight from the Old Kentuck Number 2 Mine, where he had been since before daylight. Bo still had his hard hat on, and he apparently had forgotten to put out the burning carbide light on top.

Seeing all three boys staring at his hat, Bo pulled it off and cut off the light. The carbide flame made a popping sound as it went out. He passed by the boys clustered at the flagpole without stopping. "Come with me, Cecil," he said, continuing the same steady pace, and looking straight ahead as he headed toward the school.

Cecil followed his Pa through the seven foot double doors and down the hall. It was the first time Bo had been inside the Browns Fork School.

Bo's walk slowed as he looked at the varnished wood doors lining the hallway and the globe lights hanging from the ceiling. He paused to gaze at a picture on the wall of George Washington crossing the Delaware. "Who's that man in that picture?" he asked Cecil.

Cecil breathed a little easier. If his Pa were taking time to stop and ask about a picture, he probably wasn't going to rush in and create a scene. "Why, Pa, that's the first President of the United States. That's George Washington." Cecil felt important. Rarely did he know something his Pa didn't.

"Oh, is that so? George Washington! Well, been a good while since I was in a schoolhouse. Guess I've forgot quite a bit. Ain't he that feller that chopped down that cherry tree when he was a little shaver, and better than tell a lie about it, he took a whupping for it?"

"That's right, Pa," Cecil answered.

"You know, Cecil, I think I might have liked to have known that feller." He tucked his hat a bit closer to his chest and glanced around the hallway. "Now, where's the principal's office?"

"Straight ahead, Principal Marcum. His name is over the door."

Bo picked up the pace again as they walked to the door. Bo knocked. "Yes? Who is it?" The voice came through the closed door.

"Bo Collins. I'm here to talk about my boy."

A short, robust man with thinning hair opened the door. "All right," he said. There was a brief pause as the two men sized each other up in the doorway. "I'm not sure if you remember me," the principal said to Bo Collins, "but I was in seventh grade with you over twenty-five years ago down on Quicksand Creek." He extended his hand to Bo.

Bo grasped his hand firmly. "Seems like I ought to know you," he said, studying the principal's face. "Yeah, I know who you are. You're Dale, Orville Marcum's boy." He pumped the principal's hand a few times, before releasing it. "I can't say I remember much about the seventh grade. That was as far as I got in school. I quit school to go to work in the mines. Been loading coal ever since."

"Well now, Bo, what can I do for you?" Principal Marcum asked.

"You can do something about that teacher of yours, Miss Savage."

Principal Marcum looked down the hall. Several teachers who had clustered outside a nearby classroom, pretending not to listen, dispersed and went to take their posts at their own doorways, ready to usher students into their classrooms when the first bell rang.

"Come into my office where we can sit down and talk," he said to Bo. He motioned Cecil to a chair beside the door. "Cecil, you can sit here. We won't be too long."

After Principal Marcum closed the door, Cecil leaned as close to the door as he could without falling out of his chair. The radiators were beginning to heat up, and the sound of the hot water and steam flowing from the coal furnace in the basement made it impossible to hear.

Just as the bell rang, two eighth grade girls, assuming Cecil was in some kind of trouble, grinned at each other and quickly looked the other way as they walked by. Cecil panicked. He just knew all the students who walked past him would wonder what he was doing sitting outside the principal's office. But most other students, excited about today's Christmas Parties, and getting out of school early, failed to pay much attention to Cecil. The hallway was clearing fast when Miles passed and quickly gave Cecil a thumbs-up as he went by. Once the tardy bell rang, Cecil had no choice but to sit alone in the otherwise empty hallway.

Inside Principal Marcum's office, a serious conversation was under way.

"Now, Bo, just what's the trouble between Miss Savage and Cecil?"

"Well, Dale, if my boy misbehaves, or does something he shouldn't do at school, and packs a whupping home, then so be it. If I find out about it, when he gets home, I'll give him another whupping."

"Dale, you and me grew up down on Quicksand, and I guess we were pretty much like any other boys on that creek. We worked hard to keep firewood cut, milked cows, fed chickens, carried water, and took care of pigs. What I'm saying, Dale, is many of these young boys today, particularly those who live out in the county, have a right smart of work to do before coming to school, just like we did. And, as you and I know first-hand, sometimes they're going to forget to comb their hair and wash behind their ears. But Dale, that don't give no teacher the right to take a paddle and beat'em on their knuckles 'til they turn blue."

Bo paused to get his breath, and continued. "Why, Cecil told me she beat the living hell out of the Hudson boy because he sharpened a pencil that didn't write dark enough to suit her, and because Miles wouldn't tattle on the boy, he had to take a whupping for it. Well, Landon Hudson's not here to stand up for his boy, so I'm standing up for my boy, and Landon's boy, too. I'm telling you straight out Dale, I'm not going to put up with that kind of foolishness." Bo's fist banged on the desk. "I want something done about it, and I want it done now. I've already missed a half day's work on account of this. I pay school taxes, and the school's causing me to lose a half day's pay. It just ain't right."

Bo was suddenly aware that he had leaned forward, and his fist was on the desk. He took a deep breath and straightened his shoulders, but left his fist on the desk. He stared directly at Dale Marcum. "I'm not a violent man, Dale, but I guess I could be pushed to it."

Dale Marcum leaned back in his chair and held up his hands, palms out. "Now just one minute, Bo. Let's not get carried away here. We're going to do whatever it takes to make this situation right." He massaged his forehead. He had two fifth grade teachers, so there was an easy solution available to him. Although he wasn't usually a man to take the easy way, he was responsible for the school and would do whatever it took to prevent an uproar. So it was settled. He knew what he had to do. "Bo, I'm going to have Cecil moved to Miss Turner's 5th-grade class."

"Well, that's good," Bo said, "but how about the Hudson boy?"

Dale turned toward the window. He liked Miles Hudson, and he knew Miss Savage was a problem, but he couldn't solve that entire problem right now. He turned back to Bo. "Bo, I'm going to have a long talk with Miss Savage about how she handles her entire class, but I can't move all her students to Miss Turner's class. The state only allows us a certain number of teachers for our school, and we have to make out the best we can with what the state gives us."

"Well, they didn't give you much when they gave you that Miss Savage."

"It's the best I can do. Is that going to be all right with you?" He raised his eyebrows and looked at Bo, uncertain what he would do, if Bo said no.

Bo hesitated. "Well, I guess it will. But if I hear of the Hudson boy being mistreated, I'll be taking a full day off, and I'll be going to the superintendent next time."

Principal Marcum had no reason to doubt him. If there was one thing he knew, Bo Collins was a man of his word. The two men stood and shook hands again. Then they collected Cecil, walked up the stairs and headed down the hall to Miss Savage's room.

Miles sat at his desk in Miss Savage's room staring at the presents under the tree. He was looking for a small gift wrapped in red paper and tied simply with satin ribbon, the present he had brought in earlier in the week. The week before, students had drawn names for Christmas. Miles had drawn Eugene's name and had known immediately what to buy for him - a checkerboard with checkers. The gift wasn't expensive, and didn't need to be, as no one expected an expensive present. For Miles and the other students, it wasn't cost, it was the thrill of surprise.

Now Miles noticed the other gifts, most wrapped in red or green paper, a few in papers with Santa Claus on a snow-covered roof with a bag of toys, or Santa Claus waving from his sleigh. A couple of the presents even had fancy bows. Miles wondered if one of those with bows could be his. His eyes traveled up the tree, and he watched in fascination as bubbles percolated up the multi-color, eye-dropper-shaped bulbs.

After the students had left class yesterday, the tree had been brought in and decorated, and the presents the students had been bringing in all week had been placed under it. Classes would last until early afternoon, and then the class mother would arrive with cookies and punch for the Christmas Party. Miles hoped there would be pecan cookies baked in Christmas shapes, the kind Mary Rose's mother had brought last year.

Nancy Ann kicked at Miles' foot from across the aisle, it was time for them to begin their pencil sharpening duties for the day. Miss Savage began her "visual roll call" and noticed Cecil's empty seat. "Cecil's not at school today?" she asked.

There was silence. Miss Savage turned and looked at Miles. "Miles, doesn't Cecil come to school with you every morning?"

"Yes, Ma'am, he does," Miles answered.

"Well, did he come to school with you this morning, or did he not?" she asked, anger rising in her voice.

Miles hesitated. Did she want the whole story or just the answer? With Miss Savage, he never knew. He decided a short answer was best. "Yes, ma'am, he did."

Miss Savage opened her desk drawer, pulled out her paddle, and slammed it against her desk. "Well, if he came to school with you this morning, where is he now?" she shouted.

Miles felt as if he were sitting on top of a hot stove. He took a deep breath and proceeded as slowly as he dared. No need to jump from the frying pan into the fire. "Miss Savage, after we got to school this morning, his Pa showed up." He looked at Miss Savage, to see if she were still angry, but her eyes seemed to have glazed over when Miles mentioned Cecil's Pa. Miles continued. "He took Cecil to Principal Marcum's office, and that's where they are right now."

Miss Savage's face paled. Miles held his breath as she stood and walked to the front of her desk where she stood silently for a moment and looked toward the classroom door. Then she turned, and went back to her desk. "Nancy Ann, you may call the rows to have everyone's pencils sharpened. Take out your geography books, and read the next chapter on Alaska and the Eskimos."

Everyone's eyes kept drifting from their books to the door, and then cautiously back to Miss Savage. Miles could feel the electricity in the air, and the hair on the back of his neck stuck out. For once, it wasn't a student who was frightened and in trouble. It was Miss Savage.

Suddenly Miss Savage got up from her desk and headed to her bird sanctuary, the far corner of the room where she had two small cases filled with her books on birds. She was proud of her collection of more than 200 bird books. She told the class she had been collecting these books since she was in grade school. Some were quite rare. If a student could manage to turn in all his or her homework, make 100 on the weekly spelling test, and avoid getting disciplined with her ruler or paddle, then they were privileged to spend a half hour in the bird-book sanctuary, reading any book of their choice. They could also draw a picture of their favorite bird for extra credit.

At the beginning of the school year, each student was required to pick his or her favorite bird. On a big chart in the front of the room, each student's name was paired with the bird he or she had chosen. Miss Savage referred to the chart when she deemed her students needed disciplining. Miles' name was paired with the purple martin, so if Miles made a bad grade, or was caught talking, Miss Savage went to the chart, called Miles' name, and said, "Well, Miles' favorite bird is the purple martin, but he is nothing like the purple martin. The purple martin works all day. Why, it stays so busy eating mosquitoes and insects, it hardly ever lights on a branch. You won't catch the purple martin not doing its work and wasting time." Then she would smack Miles' knuckles with her paddle. "From now on, Miles, try and be like your favorite bird, the purple martin."

Miles knew Miss Savage was nervous right now. She was dusting the bird books. She had always given this duty to one of the students. No one had ever seen her dusting or cleaning before. The students heard talking out in the hall, and all eyes turned toward the open door.

"Bo, you and Cecil wait here, and I'll have Miss Savage come out here in the hall." As though the room were contaminated, Principal Marcum stuck his head and shoulders inside the door to Miss Savage's classroom, all the while keeping his feet planted firmly in the hallway outside the door.

"Miss Savage, I need to see you out here, please."

Miss Savage folded her dust cloth and placed it on top of the bookcase. She straightened the padded shoulders of her dress, held her head high, and calmly walked over to the door and out into the hall.

Every student watched the door, disappointed when Principal Marcum closed it behind Miss Savage.

Andrew, usually the quietest boy in class, was the first one to speak. "I hope they fire that old heifer."

"Yeah," William chimed in, "she's had it coming."

"Shhhhhh!" said Sarah, who was considered the smartest student in the class, wore glasses, and usually had a pencil tucked behind her ear. When Sarah spoke everyone paid attention. "Everybody be quiet!" said Sarah.

They could hear voices, but with the door closed, at first no one could make out what they were saying. But after a short while, the voices became louder.

Bo threw up his hands and exclaimed, "God Almighty, woman! You're supposed to be teaching these children, not beating on them 'til you break their spirit. You know, Miss Savage, I've tried all my life to be a gentleman, but if I was a student in your class, and you treated me the way you do some of these children, I'd cram that paddle down your throat."

"All right. That's enough. Miss Savage, have Cecil get his belongings so he can move to Miss Turner's room. Now we've got to get back to the running of this school."

Out in the hallway, Principal Marcum turned to Bo. "Everything will be taken care of. Cecil can tell you about it when he gets home today."

"All right," Bo said. "I'm leaving it in your hands, Dale."

The door opened. Cecil and Miss Savage walked slowly back into the room. Principal Marcum stood watching from the doorway.

Miss Savage walked back to her desk, took out her grade book and marked out Cecil's name.

Cecil walked to his desk, took out his notebook and placed his Webster's Dictionary on top of it. He tightened the cap on his ink bottle and put his pen and pencils in his pocket. Miles tried to get his attention, but Cecil wouldn't look at him.

Miss Savage looked up from her desk. "Wilbur, find Cecil's Christmas present under the tree for him. We don't want him to have to come back in here again." Principal Marcum glared at Miss Savage, but said nothing.

Wilbur shuffled through the presents under the tree and handed Cecil a small box wrapped in red paper with a white ribbon on top. Principal Marcum motioned for Cecil to hurry. "Is that everything, Cecil?"

"Yes, sir, it is."

"All right. Let's go." He waited for Cecil at the doorway. "And Miss Savage? I will need to speak with you today before you leave."

The class looked with envy at Cecil and Principal Marcum as they walked out the door. Why should Cecil get to go to Miss Turner's room and not them? Miles thought about Miss Turner, the youngest teacher at the Browns Fork School. She was known for giving lots of homework, and she didn't put up with anyone misbehaving in class, but she was also a lot of fun. Sometimes during recess, when the girls were jumping rope, she would kick off her shoes, run out into the middle of the rope and jump with them. This delighted all the other students. They formed a circle and counted out loud the number of times Miss Turner could jump without missing.

The bubble lights on the Christmas tree caught Miles' eye, but he wasn't thinking of Christmas. He was thinking about late spring. All Miss Turner's students looked forward to late spring. When the temperature climbed to 85 degrees, as it often did in late spring, the heat caused the schoolroom to become unbearable. Always trying to create a favorable learning environment for her students, Miss Turner marched the children down the stairs, out the front door, and held class under the large oak tree in the school yard.

It just wasn't fair that Cecil got to go to Miss Turner's room. Miles looked at the disappointed faces of his classmates and knew they were all thinking the same thing. Miss Turner was indeed a teacher ahead of her time.

SIX

The temperature had dropped during the day. It was below freezing and more snow was falling as Miles left school and walked toward town. He pulled his toboggan over his ears and stuck out his tongue to try to catch some snowflakes.

After lunch, he had forgotten about Cecil and Miss Turner and enjoyed the Christmas Party. He ate another piece of the Whitman's chocolate-covered cherry candy Nancy Ann had given him. He sure was glad that she had drawn his name. He could hardly wait to show Evaline his present.

Miles' nose and cheeks were red from the bitter cold, and the warm air that met him as he entered the Farmer Hotel lobby felt good. But Miles knew something was not right. Mrs. Farmer was behind the hotel desk in the lobby, not in her office. She hardly ever went behind the large hotel desk, with its boxes for guest keys and mail slots. This was Mr. Farmer's domain, where he checked in guests. Mrs. Farmer kept the books in her small, enclosed office, and most of the time, the Farmers stayed out of each other's way.

Of course, staying out of each other's way didn't mean that Mrs. Farmer didn't know what went on at the front desk. Her office, directly behind the front desk, was separated from the lobby with a wall of glass, her own design, so that she could "watch over things" at the hotel. Oscar's job performance was one of the things she particularly "watched over." She knew he kept a small flask of liquor underneath the desk and had a tendency to "dram-drink," take a little nip every so often, but not so much as would make him noticeably drunk. From her glass enclosure, Mrs. Farmer could monitor Oscar's drinking.

One day after Miles had made a liquor run to the Broke Spoke for Oscar, and Mrs. Farmer was not around, Oscar mimicked Mrs. Farmer. He went inside the glass office enclosure, tapped sharply on the glass a couple of times, and shook his finger at an imaginary Oscar standing behind the front desk. "If I didn't keep an eye on you, you'd run us into the poor house," he said, narrowing his eyes to little squinty slits and leaning in until his nose almost touched the glass. Then he and Miles laughed and Oscar took another nip from his flask.

Today as he stepped into the lobby, Mrs. Farmer looked up from the stack of mail she was going through. "Hello, Miles." Mrs. Farmer didn't wait for Miles' response. She went back to her mail sorting and didn't look up again. "Oscar's not here today. He's home in bed, sick with the flu. The lobby needs cleaning, though. I've been doing my job and Oscar's, too, and I haven't had time to get around to cleaning the lobby. We're almost full up. Lots of salesmen in town right now. They're making last calls on their customers before the holidays, and everything is a mess. Why, Rachel is usually gone by two o'clock, and here it is almost three-thirty. She still has three more rooms to clean. Well, you know where everything is. Go ahead and start your cleaning."

Miles didn't respond, not even a "yes Ma'am." Mrs. Farmer was a woman used to giving orders, and having them followed with no questions asked. It took Miles about a half-hour to get the lobby cleaned and another fifteen minutes to go to the City Café to pick up Mrs. Farmer's supper. Mrs. Farmer was a good eater and the "regular" plate lunch she always ordered had to be fixed special with heaps of everything, and extra gravy on the mashed potatoes.

Finished with his cleaning and back from his errand to the City Café, Miles gathered his coat and prepared to leave. Mrs. Farmer opened the cash register and took out two quarters. "All right, here's a quarter for cleaning the lobby." She handed one quarter to Miles, then paused and held the other quarter in the air for him to see. "And, a quarter for Christmas. Merry Christmas, Miles." She presented the second quarter like a prize trophy.

"Thank you and Merry Christmas to you and Mr. Farmer," Miles said, turning and walking toward the door.

"Oh, I almost forgot," Mrs. Farmer called to him. "Oscar said for me to be sure to give you this Christmas card when you came in."

Miles went back and took the bright-green, sealed envelope Mrs. Farmer had picked up from behind the counter. Nothing rattled inside the card, so if there was money, it was probably a dollar. Mrs. Farmer had noticed the same thing. She stared at him steadily as he placed the envelope inside his coat pocket. "I sure hope Mr. Farmer gets to feeling better, and tell him I thank him for the Christmas card," Miles said.

"You can open your card here if you want to, Miles," Mrs. Farmer purred. Mrs. Farmer didn't usually purr, so Miles knew she had to be curious about what was in the card. "I didn't know Oscar had it for you until I was ready to go out the door this morning." She smiled at him. She didn't usually smile too much either.

Miles smiled right back and tried not to laugh. "Oh, that's all right. I'd rather wait until I get home."

Mrs. Farmer sniffed and lifted her chin, indicating that the conversation was no longer worth her time. "Suit yourself. I've got work to do." And with that she walked back around the counter and busied herself going through the mail she had already sorted.

As soon as Miles was out of Mrs. Farmer's sight, he took the envelope out of his coat pocket and tore it open. On the front of the card was a picture of Santa Claus getting ready to go down a chimney on a snow-covered roof. Santa was smoking a pipe and had a bag of toys on his back. Miles opened the card. A dollar bill lay inside, covering the printed greeting: "Merry Christmas." Oscar had written a note at the bottom:

Miles, I hope you and your family have a good Christmas.
Oscar

This was Miles' lucky day. For the last five weeks, he had been saving to buy Christmas presents for Drucella and Evaline. He now had six dollars—the five he had already saved tucked safely in his pocket, the dollar from Oscar, and the two quarters from Mrs. Farmer.

Miles had not intended to stop and look at the electric train as he went by the Sterling Hardware store, but he couldn't help himself. He thought for the millionth time about how lucky for any kid to wake up on Christmas morning and find an electric train under the tree. But it cost too much. Miles would be embarrassed to receive such an expensive present when his family needed the money for more important things.

As Miles continued his walk up Main Street, he heard "Jingle Bells" coming from the Salvation Army band in front of the Five and Dime. A lady in a dark navy uniform with gold buttons down the front was ringing the Salvation Army bell. "Would you please help the ones who are less fortunate than you?" she asked as people walked by. "Please help us make sure everyone has some Christmas spirit this year?"

Miles reached down into his pocket and found the two quarters Mrs. Farmer had given him. He walked over to the big red kettle and dropped them in.

"Why, thank you sir, and a Merry Christmas to you," the lady said, smiling.

Miles thought of what his two quarters might buy someone, oranges, apples, or maybe some candy. He felt good not only for giving the two quarters, but because the smiling lady had looked at him with so much respect and called him "sir." No one had ever called him "sir" before.

When Miles entered the Five and Dime, he inhaled deeply and immediately knew the special for the day being prepared behind the lunch counter was hamburger steak. Almost all the stools at the counter were taken. He scanned the long mirror that covered the entire wall behind the counter, noting who was eating at the Five and Dime today. He stopped short when he recognized Black Hart James. Black Hart was busy eating, and Miles hoped he could get out of the store before Black Hart saw him. But no such luck, Black Hart looked up, and he and Miles were suddenly staring at each other in the mirror. Miles turned away quickly.

"Hello stranger," said Black Hart as he turned around on his stool. "You getting too good to speak to your old friends anymore?"

Miles turned back to face him. "Hello, Black Hart. I didn't see you."

Black Hart cocked his head to one side and raised an eyebrow. "Why, if I didn't know better, I'd think you were trying to avoid me," Black Hart said. He bit down on the toothpick hanging from the side of his mouth.

"That's not it. I'm just in a hurry to buy some Christmas presents."

"Well, is that so? What did you think I was going to do? Hold you up and socialize with you all day? You think I can't tell when someone is ignoring me? Do I look dumb to you, boy? Miss Queen Bee been telling you to stay away from me? Is that it?"

Black Hart's face and neck were turning red. Beads of sweat had popped out on his forehead. Miles took a deep breath and exhaled slowly. Everyone was looking at him. He was scared of Black Hart, but no one else had to know that. It was time to make a clean break like Evaline had told him.

"I'm not going to run bets for you anymore. I don't think it's right and besides, you never want to pay me anyway."

Black Hart slid off the stool. He towered above Miles and said angrily, "If we weren't at this lunch counter, your ass would be mud. Hell no, I'm not going to pay you! You think I'm going to pay a little smart ass like you anything? When you see that sister of yours, you can tell her she can go to…"

Miles stared straight into the angry heat of Black Hart's face. "Damn you! If I ever hear you mention my sister again, I'm going to Sheriff Sizemore, and we'll see what he can do about it. In fact, I think I'll go right now!" Miles' voice broke just a little and neither he nor Black Hart could tell if it broke from fear or anger.

Black Hart reached out for Miles shoulder. "Now hold on, boy. You don't have to do that." Miles never glanced away and his cold stare unnerved Black Hart. He took his hand away. "I guess I did get carried away a little. No need for us to get all upset. Hellfire, it's Christmas! Everyone ought to be getting along, not fussing and fighting with each other. Just to show you my heart's in the right place, why, I'm going to go ahead and pay you that seventy-five cents I owe you." Black Hart reached into his hip pocket. He realized that everyone around the lunch counter had stopped eating. They were all quiet, looking at him and Miles and listening to everything being said. This kid was showing him up.

Miles had noticed the attention, too, but he was embarrassed to have lost his temper in front of everyone. He certainly hadn't meant to challenge Black Hart. "I don't want your money. I just want you to leave me alone." Miles turned to look at the comic books in the rack behind him.

"Sure boy! Sure thing! I'll be seeing you around."

"Don't bother," Miles said. "Just stay away from me."

"No problem there," Black Hart said, turning and walking over to the cash register. He took out his billfold, pulled out a five-dollar bill and handed it to Nell, the head waitress who was never at a loss for words.

Nell took her time handing over the change to Black Hart. "You know, Black Hart, next time, why don't you try picking on someone smaller than you." She leaned toward him with a smile and popped her gum in his face. "You big bully."

"When I want your opinion, I'll ask for it, Toots." He winked at her, grabbed the door and gave it a hard pull and quickly stepped outside. He strode down the street so hard and fast, the metal taps on the heels of his wingtip shoes made sparks as they clicked on the pavement. He cussed Miles under his breath. The one person Black Hart feared most in the small town of Hazard was Sheriff Sizemore.

Sizemore was a no-nonsense Sheriff when it came to enforcing the law. Most of the time, Sizemore tried to stop trouble before it started, and Sizemore had already had several talks with Black Hart about his gambling. "If that kid gets me in trouble with Sheriff Sizemore, I'll break his scrawny little neck," Black Hart mumbled as he hurried down the street.

Back in the Five and Dime, Nell walked around from behind the counter and over to the comic-book rack where Miles stood. "Hey kid. Don't let that big bully get to you. He's bad news, and sooner or later he'll get what's coming to him. Just stay away from him."

"Yeah, I'm going to do that," Miles said. He stood up a little straighter, determined to look calmer than he felt. "But I'm glad it happened. Now I don't have to have anything to do with him anymore."

Nell looked back toward the door and gave her gum a loud pop. "I wouldn't be so sure about that kid." She looked back at Miles. "Just stay out of his way, and everything will be all right. Don't let this squabble ruin your Christmas."

"I won't," said Miles. "Christmas" was the magic word. He was smiling now, already forgetting about the show-down with Black Hart that had just occurred in front of a lunch counter full of people. "I think this is going to be my best Christmas ever. Why, I've saved six dollars to buy Ma and my sister Christmas presents. I can hardly wait for Christmas morning!"

Nell took a good look at Miles. He had inherited his mother's black hair and dark eyes. He always said, "Yes, ma'am" and "No, ma'am." Looking at him, Nell, who was in her late thirties and never married, thought about some of the things she had missed in life. She smiled admiringly at the 11-year-old boy, all excited about spending Christmas with his mother and sister, her eyes becoming moist as she placed her hand on Miles' shoulder. "You know, you're a good kid. You know that, don't you, kid?"

"Thanks," Miles said, his face turning red.

"Hey, you're going to make me cry," Nell said, patting Miles on the head. "Now, you better get busy if you're going to buy those Christmas presents. I hope your mom and sister have a Merry Christmas."

"Thanks," Miles said, "and a Merry Christmas to you."

SEVEN

Drucella set her alarm for four-thirty Christmas morning. The first thing she did when she got up was start a fire in the cook stove and get the coffee perking. On this morning, she mixed green oak with seasoned oak to create a fire hotter than usual. The oven temperature rose quickly to nearly 350 degrees, perfect for baking a golden-brown turkey and dressing.

Mr. Herd, who raised and sold turkeys on his small mountain farm in the hollow, had delivered Drucella's Christmas turkey on Christmas Eve. The Christmas turkey was partial payment for the wedding gown Drucella was going to make for Mavis, Mr. Herd's daughter, a wedding gown just like the one in the picture Mavis had cut out of a magazine. Drucella had looked at the picture, taken Mavis's measurements, and given Mr. Herd a price for the wedding gown--two turkeys, one for Thanksgiving, that she had already received, the other for Christmas Day, which he had delivered as promised on Christmas Eve, and five dollars cash to be paid in May when the gown was completed for Mavis' wedding to Elmer Wiggins.

Drucella and Mr. Herd had not formalized their agreement with a signed document. The mere mention of such a thing by either would have been an insult to both. As they shook hands, each was acknowledging to the other, a commitment to honor the agreement. The handshake was their bond, and each knew that no self-respecting mountain person would ever fail to honor a handshake.

The Christmas turkey, a plump 20-pound hen, had been baking in the oven for over an hour. With its delicious aroma and the smell of coffee circulating throughout the house, Miles began to awaken from a deep sleep. He rubbed his eyes and turned over on his pillow, taking in the rich smells filtering throughout the house. He sat up in bed and looked out the window. All at once, he realized, it was Christmas morning! He jumped out of bed and headed to the kitchen.

"Land sakes alive! You out of bed already?" Drucella asked, sifting the last of the flour for her pie crust into the bowl. She brushed aside a stray lock of hair with her left hand which left a streak of flour on her forehead.

"Merry Christmas, Ma! It's finally got here! I can't believe it's finally Christmas morning!" Miles jumped up and down. He grabbed Drucella's arm, pulling her toward the living room and the presents under the tree.

Drucella didn't budge. "Miles, it's only a little after six o'clock, so don't go waking up your sister. This is one of the few days out of the year when she gets to sleep late."

"But Ma, don't you think she would want to be awake? Christmas only comes once a year," Miles pleaded, looking longingly toward the living room. When he turned to give Drucella another hopeful look, she had already returned to making her pie crust.

"Well, you can help me in the kitchen another hour or so, and then maybe you can wake her up."

"But, Ma! I want to see what…"

"It's all right, Momma." Evaline stood in the doorway, rubbing her eyes sleepily. "With all the stomping around, and all the talking going on, I'm wide awake." She smiled at Miles.

"Well, since everyone's out of bed, we may as well have breakfast," Drucella said. "I've got biscuits and gravy already fixed."

"But Ma, can't we open our presents first, and then have breakfast?" Miles pleaded, turning toward the living room and the Christmas tree again.

"Don't take another step, young man. We'll eat, and then we'll open our Christmas presents."

"But Ma!"

"Don't 'But' me or you'll spend Christmas Day in your room. Do you understand?"

"Yes, ma'am."

"Well then, the sooner you sit down and start eating," Drucella said, "the sooner you'll get to open your presents." Evaline shrugged her shoulders and picked up the bowl of gravy, waving it under Miles' nose a few times as she headed toward the dining room. Miles, who was always hungry, followed the scent of the gravy, and Drucella brought up the rear carrying the bowl of buttermilk biscuits.

With everyone finally seated in the dining room, Evaline and Drucella had hardly started eating before Miles had cleaned his plate. Drucella's biscuits and gravy were so good, Miles wondered how anyone could eat them slowly. It looked like Evaline and Drucella were going to take their time as they talked first about Charlie Wills, then about Mavis's wedding gown, and then about the Thomas family.

"Mr. Thomas lost his job at the Piggly Wiggly almost a year ago," said Drucella, "and still hasn't found another one, so the Thomas family won't have a very merry Christmas. Maybe after dinner we should send them some of the left-over turkey."

Evaline nodded her agreement. "And the children won't be getting much either. Maybe we could send the Thomas boy one of Miles' presents." She looked at Miles. Now she had his attention.

"How about that lump of coal you're getting? Could we give that to the Thomas boy?" She reached over to ruffle his hair and gave him a sly grin. "Miles, would you like another biscuit?"

"No thanks," Miles replied with a sigh. He slumped in his chair.

"Well then, I think I'll have one or maybe two more," Evaline said, reaching into the bowl for another biscuit. Evaline loved Miles, but she also enjoyed teasing him.

Drucella looked at her children and smiled. "Let's all take our coffee into the living room and open our presents."

In the living room, Miles stretched out on the floor beside the tree. "All right, who's going to open the first present?"

"Miles, let Momma open the first present, the one I got for her," Evaline said. "It's the one wrapped in white tissue with red ribbon." Evaline settled into the rocking chair, situating herself so she could see Drucella's face clearly.

Miles rose to his knees and crawled over to the present Evaline had indicated. He picked up the present and his eyes widened with surprise. "What's in here? A block of No. 9 coal? It weighs a ton!" He crawled over to the stuffed chair where Drucella sat and placed the gift in her lap.

Drucella, held the box, lifting it up and down, weighing it in her hands. Careful not to destroy the ribbon, she tore the wrapping off the package. She gasped as she held the small Philco Radio up for everyone to see.

Miles had crawled closer to Drucella as she fussed with the ribbon, eager to see the first present. Now he fell back, his arms stretched wide as he stared at the ceiling in disbelief. "Wow, a Philco Radio! Now we can listen to The Lone Ranger and Tonto!"

"And to Bing Crosby," Evaline said dreamily.

"Yeah, and to Jack Benny and Charlie McCarthy. Wow!" Miles jumped to his feet. "Let me plug it in. I can tune it in to WCKY. They're playing Christmas music all day long."

Drucella tried not to show her own excitement. "Evaline, just how much did you pay for this radio, anyway?"

"Well, Momma, it doesn't matter how much I paid for it." Evaline sighed. Drucella was always worried about money and she would find out how much Evaline had paid whether Evaline told her now or not. "But if you must know, it was nineteen dollars and ninety-five cents, on sale at the Star Furniture."

Drucella's jaw dropped. Surely Evaline hadn't spent a whole nineteen dollars and ninety-five cents on Drucella's Christmas. "I mean, how much did you pay down on it?"

"Momma, I didn't pay down on anything. It's paid off in full. I don't owe one brownie on it. Now, you know you always wanted a radio to listen to while you worked at your sewing machine. Why won't you just settle down and enjoy it?" Evaline asked tilting her chin up proudly.

Miles plugged in the radio and tuned it in to WCKY. He had listened to the radio at Cecil's house many times, but now the radio sounded so much better. Just knowing that it belonged to his family, and that it was playing in their house, made all the difference.

During the next half-hour the family enjoyed Christmas music as they unwrapped presents. In addition to the radio from Evaline, Drucella opened three packages from Miles: a music box, a set of six orange-juice glasses, and a pitcher to match the glasses. Miles had wrapped the glasses and pitcher separately so that Drucella would have more presents to open.

From Drucella, Evaline received a Sure Shot Camera and two rolls of film, and in her stocking was a gold ring that had belonged to Drucella's grandmother. Miles gave Evaline a leather billfold and a *Photo-Play* movie magazine.

Miles opened a chemistry set from Drucella, and he was thrilled to find in his stocking the Case pocket knife that had belonged to his father. Finally, the only present still under the tree was a small box that appeared to be only about an inch wide and maybe three inches long. It was Evaline's present to Miles.

"Gee, Evaline, it sure looks small," Miles said.

Evaline was teasing again. "Well, I decided you weren't worth that lump of coal, so I got you something else."

Something this small can't be worth very much, he thought as he took the box and began removing the white paper. The box beneath the wrapping had no writing on it. Still uncertain as to what he was getting, he opened the box. As soon as he saw it, he let out a scream. "Oh my Lord! A wristwatch! Oh my Lord! I can't believe it! Just how much money you got hidden in your mattress, Evaline?"

Evaline stood by the fireplace beaming over Miles' reaction to her present. "Well, it didn't cost anything like Momma's radio, but it does have a year's guarantee on it. And Miles Hudson, don't you be worrying about my money. You stay out of my room. That's private."

Miles wound the watch and held it to his ear, listening to the quiet, steady ticking. He set the time, put it on, held his wrist to his face and checked the time. He listened once more to make sure it was still ticking and checked the time again. When he realized that Drucella and Evaline were watching him, he tried to shift the attention to Drucella. "Ma, you sure 'cleaned-up' this Christmas."

"Lord, Miles, I know. And you didn't need to get me three presents! One would have been plenty. Why, I feel like you children just spent way too much money on me," Drucella said, but her voice was happy.

With all the presents opened, and the radio playing Christmas music, Drucella went back to the kitchen to check on the turkey and tend the fire in the cook stove. It wouldn't do to burn her dinner on Christmas Day. Miles followed her a few steps toward the kitchen and called after her, "Mama, if you ever want to know what time it is, you can just ask me. It is now 7:30."

Evaline laughed, "Miles, you are going to stare at that watch until the hands fall off it. I'm sure glad you like it."

A few minutes later, Miles lay asleep by the fireplace, and Evaline sat in the rocking chair reading her movie magazine. Around eight o'clock, someone knocked on the front door.

Evaline put down the magazine, and Miles rolled over and stood up.

"Miles," Evaline said, "can you tell who it is?"

Miles peered through the curtains. "Yeah, it's Charlie."

"My Lord! What in heaven's name is he doing here this early? Doesn't he know it's Christmas morning? I'm still in my robe, and my hair is a mess!"

Drucella came in, drying her hands on her apron, just as Evaline stood up to leave the room.

"Well, Evaline, where are your manners? Open the door and let him in," Drucella said.

"Open the door and let him in? With my hair looking like a bird's nest? He should know better than to come here this early in the morning. I'm going to my room!" Evaline was already in the hall now. "You all can open the door or let him stay outside and freeze. Why, if I live to be a hundred, I don't believe I'll ever understand Charlie Wills." The door to Evaline's room slammed.

"Miles, be sure to ask him if he would like a cup of coffee," directed Drucella, turning and going back into the kitchen.

Miles opened the door. Charlie stood in the doorway in his gray overcoat holding an armful of gifts. "Hello, Miles. I hope I'm not disturbing you all by stopping so early, but I had these presents to deliver. I thought you all would be up."

"Sure. Come on in." Miles nodded to the fireplace and watched Charlie unload the presents on the hearth. "No, Charlie, you're not disturbing me," Miles said. He wondered which of the three boxes would be his. "Why, I've been up since six o'clock. Would you like a cup of coffee?"

"I sure would. The heater went out in my pickup last night, and it feels like an ice box. I'm nearly frozen to death," Charlie said, walking over to the fireplace and warming his hands. He checked the room out, obviously looking for something.

Drucella called out from the kitchen, "Charlie, I'll have your coffee in just a minute. Just make yourself at home, and Merry Christmas!"

"That's fine," Charlie called back. "Merry Christmas to you, too!"

Drucella walked through the hallway where Charlie couldn't see her, opened Evaline's door, and closed it behind her.

In the living room, Charlie turned his back to the fireplace to warm it, and said, "Did you have a good Christmas, Miles?" Charlie checked out the room again and saw the opened boxes under the tree which displayed some of the gifts the family had opened. He heard Christmas music playing from a small radio that hadn't been there when Charlie helped the family decorate the tree. But he still did not seem to find what he was looking for.

"Yeah, I sure did! Look at the watch Evaline got me." He thrust his wrist into Charlie's face, but didn't stop talking. "I got a chemistry set and my Dad's pocket knife, too!"

Charlie wasn't really listening. "Oh that's nice Miles." He peered down the hallway. "Is Evaline taking a nap or something?"

"No," said Miles in a low voice. He glanced back cautiously toward Evaline's room.

"What is it, Miles?" Charlie whispered.

Miles, feeling wiser than his years, looked up at Charlie. "Come here, Charlie," he said, putting his finger to his lips. This was something that needed to be talked about quietly. When Charlie lowered his head to Mile's level, Miles whispered, "Well, you know how girls can be sometimes. Seems like they always want boys they like to never see their hair all messed up, or them not looking pretty all the time."

Charlie turned red and smiled sheepishly. "Do you think Evaline really likes me? Did she ever tell you she likes me? What did she say that makes you think she likes me?"

"Well, she never really came right out and said it, but you know... well...you know, she looks at you a little differently than she does Ma and me."

"Gee whiz! Maybe she does like me and just doesn't want me to know it. Wouldn't that blow the roof off the barn?" Charlie said, ignoring Miles.

In Evaline's room, Drucella sat on the bed watching Evaline brush her hair with furious strokes. "Evaline, now you listen to me," Drucella said. "Charlie came here to see you, and you will go out there and be polite to him."

"Momma, I'm not going out there," Evaline protested.

"You get yourself ready and get out there in the next two minutes, or I'll drag you out there. You know I'll do it." Drucella met Evaline's eyes in the mirror. They stared each other down. Evaline blinked first.

"Okay, Momma. If it will make you happy, I'll be out in a few minutes." She put down the brush and stood up. Drucella noticed for the first time that Evaline had already changed into her Christmas clothes. She left, shutting the door quietly behind her, then went to the kitchen, got Charlie his cup of coffee, and headed back into the living room.

Charlie turned expectantly when he heard the footsteps from the hall. He hoped he didn't look disappointed when Drucella handed him his coffee. "Sorry about barging in on you all so early," he said to her, "but I wanted to give you these presents."

"Why, that's awful nice of you, Charlie Wills! I'm sorry we didn't get you something, but we've all been so busy. I guess we just plum forgot. We would consider it a real honor if you would eat Christmas dinner with us. You know you are more than welcome. We'll eat around one o'clock."

That'll give me a chance to see Evaline again today, Charlie thought. "Yes ma'am. I'm happy to do that, but I can't eat much. I'll have to eat again with my folks at four."

Miles eyed the presents Charlie had brought. He wondered how he could work them into the conversation without appearing too anxious. He checked his new watch again. "According to my Bulova wristwatch the time is now a quarter till. Charlie, do you think this would be a good time to open our presents?"

"Sure, Miles. I can't think of a better time to open them than on Christmas Day!"

The presents were still on the hearth where Charlie had placed them. He reached down and handed one to Miles and another to Drucella. Miles' present was small, about the same size as the box his watch had come in. He quickly opened it and threw the paper in the fireplace.

"Wow! Thanks, Charlie! Thanks a lot!"

"Well, you can't learn to play the harmonica if you don't have one, can you?"

Miles placed the brand new harmonica to his mouth and blew softly, testing it out. It didn't sound at all like Charlie's harmonica had sounded. He grinned at Charlie. "It's not as easy to play as I thought it would be."

Drucella was beginning to enjoy receiving presents. She was almost as excited as Miles. "Why, Charlie! A box of candy! How nice of you to think of me. It's been years since anyone gave me a box of candy."

"Ma, are you going to open your candy now?" Miles asked, looking at the box hungrily.

"Why, sure. We'll let Charlie have the first piece." Drucella took off the lid and handed the box to Charlie.

Charlie looked down into the box. "Let me see. I don't like those gooey pieces. I sort of like the ones that have the nuts inside."

"Well, would you look at this? There's a picture inside the box lid that shows what's inside every piece of candy," Drucella said and she handed the top of the box to Charlie.

Miles thought Charlie had studied the diagram of the chocolates for a long time before Charlie slowly reached down into the box. "Why, I think I'll have this one right here. It has a walnut inside it. Yeah, I'll have this one. I just love walnuts."

When the box and lid were finally passed his way, Miles took only the box. Candy is candy, he thought. He reached into the box and picked out the largest piece he could find.

Evaline, who had been watching from the hallway, came into the room in time to see her mother open the candy. She announced her presence as she stepped into the room to join them. "Decisions,

decisions! Seems like everyone's always making these important decisions. I'm sure glad President Roosevelt doesn't have important decisions like this to make every day!"

They all looked up at Evaline. She wore a plaid skirt, white blouse and red button-up sweater. Her long dark hair shone, and her cheeks were rosy from the cool spring water she had used to wash her face.

"You sure look pretty," Miles said.

"Yeah, you sure do," Charlie agreed. "Why, you look as pretty as a speckled pup hiding under a red wagon with yellow wheels on it."

"Well, I don't know whether that's a compliment, or not. I don't think I've ever been compared to a speckled pup, or a red wagon," Evaline said playfully. "Why don't you go ahead and get me a speckled pup so I can see just how cute that is?"

"I don't think we need a dog here," Drucella said. "You know, we like to have never got rid of that one-eyed cat that Miles kept feeding." No one was paying attention. Charlie and Evaline were smiling at each other, and Miles was eyeing that last present, still wrapped on the hearth.

"Evaline, Charlie brought each of us a Christmas present," Miles said. "I got a harmonica and Ma got the box of candy. Your present is by the fireplace. Are you going to open it?"

"Yes, if that's okay with Charlie."

"Well, sure it's okay. That's why I came by so early. I couldn't wait to see you open it."

Charlie handed Evaline a small box wrapped neatly in white tissue paper, probably wrapped by Charlie's mama. Drucella leaned forward in her chair and smiled at Evaline. Evaline opened the box, her eyes widening in surprise and delight. She held up a bracelet, one end in each hand, and stretched it before her face. "Why, Charlie

Wills! This is the most beautiful bracelet I ever saw!" Then she turned the bracelet so everyone else could see. "Look, Miles, it has my name engraved on it!"

"It sure does. It's an ID bracelet, and my name's engraved on the other side," Charlie said quickly.

"Well, Charlie," Evaline teased, "you didn't have to do that. I know how to spell your name."

"And it's gold-plated, too," Miles said.

"Look, Momma!" Evaline said to Drucella. "Look what Charlie got me. Do you like it?"

"I sure do! It's awfully pretty, but I wish Charlie hadn't spent so…"

Charlie interrupted, "Oh, don't go worrying about that, Mrs. Hudson. My Pa's sawmill had a good year, and he gave me and my brother Adam thirty-dollars apiece for a Christmas bonus. That's not even counting our paychecks!"

"Wow! Thirty dollars apiece!" Miles exclaimed. "I sure wish I worked for your Pa!"

Evaline, thought suddenly about Katherine Hepburn, the actress she had just been reading about in her movie magazine before Charlie arrived. Evaline admired the actress' boldness. She wondered just what Miss Hepburn would do in a situation like this. Whatever she did, it would be bold.

Evaline held her head back, smiled and walked over to Charlie. She put her arms around his big shoulders, stood on her tiptoes and kissed Charlie right on the lips.

Drucella quickly turned and walked back into the kitchen. This could be serious.

For the first time all morning, Miles was at a loss for words. He just stood there with his mouth open, blushing with disbelief.

Charlie tried to say something, but he could not speak either. His mouth moved, but no words came out.

"Well, that's my present to you, Charlie Wills. I hope you liked it," Evaline said, taking one step back and looking Charlie in the eye.

Charlie finally composed himself enough to speak. "Holy cow! I think I just got the best Christmas present of my life!" Charlie looked at his watch. It was eight-fifteen, and he felt if he didn't leave now he might wake up and find out he was only dreaming. He wanted to be by himself and think about what Miles had said about Evaline liking him. He wanted to remember the look on her face when she opened her present. Most of all, he wanted to remember the kiss she had just given to him.

"This has been some Christmas," he said, opening the door. "I'm going to check on the heater in my pickup, but I'll be back by twelve-thirty for dinner."

Charlie was as good as his word. At exactly twelve-thirty, he crossed the swinging bridge, walked up the wooden plank steps and knocked on the Hudson's door.

When Evaline opened the door, the aroma of turkey and dressing surrounded him. Evaline was wearing her bracelet. She kept looking down to make sure it had not fallen off.

Miles had the harmonica in his hands when he greeted Charlie. "Maybe I could get a lesson on my harmonica after dinner."

Drucella, drying her hands on a dish towel, came to the door to welcome him. "I'm glad you're back," she said.

Charlie felt warm. This felt like family.

After dinner Charlie sat down in the rocking chair by the fireplace, and Evaline sat on the hearth beside him. She put her hand inside Charlie's, and they watched the fire. They did not speak. There was no need.

Miles sat on the couch, content with everyone around him. This was his best Christmas ever.

EIGHT

Y es, it had been a wonderful Christmas morning, but the best part of Christmas is still ahead of us, thought Drucella, as she turned her collar up and placed her ear muffs over her ears. She had wrapped the left-over string beans, and the turkey and dressing, in wax paper and placed the food in a paper box. She also placed in the box the rag doll she had been working on for the last month. The rag doll, which was for Gloria Thomas, age 6, was nearly identical to a Raggedy Ann doll she had recently seen in a store window. The "Raggedy Ann" Drucella had made had red hair, the same color of Gloria's red hair, and the same color of the hair of the Raggedy Ann in the window. Drucella was excited and couldn't wait to see Gloria's face when she opened the box. In order to also have a gift for Jack, Gloria's brother, Drucella had gone to Miles' room and got from his closet a toy Gun and Holster, a gift he had received last Christmas, but had never played with because he felt he'd outgrown toy guns.

Even though very eager to deliver the gifts to the Thomas family, Drucella took time to invite all the family to go with her. As soon as Charlie, now feeling part of the family, heard Evaline say she was going with Drucella, and mostly because he wanted to be with Evaline, he said he also wanted to go. Miles was still considering the invitation, but once he realized they'd be going in Charlie's pick-up truck, and since only three could fit in the cab, he'd have no choice but to ride in the back of the truck in icy cold weather, he told Drucella he'd decided not to go.

When Charlie, Drucella, and Evaline, pulled up in front of the Thomas house, Mr. Thomas came out to meet them. Drucella spoke first. "Hello Mr. Thomas, sure hope you won't be insulted with all this left-over turkey and dressing!"

"Thanks, but we don't accept charity."

"I knew that already," said Drucella, "and that's why I brought you a bill. It's for $5 to be exact, and I expect you to pay me when you get work, or you can pay me now, either way's okay with me."

Mr. Thomas looked back toward his house, then at the box, then at Drucella. "Be glad to make that deal, Drucella, and I will pay you back."

Drucella saw that Gloria and Jack were watching everything from the Thomas living room window. Mr. Thomas didn't speak, just looked back once again at Gloria and Jack, and realizing they had no idea he had agreed to accept the gift, he nodded yes.

Just as Drucella had planned, the Raggedy Ann doll went to Gloria, and the Gun and Holster set went to Jack. Gloria, who seemed thrilled beyond words, put both arms around the doll and held it close to her chest. Jack, equally thrilled, buckled the Gun and Holster around his waist, and wandered up to his room to play.

Charlie, feeling somewhat left out, told Mr. Thomas he had been asked to deliver a message. "Mr. Thomas, my dad's been thinking about hiring another man to help at the sawmill. He said it would be part-time, but if you were interested, he'd like very much to talk with you about coming to work for him."

For the first time since they'd arrived with the gifts, they saw Mr. Thomas smile, ever so slightly, but it was a smile. "If he hires me, Charlie, I won't let him down, you can be sure of that."

On the ride back, no one spoke. Finally, and just before they arrived back home, Drucella, who seemed to sense what she, Charlie, and Evaline had been thinking, put their thoughts into words.

"This must be the true feeling of Christmas!"

NINE

The storm clouds of war were now racing across Europe. Britain had declared war on Germany, and everyone wondered how long it would take before the United States would have to enter the conflict. The country had taken on a somber mood. Yet people still went to movies, listened to their favorite radio programs, laughed, talked and tried to forget their concerns over the United States having to fight a Second World War.

The last days of Miles' vacation rapidly slipped away. As he prepared for bed Sunday night, he dreaded getting up early and going back to school the next morning. Lying in bed, he thought about the Christmas vacation. He remembered all the delightful mornings sleeping until eight o'clock in his feather bed with the warm covers piled up under his chin. It seemed like he had no more than closed his eyes when his 7 a.m. alarm sounded.

As Miles reached over to turn off the alarm, a severe pain shot through the middle of his stomach. Fighting body aches he hadn't noticed last night, he pulled himself into a sitting position. The pain intensified. He shivered as he wrapped the blanket around his arms and legs to keep warm.

"Time to get up, Miles," Drucella called out from the kitchen.

"Ma, I don't feel good."

"It's a funny thing that you don't get sick until the day you have to go back to school," she said.

"I'm freezing one minute, and burning up the next. I feel sick at my stomach, too."

Drucella came in and placed her hand on Miles' forehead. "Evaline, honey. Come in here and feel his forehead. Why, his head's hotter than blue blazes!"

"Ma, my stomach hurts, and my legs and arms are aching all over." He moaned and shivered, pulling at the covers again.

Evaline, already dressed for work, was having a last cup of coffee. She hurried in and sat beside Miles on the bed. She frowned the moment she laid her palm across his forehead. "Momma, he's bad sick. What are we going to do?"

"The first thing we are going to do is try to get his temperature down," said Drucella. "Evaline, get me some washcloths and a pan of cold water. I'll take his temperature."

Evaline moved quickly. Upon returning, she handed Drucella the thermometer and placed the pan of cold water, containing the wash cloths, on the little table by Miles' bed. Drucella placed the thermometer under Miles' tongue, and wrung out one of the cool washcloths and placed it on Miles' forehead. Upon removing the thermometer, Drucella exclaimed, "Lord, have mercy! His temperature is a hundred-and-three!" She then shouted, "Evaline!" Looking up, she saw Evaline and seemed to have forgotten that Evaline was right beside her. "Thank God you're ready. Go on to work and call Doc Riley. We need him to come to the house as soon as he can get here."

Evaline didn't need any urging. She was out the door and headed for the store almost at a run.

Drucella knew that it would be a while before Doc Riley could get to their house. She didn't begin watching for him from the window until ten o'clock, but when he finally arrived at almost noon she was put out by the wait. She saw him take his small black bag from his car. He crossed the swinging bridge and walked up to the door. He didn't have to knock.

"Sorry I'm so long in getting here," Doc Riley said as Drucella held the door open, "but this flu is all over town. I was making house calls last night at ten o'clock."

"Well, my boy is awful sick, Doc. Just how bad is it?" Drucella wrung her hands and glanced toward Miles' room.

"Drucella, I'm not going to lie to you. It can be really bad. It makes some folks sicker than others. Nobody rightly knows why."

"Do you know of anyone dying from it?"

"I'm afraid I do, Cella. Two older people died last week up on Mason's Creek, and a little feller about six years old down on Walker's Branch didn't make it either." Doc Riley took off his hat and put it on the chair. He clutched his bag under one arm and nodded toward the hallway. "Is he in his room?"

Drucella led Doc Riley to Miles' bedroom. The boy's face was flushed and his undershirt soaked with sweat. Doc sat on the bed and opened his bag beside him. "Now Miles, hold out your tongue," Doc Riley directed, placing his thermometer underneath it. After a minute or two, Doc Riley removed it. "This boy has a bad case of the flu. His temperature is a hundred-and-three. That's way too high. I think he needs to go to the Mount Mary. We need to get his fever down. Get a blanket and wrap it around him. I'll take him in my car," said Doc Riley, as he stood up and was closing his bag. Drucella was silent. He turned to look at her.

Drucella's chin was stuck out stubbornly, and her mouth was closed in a tight line. She shook her head back and forth. Finally she spoke. "No, Doc. He won't be going to no hospital. That's final."

"But, Cella, this boy could…"

"No, he's not going. I've seen too many people go to hospitals, and most of the time they end up dying there. He is not going, and that's the end of it."

"Now, Cella, I can't make you put him in the hospital, but if his fever doesn't come down soon you're going to be running a big risk."

Miles raised his head up. "Ma, I don't want to go to the hospital," he said weakly. "I'm feeling a little better." Slowly, he put his head back down.

"How much do we owe you, Doc?" Drucella asked.

"If you don't take my advice, I can't do you any good." Doc Riley shrugged, his hands open, palms up, in front of him. He paused a moment, hoping Drucella would change her mind. Finally he sighed. "I'll only charge you a dollar for making the trip up the hollow. But Drucella, you must keep putting those cold towels on his head, and be sure he drinks plenty of water."

Doc Riley closed his bag and walked out the bedroom door.

"Doc, would you please stop by Anderson's Store and tell Evaline I need her to come home," Drucella said, sinking back down onto the edge of the bed, and never taking her eyes off Miles' face.

"Yes and maybe she can talk some sense into your head. I sure can't."

Evaline had made several mistakes that morning as she went about her work in the store. She couldn't think about anything but Miles. She had told Doris about the fever and Miles' aches. After Doc Riley delivered Drucella's message, Doris said, "Evaline, honey, why don't you get ready and go on home. I know you're worried to death about your brother. You can help Drucella. We'll be okay without you."

For the second time today, Evaline ran down the road between the store and her house. When she came to the front door she was out of breath. She went straight to Miles' room.

Drucella heard her come in. "Evaline! Miles' temperature is still a hundred and three. It just won't come down." Drucella was sitting beside Miles, wiping his forehead with cold cloths and looking frightened just as she had been when Evaline left earlier. But now she looked tired, too.

Evaline felt Miles' forehead again for herself. "Momma, Doc Riley says he needs to go to the hospital."

"I know what Doctor Riley said, but Miles is not going to the hospital." She stood up and faced Evaline. "Now you listen to me! I want you to sit down, drink a cup of coffee and rest. After you get rested, I want you to go to the top of the mountain and get Silver-Eyed Jane to come and get rid of this fever."

"Silver-Eyed Jane?" Evaline cried. "Momma, I'm afraid of her! I've never been to the top of the mountain before!"

"Don't you be afraid of Jane." Drucella put her hand on Evaline's shoulder. "She won't hurt you. I've known her since grade school."

"Momma, couldn't we get Charlie to go to the top of the mountain and tell her we need her?" Evaline pleaded.

"You've got to listen to me," Drucella explained. "We don't have much time left. I didn't tell you, but Miles has been talking out of his head. He said something about a train with a red caboose. We don't have any time to waste. Now you got to have faith in me like I have faith Jane can break this fever!"

"Are you sure it's the right thing to do?" asked Evaline quietly. She heard Miles moan, and she and Drucella both turned to look at him.

"I'm not sure of anything except what I have seen with my own eyes when Jane was a little girl," Drucella said. "She has powers that are not of this world, ones that normal people just don't have."

"Okay, I don't need the coffee. I'll go, but if I'm not back in an hour, you better come looking for me."

"Land sakes alive, child! Do you really think I would send you to the top of that mountain if I thought anything would happen to you? Jane just acts mean so people won't come around and bother her. I guess she's afraid someone will find out where she stores all that moonshine she sells."

Drucella followed Evaline to the door and gave her a quick, fierce hug before she left. As she watched Evaline heading up the path toward the barn and the mountain, she remembered the first miracle she had ever seen Silver-Eyed Jane perform. There had been a logger cutting timber who cut his foot nearly off. The doctors brought him out of the woods on a blanket. Drucella's Pa's house was close by, so they brought the logger to their place to try and stop the bleeding. They were about to take him to the hospital when his wife showed up. She told the doctors he wasn't going to no hospital because he would bleed to death before they could get him there. She also told the doctors she was going to send for that little girl who could see people no one else could see, the little girl who had powers and could stop the bleeding.

Later, while the two doctors watched, Jane had laid hands on that logger's foot and said, "This bleeding will stop before I get back home." And the bleeding completely stopped before Jane was out of sight. The doctors hadn't known what to say. They just shook their heads and said they had never seen anything like it. That evening, those doctors had gone to Jane's house and offered to pay her Ma and Pa if they could get Jane to tell them how to stop bleeding. But Jane hadn't told them anything—only that if she did tell them, the Lord would take her powers away.

Remembering the story, Drucella bowed her head and said a little prayer: "Lord, please guide her through this journey." As she did so, she realized that she was praying for Evaline in her journey up the mountain, and for Silver-Eyed Jane in her journey to cure Miles.

Evaline hurried up the path past the barn. She paused at the open gate and looked up the mountain. Brownie, their Jersey milk cow, grazed at the foot of the path just outside the gate. "Brownie, I wish you were a person and not a cow. If you were a person, you could go with me to the top of the mountain. I bet you would protect me, wouldn't you old girl?" She petted Brownie's nose and passed through the gate.

Saw briars clung to the sleeves of her dress as she pushed through the undergrowth on the seldom used path. Occasionally, she stopped to pick off a saw briar which made it through her sleeve and pricked into her arm. She pushed away low hanging branches that lashed back into her face. With every step she took, she had to be careful not to step on the glass from broken moonshine jars. She felt the cold wind on her face as she reached the top of the mountain. As she looked down, she could see white smoke coming from the chimney of her house in the valley below, and was amazed at how small her house looked from the top of the mountain.

She followed a small path that led around the ridge. It was a narrow ledge wide enough to walk on, but not wide enough to walk on if you were in too big a hurry or got careless. She wondered how Jane's customers got their jars of moonshine past this point and how did Miles get their beautiful Christmas tree around the ledge? She walked slowly over the ledge, not daring to look down at the jagged cliff below her.

Safely past the ledge, she could see Silver-Eyed Jane's house. Evaline had heard stories about how birds and raccoons let Jane know if someone was approaching her cabin. Evaline's fear of Silver-Eyed Jane grew with each step she took. To combat her fear, she began to softly sing to herself.

The barking of two chained dogs interrupted Evaline's singing. A thin, little lady wearing a long gray dress, and a black apron tied around her waist, stepped out from behind a pine tree. It was Silver-Eyed Jane. Her shoes looked worn, and they were strung up past her ankles. She was smoking a corncob pipe, and she had a rifle pointed straight at Evaline's heart.

"Don't take another step, girl. I got a bead on you. What business you got coming up here on my mountain? Only two reasons a body comes up here. One is to buy moonshine. Another is to have their fortune told. Give me some answers before I get an itchy trigger finger, girl."

Evaline froze, staring straight at Silver-Eyed Jane. She knew Jane was her momma's age, but with Jane's wrinkled, weather-beaten face, Jane looked much older. Her left eye was almost completely shut, and with the silver color that encircled it, she was a frightening sight.

Evaline was ready to turn and run back down the mountain when a black crow flew out of the top of the pine tree. It lit on the barrel of Jane's rifle. "Damn you, Timmy! Get the hell off my gun!"

The crow flew from the barrel of her gun and landed on Evaline's shoulder. Evaline quickly turned her head away from the crow, in case it tried to peck her cheek.

"Don't worry, honey, he won't hurt you," Jane said. "He won't land on anyone he doesn't trust. So, I'm asking you again, what business do you have on my mountain?" The gun was still aimed at her.

Scared and confused, Evaline lashed out. "I'll tell you something, Miss Silver-Eyed Jane! I never wanted to come up here on your mountain in the first place, but my momma sent me here!"

Jane lowered the gun. "What did she send you here for?"

"My brother's got a fever that won't go away, and his temperature is a hundred-and-three. Momma says he's talking out of his head, and you're the only one who can take his fever away."

"She's right about that. So, who's your momma, girl?"

"Drucella Hudson. I'm Evaline."

"I know your momma! I've known her since I was a little girl. I always liked Cella. She never said mean things about me or passed judgment on me."

"Can you make his fever go away?" She thought of Miles, burning with fever and of Doc Riley saying he needed to go to the hospital.

"Why, as sure as you're a foot high I can take a fever away. If I have a mind to do it. Go home and tell your momma not to worry none. I'll get some things from my cellar. Timmy and me won't be far behind you."

Evaline jumped as Timmy flew off her shoulder and into the woods. When Jane saw that Evaline was afraid of the crow, Jane thought no need for that, and decided to do something about it. Looking at Evaline, Jane nodded in the direction Timmy had just flown away. "Now, let me tell you about Timmy. Well, I found him early one morning after a bad storm came across Jack Lot Mountain. He had a broken wing and was almost dead. I healed him up, and now he follows me everywhere I go." Silver-Eyed Jane took a puff from her corncob pipe and walked back toward her cabin.

"I'll go tell my Momma you're coming," Evaline said and she turned toward the Path that led down the mountain. She hoped the faith her momma had in Silver-Eyed Jane's powers was justified, and she prayed those powers could save her brother.

TEN

rucella was sitting on the edge of Miles' bed when she heard Evaline burst in the back door. Drucella rushed to the kitchen. "Thank God, you're back! His temperature is still a hundred and three. He's been sleeping ever since you left, except when he wakes up and talks out of his head. Did you see Jane? Is she coming down from the mountain?"

"Yes, Momma, she's coming. It won't be long now. I just saw Timmy, her pet crow, light on the porch rail. Timmy follows her everywhere she goes."

In no more than 10 minutes or so Drucella and Evaline were startled by a loud knock at the front door. "Thank God!" Drucella exclaimed. "I don't think I could take much more of this! Open the door Evaline, and be sure to do everything she tells you."

"Don't worry, Momma," said Evaline. "Whatever she says, I'll do!"

Silver-Eyed Jane was a scary sight as she stepped inside. Her gray hair hung over her forehead and eyebrows. Smoke curled out of the corncob pipe stuck in her mouth, and a burlap bag hung over her shoulder. She slowly looked around the room as she placed her bag on a chair. She turned and looked at Drucella and Evaline. "Lord, honey, it's been years since I saw you, Cella. Why, you got a right nice place here."

"Thank you, Jane. Thank you for coming to help my boy," Drucella said.

"That's all right, honey. You and your girl warm up that cook stove. I'm going to make him some sassafras tea to cleanse his body after I take away his fever. Have your girl get me the biggest pan you got, and fill it up with cold water. I'll need it after I take away this fever!"

Drucella and Evaline filled the stove with firewood. The flames flared, and soon coffee began perking in the metal pot.

In his bedroom, Miles tossed and turned, talking out of his head. The fever had a firm grip on his body now. His fate rested in Silver-Eyed Jane's hands.

Evaline brought the large pan of cold water and placed it on a cane bottom chair beside the bed. Drucella watched near the doorway. She covered her mouth with her hand, worry and concern blanketing her face. Drucella realized that the next few minutes would decide whether Miles would make it through the night. She was afraid she might do or say something that would prevent Jane's healing powers from working. She closed her eyes and softly whispered, "Please, God. Please!"

Jane encircled Miles' head with her palms. Miles shivered out of control as she put her hands on his face and began to speak.

"Fever that has possessed this body all day, I command you to go away. Let go of his soul and come into my hands. Fever! You have heard my command."

Miles' head turned back and forth. He groaned as Silver-Eyed Jane's hands moved across his face.

Evaline could see the color of Jane's hands changing from soft brown to bright red. Silver-Eyed Jane closed her eyes and held her hands on Miles' face for another minute or so. When she removed them, her hands were now blood-red. She placed them in the large pan of cold water. The water made a hissing sound and steam rose from the pan.

Evaline gasped. Drucella wrung her hands silently.

"Now, girl," Silver-Eyed Jane said to Evaline, "take this pan of water outside and throw it out." She took a small towel from the foot of the bed and wiped her hands and face dry.

"The fever is gone, and it won't come back," Jane proclaimed as Evaline came back into the room.

Evaline and Drucella looked at each other in relief and disbelief. Drucella walked to Miles bed. She took his hand, sandwiched in between her hands and squeezed it lightly. "I love you," she whispered.

Evaline's hand was on Drucella's shoulder. Evaline looked down at her brother, his face pale, but his breathing normal and his body more relaxed than it had been for hours. Gently, she pulled the covers up over his arms.

Evaline and Drucella followed Silver-Eyed Jane into the kitchen where she took a large wooden spoon and began stirring the sassafras tea. She reached into her bag and took out a small jar and poured the contents into the tea. "Now, Cella, don't let this boy out of the house for the next two days. Make him drink two cups of this tea each day for a few days. It will give him strength and cleanse his blood."

"I'll sure do that, Jane, and I want to pay you whatever you want for what you've done for us."

"Pay me?" Silver-Eyed Jane exclaimed. "Why, Cella, don't you know you been paying me for years? You paid me when you spoke to me on the street while other people were crossing to the other side so they didn't have to look at me. You paid me when the children called me names at school, and you came over to put your arm around me.

You've been paying me for years, and now I got to do something for you." Jane walked to the door and opened it to step outside.

"Thank you, Miss Jane," Evaline said. "Thank you for giving Miles back to us."

"You're welcome, girl. You can come up on my mountain anytime." Jane smiled.

"Thank you, Miss Jane," Evaline said again. "I need to know one thing though. Would you have shot me for coming up on your mountain?"

"Now, don't you go and tell anyone, girl, but that old gun hasn't been loaded in years! My great-grandfather brought it home after the Civil War. It's been hanging over the fireplace ever since. Why, if people knew that, they would be all over my mountain. Picnicking, shooting birds, starting fires. It would be the worst mess you ever saw!"

"Well, if you wouldn't have shot me, then I would love to come visit you sometime. Could I ask one other thing of you before you go?"

"Why, I guess so. What is it?"

"Could you call me Evaline once before you go?" Evaline asked. "And could I give you a hug?"

Silver-Eyed Jane looked confused. For the first time in her life she didn't know what to say. She couldn't imagine anyone wanting to give her a hug. She didn't look at Evaline. She looked down on the pine floor of the kitchen. "Well, Evaline, I guess that would be all right," Jane answered.

Evaline hugged Jane and patted her thin back. "Thank you, Miss Jane."

Silver-Eyed Jane opened the door and stepped outside onto the front porch. Her hand was holding the door handle. The cold wind rushed inside the house. She appeared to be undecided whether to say anything else, or just close the door and leave. As the door slowly closed behind her, she said softly, "Goodbye, Cella, and thank you for the hug, Miss Evaline."

Drucella and Evaline watched through the window as Timmy flew down from the top of the porch and landed on her shoulder. The two slowly disappeared into the evening shadows.

Miles soon awoke with his fever completely gone. Although he was still weak, his face was no longer flushed and his skin no longer clammy.

Drucella fell asleep in the rocking chair by the fireplace. It had been one of the worst days of her life. But the danger had passed.

ELEVEN

I t was one of those winter evenings when the clouds dropped down between the mountains. The air was warm with a misty rain.

Evaline walked hurriedly over the road and into Jack Lot Hollow, eager to get home to the glow of the fireplace and the hot supper she knew awaited her. There would be pork shoulder, biscuits and the last of the beets and corn that she and Drucella had put up last summer. Evaline placed her hand inside her coat pocket to make sure she hadn't forgotten the two Baby Ruth candy bars she was taking home to Miles.

Darkness had settled in, making it hard for Evaline to see the road in front of her. She approached the old, abandoned coal tipple in the distance. The tipple was a processing plant, built many years ago by Jack Lot Mining, for sizing and loading coal into railroad cars to be shipped to Jack Lot's customers in Ohio and Michigan. The wooden structure was three stories high, with chutes that funneled the coal into the rail cars on the tracks below.

As Evaline got closer to the tipple, she heard a clanging noise that seemed to be coming from inside. It sounded as if a piece of the old tin roof had come loose, and the wind was moving it back and forth.

Evaline looked high up into the sycamore tree and saw the branches weren't moving. The wind wasn't blowing. She quickened her pace. She glimpsed a movement out of the corner of her eye, but before she could turn her head to see what it was, someone gave her a hard push from behind. Surprised, she stumbled and hit the gravel road on her hands and knees.

Before she could recover, her attacker reached down, placed his hands around her neck and began choking her. She could smell alcohol as she tried to turn and fight off her aggressor, but he had the advantage. As Evaline searched for some way of defending herself, her fumbling hands came into contact with a rock. Evaline was strong and athletic, a fighter, and now she had a weapon within reach. The tables had turned. Now she had the advantage. She made another futile effort to turn and see her opponent.

His hands tightened around her throat. He wasn't about to let her turn and get a look at his face. Putting her weight on her left forearm, Evaline picked up the rock with her right hand. She thrust her arm back and up and delivered a sharp blow to his ribcage. Once, twice, and then a third time. His stranglehold loosened as he gasped for air. Then he released her entirely and tried to grab her arm.

But Evaline had anticipated his reaction. Now she saw her chance. She slammed the rock against the side of her attacker's head. He fell to the ground. By the time he pulled himself up on all fours, Evaline was on her feet. He began crawling away. Evaline found another rock, heavier than the first, and staggered within a few feet of the man. She drew back and threw the rock into his back with all her force. He gave out a groan, got to his feet and disappeared into the night.

Evaline staggered to the side of the road and found her handbag. She reached down to her wrist to make sure her bracelet was still there. She picked up another rock and put it inside her coat pocket in case the man decided to return. Her throat felt sore. Her knees and hands stung from the scrapes and cuts from the gravel road.

She pushed her fear down deep inside and focused on getting home, one step at a time.

It was almost impossible to follow the small road home in the dark. Evaline walked very slowly, waiting for the moon to come out from behind a cloud. Once the moon appeared, she walked as fast as she could before the moon found another cloud to hide behind.

As she walked around the last bend in the road, she saw her house. The front porch light shone brightly. As she crossed the swinging bridge, she could see Charlie Wills' pickup parked beside the road. She could hear voices coming from the front porch, and knew Charlie, her Mom, and Miles, were no doubt very worried about her. "Momma, don't worry. I'm all right," Evaline called out as she hurried up the path.

Charlie and Miles ran down to meet her. "Are you sure?" Miles asked. "You sure you're all right, Evaline?" Charlie couldn't see the cuts and bruises in the dark, but he knew her voice didn't sound exactly all right.

Charlie picked her up in his arms and carried her the rest of the way to the house. Evaline didn't resist. She was too tired from the fight and the long walk home.

"Evaline! Good Lord, what happened to you?" Drucella asked from the porch. "Why, we've been worried sick! Charlie just came by, and he was going out to look for you."

With Evaline in his arms, Charlie stepped onto the porch. Drucella gasped. Miles jumped ahead and opened the door. Inside the house, Evaline began to protest. "Put me down," she said. But Charlie had seen the cuts and dirt on her, too. He took her directly to the kitchen and put her down by the sink.

"Evaline, what happened to you?" Drucella asked again as she got out a clean towel.

Evaline splashed water on her hands and face and patted herself with the towel. "Momma, some lowdown coward jumped me from behind as I walked by the coal tipple. Don't worry. I'm all right, and I'll be a lot better as soon as I find out who the coward is!" Evaline began washing the dirt from her knees and told them about the attack.

Although Evaline insisted that she really wasn't hurt, Drucella worried. "Why don't you go lie down on the couch?" Drucella suggested. "And I'll bring in the smelling salts, just in case you get to feeling faint." She headed to the kitchen cabinet where they kept the smelling salts.

"Don't get those out. I won't need smelling salts," said Evaline, getting to her feet.

Charlie came to Evaline's side and she thought he might just try to pick her up again and carry her to the couch, so she shot him a fierce, independent look and walked to the living room on her own power. Charlie followed close behind.

"I'll go get your pillow for you," Miles volunteered and turned down the hall toward Evaline's room. He retrieved the pillow and handed it to Evaline, who settled herself onto the couch.

Charlie looked down at Evaline lying on the couch. Her cheeks were bruised, and there were red handprints on her neck. Her hands and knees were pitted from the gravel road. Charlie put his hand on Evaline's shoulder. She flinched involuntarily.

"I'll be okay, Charlie," she said, trying to smile at him. "I'm just so damned mad, I could spit."

Charlie tried to smile back, but he turned away so that Evaline would not see the rage toward her assailant that bubbled up inside of him. Finally he said, "I'm going to drive out of the hollow and see if I see any hint of anyone who looks or acts suspicious. Then I'm going to report this to the Sheriff."

"I'll go with you," Miles said, jumping up from his chair.

"No, you won't. I need you to stay here with me," Drucella said.

"But, Ma! I want to go." Like Evaline, Miles was a fighter when he was angry. He would be proud to confront her attacker and avenge his sister.

"You're not going, and that's final." Drucella stared sternly at Miles until he sat down. Then she turned back to Charlie who had already crossed to the door. "You go ahead, Charlie. Let us know what you find out."

"I'll do that, Mrs. Hudson, but if I find out who did this, there won't be much to let anyone know about. I'll take care of him myself!"

"Now, Charlie, we got to let the law take care of the varmint who did this! There's no sense in you doing something and getting into trouble when the law can handle it," Drucella warned.

Charlie opened the door to his pickup and slid across the leather seat and under the steering wheel. He reached under his seat and felt his thirty-eight Smith & Wesson pistol in its holster. He pulled it from under the seat and released the button on the side. He flipped out the cylinder to make sure it was loaded. He placed the gun on the seat beside him and slowly drove out of the hollow.

Charlie kept moving his eyes back and forth to both sides of the road to make sure he didn't miss anything unusual. He stopped at the coal tipple, took out his flashlight and shined it all around the inside of the tipple. Satisfied the attacker was out of the hollow, Charlie drove into town.

Hazard seemed darker than normal as Charlie drove down Main Street. The flashing red-and-orange neon signs reflected off the wet pavement. Charlie couldn't help but view everyone on the street with suspicion. He pulled into a parking space in front of the courthouse.

He reached down into the seat, picked up his pistol and placed it back in its holster under the seat.

After locking the doors to his pick-up, Charlie hurriedly climbed the steps to the courthouse. He opened the heavy door and proceeded down the long hall. All the doors on either side were closed and locked except the one at the end. That door was partly open, and a light glowed from inside. A sign printed on the glass window of the door read, **Sheriff of Perry County, Coleman Sizemore**.

Charlie walked over and lightly tapped on the glass window. A voice from inside said, "Come in. The door's open."

Sheriff Sizemore sat at his desk. He was a stout, heavyset man in his late forties, wearing a khaki shirt and khaki pants—the uniform he always wore. His black shoes were always shined and his gold badge was pinned just above his left shirt pocket where he routinely kept a pack of Camel cigarettes.

"Well, Charlie Wills. What in heaven's name brings you to my office this time of night?" Sheriff Sizemore inquired. He knew from the look on Charlie's face that this was no social call.

Charlie stood in the doorway and took a deep breath. "Sheriff! Some lowdown skunk attacked Evaline Hudson at the Jack Lot coal tipple tonight while she was on her way home."

"That sounds pretty serious. Is she okay?"

"Yeah, she's okay. She fought back, and from what I understand from Evaline, it sounds like her attacker got the worst of it!"

"Why don't you sit down?" the Sheriff asked, nodding to the chair in front of his desk. He then reached into his shirt pocket, took out a small black notebook and began writing as Charlie crossed the room and sat on the edge of the chair.

"Charlie, I need to talk to Evaline. For the time being, though, why don't you tell me exactly what she said?"

Charlie relayed what Evaline had told him.

"Well, I'll be damned!" exclaimed the Sheriff when Charlie finished. "God Almighty! She must take after her Pa! Why, I was in the war with Landon, and he was one of the toughest SOBs I ever saw. Sounds like the attacker must have jumped on a mountain lion to me! You sure she's okay?"

"She's doing all right," Charlie answered. "But she has some bruises on her neck and hands. Her knees are scratched up pretty good. Other than that, she's fine."

The Sheriff picked a book of matches up off his desk, lit up a Camel and leaned back in his chair. He puffed on the cigarette, and seemed lost in thought.

"Charlie, are you aware of an argument young Miles had with Black Hart James a few days before Christmas in the Five and Dime?" he asked.

"No," Charlie answered, surprised. "I didn't know anything about that."

"I haven't gotten around to looking into it yet, but from what I heard through the grapevine, they had a pretty good screaming match." He didn't say that someone had told him Evaline's name had come up during the screaming match. "Something about Miles not wanting to run bets for Black Hart. I never cracked down on Black Hart before because two and three dollar bets don't amount to much, but if I find out he's been using children to run bets for him, he's in big trouble."

"I'll ask Miles about this," Charlie said, getting up from the chair. "But for the time being, I want to see the low-down skunk who attacked Evaline behind bars. You've been a good friend to the Hudsons and I know you're going to do what's got to be done."

"Charlie, you can count on that." Sheriff Sizemore stood and the two men shook hands. "I'll be talking to everyone before this is said and done. Feel free to check back with me from time to time, and I'll keep you up to date."

"Okay, I'll do that." Charlie said. He walked to the door and stopped. He turned back to Sheriff Sizemore who had already sat down and begun reviewing his notes. "Sheriff, I quit smoking two years ago, but after all that's happened, I could sure use one of those Camels."

"Help yourself, Charlie." Sheriff Sizemore tossed the open pack onto his desk.

The following morning, the Sheriff was up early. He had his breakfast at the Bus Station and then drove up Jack Lot Hollow to the Hudson home.

It was around seven o'clock when he knocked on the front door. When Drucella saw the Sheriff, a smile came across her face. They had known each other since grade school.

"Why, Sheriff Coleman Sizemore, won't you come in?" Drucella said sweetly. "It's a real honor to have you here. I just wish it was under better circumstances."

"I do, too, Cella. I know it's early, but I was thinking you all are early risers. If you can give me a few minutes of your time, maybe I can find out who's to blame for all this grief you've been put through."

"Thank you for coming," Drucella said holding the door open. "Evaline and Miles are at the kitchen table." The Sheriff followed Drucella as she led the way. "Come on in the kitchen. Sit down and I'll get you a cup of coffee."

Evaline and Miles sat eating their breakfast silently. Evaline had circles under her eyes. She hadn't slept all night. She kept replaying the attack over and over in her mind as her anger built.

"Morning, folks," Sheriff Sizemore said, pulling a chair out from the table and sitting down. "How are you feeling this morning, Evaline?"

"I'm okay. Just a little sore and scratched up, but I'll be fine."

"Evaline, I talked to Charlie, but now I need to have you tell me exactly what happened at the tipple last night."

Embarrassment and anger reddened Evaline's face as she recalled the attack. Drucella and Miles hung on every word. Their faces were somber; their eyes, hostile. Sheriff Sizemore was well aware that in the southern Appalachian Mountains "blood-kin" ran as deep as the coal embedded in the mountains. Grudges and feuds had been known to last for years, or until settled by a lone gunman's bullet on a dark night. Sheriff Sizemore knew his people, and he could feel the anger in the room.

When Evaline finished, the Sheriff didn't say anything for a minute or two. He simply wrote in his black notebook. Finally, he said, "Charlie told me pretty much the same things you just told me. Is there anything you might have forgotten?"

"No, that's it. Except that I hope you catch that lowdown varmint. I would love to pull his hair out!" Evaline exclaimed.

"It's a shame that you didn't see his face. It's going to make it hard to arrest someone," the Sheriff said.

No one spoke. Everyone was lost in their own thoughts. Sheriff Sizemore took another sip of coffee and then looked Miles in the eye.

"Now, Miles, what's this I hear about you and Black Hart having a big argument in the Five and Dime?"

Miles looked dumbfounded. His face paled. Evaline looked open-mouthed at Miles.

"Black Hart James!" she cried. "I never thought about him, but it could have been him! He's tall and thin, and he's always giving me dirty looks!"

Drucella broke in, "Miles, you better tell us what this is all about. What's with you and that gambler?"

Miles looked at Drucella and then at the Sheriff. He decided he had better confess to Drucella first. "Momma, I know my running bets for Black Hart I was breaking the law, and I promise I'm never going to do that again." Now he looked at the Sheriff. "But, Sheriff, what really started our argument was what Black Hart said about Evaline."

"So tell me what happened in the Five & Dime," Sheriff Sizemore said calmly.

Miles repeated the entire story. By the end, Miles knew from Drucella's reaction that although Drucella might not completely let him off the hook for running bets, for now she was concentrating on Evaline.

Drucella didn't want Evaline to go to work at the store. She said she should stay home and rest at least one day, but Evaline said she wasn't about to let that skunk keep her from going to work. She got ready and rode out of the hollow with the Sheriff.

After dropping Evaline off at Doris Anderson's store, the Sheriff went back to the Bus Station and waited until the nine-thirty bus arrived from Lexington. Part of his morning routine was to meet the Greyhound every day and see who was coming into his town.

It was almost ten o'clock, and most of the breakfast crowd had left when the Sheriff crossed the street to the Five and Dime. Everyone turned to look as he walked into the store and took a seat at the lunch counter.

Al, the short-order cook, was polishing the large silver coffee urn with a white cloth. Nell was wiping down the counter. When she saw the Sheriff sit down, she looked up and smiled.

"Well, hello handsome," Nell said. "Haven't seen you in here in a while. What are you having today?"

"Just a cup of coffee will be fine," he answered.

Nell looked into Sheriff Sizemore's bright blue eyes and handsome face and thought what a damn shame it was that he was married. "Okay, one cup of coffee." She poured a cup and set it in front of the Sheriff. "Sugar's in the bowl, and there's cream in the pitcher. Help yourself."

"Nell, I have a few questions for you, if you don't mind," the Sheriff said.

"If it has anything to do with the little Hudson girl being attacked, I'll be happy to answer questions all day to help find out who did it," Nell said.

"Well, yes, that's what it's about. Man alive! News travels fast in this town." The Sheriff smiled ruefully.

"Well, we pretty much know what's going on," Nell explained, setting the coffee pot down on the counter. "It seems like everyone in the whole town comes in here at least once a day."

"Do you remember young Miles and Black Hart having an argument in here a day or two before Christmas?"

"Yes, they sure did, and that little fellow really stood up to Black Hart. He told him he better never say anything about his sister again, or he would see what you had to say about it."

"Just what was it that Black Hart said about Evaline?" the Sheriff asked.

Nell picked up the coffee pot and refilled the cups of the last two customers remaining at the counter besides Sheriff Sizemore. She talked as she worked. "The best I remember, he was mad because Miles didn't want to run bets for him anymore. Then he called Evaline 'Miss Queen Bee' and said she was the one who was telling Miles to stay away from him."

Al stopped polishing the coffee urn and broke in. "That's right, Sheriff. Black Hart got shook up when the little fellow told him if he talked about his sister again, he was going to come see you about it. Why, Black Hart even offered to pay him some money he owed him, but the little fellow told him to keep it. Said he just wanted Black Hart to leave him alone."

"Is Black Hart under suspicion?" Nell asked.

"No more than anyone else," the Sheriff answered as he raised up off the stool at the counter. "I'll be talking to him, and I'll be talking to quite a few people in the next few days. What do I owe you, Nell?"

Nell smiled. "Not one copper! Coffee is always on the house for you, handsome!"

"Well, that's awfully neighborly of you, Nell. Thanks."

"You're welcome! Just try and not be a stranger in the future," Nell laughed.

Sheriff Sizemore's next stop was the Taylor Hotel across from the Bus Station. It was a second-class hotel that had only twelve rooms, three floors with four rooms each. There was no private bathroom in any of the rooms, just one at the end of the hall on each floor.

In the cramped lobby, a hotel desk sat under the stairs that led up to the second floor. Three straight-back chairs, a sofa and a pinball machine, tucked into the corner, were the only other furniture.

When Sheriff Sizemore walked into the lobby, Eli, the desk clerk, was not behind the hotel desk. He was in the corner playing the pinball machine. As always, a half-eaten Moon Pie lay on the corner of the pinball machine within Eli's reach. Eli, a short, balding, rotund man had a fondness for cakes and pies of every kind, but he was extremely neat. Every day, his shirt was perfectly pressed, his shirtsleeves crisply folded up twice. Eli quickly glanced at the Sheriff and then back to the pinball machine. He pushed the buttons to flip the steel ball back at the colored lights, but with the distraction of the Sheriff, he missed, and the game was over.

"Dagnabit, Sheriff!" Eli complained. "If you hadn't come in when you did, I would have beat this damn machine! I only needed fifty more points to win! I been trying to beat this blasted machine for over a year now, and this is the closest I've ever come to beating it. If you hadn't come in and caused me to lose my concentration, I would have won. Well, so much for that."

"Sorry I messed up your game," the Sheriff said.

"Oh, that's okay. I guess if I ever did beat that machine it would take all the fun out of playing it. Wouldn't have anything to occupy my mind if I ever beat it."

Eli walked Past Sheriff Sizemore to his place behind the front desk. "Sheriff, what can I do for you?" he said.

"Does Black Hart still rent a room here?"

"Yeah, sure does. He's been renting the same room on the second floor for over three years. Why?"

"I need to talk to him. Have you seen him today?"

"Nope. I hardly ever see Black Hart. I come in at nine, and he's usually gone by then."

A door opened and closed on the second floor. Eli and Sheriff Sizemore looked at each other curiously and then toward the stairs.

"I wonder who that could be." Eli said. "I didn't know anyone was upstairs. I thought all the transient people had checked out."

Black Hart inched slowly down the stairs. He held tightly onto the rail and walked sluggishly as though each step caused excruciating pain. The hair on the right side of Black Hart's head was matted. It looked almost as if it had dried blood in it.

"Black Hart! What in the world is wrong with you? You're walking like you got run over by a ten-ton coal truck!" Eli said.

Black Hart looked surprised to see the Sheriff and Eli staring up at him. He did his best to compose himself. "Well, to tell you the truth, I was in a little poker game last night at the Palace Hotel. I had a little too much to drink." Black Hart descended the last few steps and stood, still holding the rail for support, at the bottom of the stairs.

"Looks like you had a bad fall." The Sheriff gave him a thorough visual inspection. "Your face has a pretty bad bruise on it. I can tell by the way you're walking that your back must have taken a hard lick, too."

"Yeah, I guess I'm getting too old to get drunk and fall down a flight of stairs," Black Hart responded airily.

"I'm going to need for you to take a ride with me. I've got a few questions to ask you."

"To tell you the truth, Sheriff, I was going to the doctor, but I could get with you later." He was defensive now. He headed to the door.

The Sheriff crossed to the door to intercept him. "How about you going with me right now, and I'll drop you off at the doctor's later?"

"Sure, Sheriff. No problem," Black Hart conceded. "No problem at all."

Eli watched Sheriff Sizemore and Black Hart walk out the door and down the street. He reached down to the windowsill and picked up his gray cat, Whiskers. He held Whiskers in his arms and lightly rubbed the back of his neck as he went back to the pinball machine. Whiskers made a low purring sound.

"You know, Whiskers, there's something rotten in Denmark. Now, why in the world would the Sheriff want to take Black Hart for a ride in his car just to ask him some questions? I wonder what he's been up to. We better start watching him more closely, Whiskers." He put Whiskers down on the floor.

"Now, let me see if I've got another nickel to put in that pinball machine." Eli reached down into his pocket and pulled out some change—a quarter, a dime and a nickel. He dropped the nickel into the slot and the other two coins into his pocket. The steel balls fell through the hole to the bottom of the pinball machine. The bells rang and the colored lights came to life. Eli pulled the spring plunger back and released it. A steel ball quickly rolled to the middle of the machine, lighting up a red light as it hit it and made a ding-ding-ding sound. One hundred points registered on the face of the machine. Eli was entranced once again. "I'm going to beat this dad-gum machine this time, Whiskers. Just you watch and see, even if it kills me!"

Outside in the parking lot, Sheriff Sizemore opened the door of his 1936 Ford Coupe, and Black Hart carefully slid into the seat. "Looks like you're going to be sore in your back for quite a while," the Sheriff observed.

"Yeah, looks that way," Black Hart snapped back.

They drove down Main Street past the Five and Dime and then on past the Virginia Theater. They turned onto High Street by the Mount Mary Hospital and continued on down to Newland Street. The Sheriff noticed Black Hart's reaction as they turned onto the road that led into Jack Lot Hollow.

"You haven't had much to say. Aren't you interested in where we're going?" the Sheriff asked.

Black Hart just looked straight ahead. "You're doing the driving, Sheriff. I'm just along for the ride. I'm still waiting to see exactly what you want from me."

"Well, Black Hart, I've got a problem."

"Oh, is that so?"

Sheriff Sizemore pulled his Ford off the road and stopped by the tipple. "Evaline Hudson was attacked on her way home last night. It happened right here in front of this coal tipple."

"Is that right, Sheriff?" Black Hart responded. "What's that got to do with me?"

"The thing it's got to do with you, is you're my No. 1 suspect."

Black Hart sat back in the seat. He turned to face Sheriff Sizemore. "Whoa! Now, just wait just a minute. You're not going to try and pin this on me, are you?"

"Yep, that's exactly what I'm going to do," said the Sheriff calmly. "You know you did it. I know you did it. You're guilty as sin."

"You listen to me, Sheriff. I've got eyewitnesses who will swear in a court of law as to where I was last night," Black Hart said sharply.

"Oh, I'm sure you do. I'm certain your two cronies, Will Price and Noah Brewer, would be happy to swear any lie you choose to tell." The Sheriff stared at Black Hart waiting for more reaction, but Black Hart was silent now, "You see, you're the only one who had a motive to do this. Everyone in the Five and Dime heard the argument you had with Miles Hudson. They all heard you bad-mouthing his sister. You were using an eleven-year-old boy to run bets for you, and you weren't even paying him. You told him his sister thought she was Miss Queen Bee. Admit it. You got to drinking last night, and you hid in the tipple until she came by, and then you attacked her." He paused again for a reaction, but Black Hart did nothing. "You're a gambler, Black Hart. You should know you're holding a losing hand."

Black Hart eyed Sheriff Sizemore cautiously. "Yeah, I had an argument with Miles, and I think his sister is a stuck-up bitch, but that doesn't prove I did that to her." Black Hart squirmed in his seat and continued to stare at Sheriff Sizemore. Finally he said, "You don't have any evidence."

"You're right. I don't have evidence. That's why I'm running you out of my town. I'm fed up with your gambling and using children to do your dirty work. The Greyhound Bus leaves Hazard tomorrow evening at six o'clock. Be on it."

"You can forget about that, Sheriff. I'm going to get Sam Moore for my lawyer, and I'm going to fight this."

"Bad mistake, but if you're not on that bus tomorrow evening, then I'm going to take a trip down to Breathitt County. I'll go see Mason Hudson. I'm sure you've heard of Mason Hudson from 'Bloody Breathitt'?"

For the first time that day, Black Hart felt fear.

"You see, Mason is Landon Hudson's brother. When I tell him what you did to his brother's daughter, I don't think he'll take it well. When I let him know I plan to be out of town for a couple of days next week, I don't think I would want to be in your shoes."

Black Hart didn't say a word on the drive back to town. Sheriff Sizemore pulled his Ford alongside the curb and stopped in front of Doc Riley's office. "You better get your face and back looked at. I think you'll get a lot worse before you get better."

Black Hart gritted his teeth, opened the door, and slowly climbed out of the car. He closed the door behind him, never looking back at the Sheriff. He walked toward Doc Riley's door. Before Black Hart could open the door, the Sheriff called out, "Hey, Black Hart. Don't forget your bus leaves tomorrow evening at six. Be sure you're on it."

TWELVE

B y the following morning, the rumors had spread across town. The gossip had started in the Underworld Pool Room with Noah Brewer, Black Hart's associate. "It's just not right that the Sheriff can tell someone to leave town without having proof he's done something wrong," Noah had told anyone who would listen.

The gossip spread from the pool room to the Five and Dime. From there, it engulfed the entire community. The Sheriff first got the news of all the talk going around town when he walked through the door of the City Café for lunch. Manuel, who worked at the Broke Spoke Liquor Store, was on his way out the door as the Sheriff was coming in. "Sheriff, is it true what I hear about you and Black Hart?" Manuel said.

"Well, just what is it you're hearing?" the Sheriff replied, irritated by the rumor mill.

"It's all over town!" Manuel exclaimed. "Everyone's talking about how you told Black Hart to be on the six o'clock Greyhound bus leaving today. It's just like one of those cowboy picture shows where the Sheriff gives the bad guy until noon to get out of town. Then the bad guy decides he's not going to leave. He's going to stay and shoot it out with the Sheriff."

"And then what happens?" the Sheriff asked, his irritation turning to amusement.

"The streets are deserted," Manuel went on excitedly. "Everyone's inside watching from their windows. Noon rolls around, and the bad guy walks up the street to meet the Sheriff. They stop fifty feet apart. The bad guy is scared, so he goes for his gun first. But as it so happens, the Sheriff is a little faster. He outdraws the bad guy and shoots him down dead in the street. Hell, Sheriff, this is the most exciting thing to happen around here in a long time."

The Sheriff laughed. "God, Almighty, Manuel! Are you losing your mind? You've seen too many Western picture shows."

Manuel grinned. "But you've got to admit it's as exciting as hell."

"Manuel, you've got a big imagination. There's not going to be a gunfight at the Bus Station. All that's happened is an undesirable character has been told to leave town. If he doesn't leave, then the Sheriff's office will do what's necessary to put him out."

Manuel's balloon had burst, and the excitement drained from his face. "Oh, hell, Sheriff. I know there won't be a gunfight at the Bus Station." Then he smiled again. "But you've got to admit that it does remind you of a good Western picture show."

The Sheriff smiled. Manuel added, "Black Hart is unpredictable. Just not knowing what he'll do makes it exciting!"

The Sheriff's smile was gone. "Man alive! I've never seen a town like this before! We don't need a newspaper. Everyone knows what's going to happen before it even happens!"

Sheriff Sizemore walked to the counter, but had lost his appetite. Instead of having his usual quiet meal in the corner, he ordered a pimento cheese sandwich and a cup of coffee to go. As he left, he thought to himself, "Damn that Black Hart! I should have run him out of here a long time ago."

By five o'clock that afternoon, the gawkers, loafers, drugstore cowboys and the curious began to gather at the Bus Station. And by 5:45, it looked like a Fourth of July Parade was getting ready to take place.

The crowd had backed up in the front of the Taylor Hotel, and Eli could no longer see through the plate-glass window. Eli placed a chair in front of the window and stood on it when he heard someone coming down the stairs. He quickly turned and felt a little embarrassed as he saw Black Hart and Noah Brewer come back into the lobby. Noah was carrying two large brown suitcases, one in each hand. Black Hart was wearing his blue suit with his black overcoat draped over his shoulder. His face still showed pain with each step he took.

Black Hart gave Eli a chilling stare. "If you can get down from that chair and stay away from that damn pinball machine a minute or two, I'll settle my bill."

"Okay, sure. Sure thing." Eli stepped off the chair and walked behind the desk. "Whiskers, you know you're not supposed to sleep on my ledger book. Scat! I need to take care of some business. Go find another place to take your nap." Whiskers jumped from the counter and found the nearest chair to continue his nap.

Eli continued, "Let's see now. You paid last week, and this is the third day of this week. That will be fifteen dollars. After this, your account will be closed."

Black Hart took a deep breath, held it a few seconds and then exhaled. He reached into his wallet and placed a twenty-dollar bill on the desk. Anxious and nervous to have his business with Black Hart finished, Eli counted out five one-dollar bills.

Black Hart straightened the money and placed it in his wallet. Noah picked up the luggage and followed Black Hart to the door. Eli was trying to think of something appropriate to say. After all, he thought, he's been a regular for three years.

"Good luck, Black Hart," Eli said.

"Thanks. I need a streak of good luck. It's been all bad the last few days," Black Hart said as he stepped out into the waiting crowd.

Eli locked the cash register and put the key in his vest pocket. He reached down and picked up Whiskers. He took a straight-back chair from the lobby and carried it up to the second floor. "Now, Whiskers, we got the best seat in the house. We can see the bus and all the passengers. I can even see the Sheriff standing by the bus-station door. It's ten minutes 'til six. It won't be long now, Whiskers."

On the street, a hush fell over the crowd as it parted to make a path for Black Hart and Noah. Everyone knew by the way Black Hart was dressed that he would be leaving town. He looked almost elegant in his new blue suit and gray tie. His dark hair and pencil-thin mustache were as black as coal. He looked straight ahead, his eyes unwavering. With Noah walking behind him and carrying his luggage, he gave the appearance of an English nobleman.

Whispers ran through the crowd.

"You know, Sheriff Sizemore is a man who means what he says."

"I told you Black Hart would be leaving."

"He ain't gone, yet ..."

"Could be some fireworks before he goes ..."

As Black Hart entered the Bus Station he saw Sheriff Sizemore standing just inside the door. He stopped and looked at the Sheriff with a sneer. Noah walked around the two men and set the suitcases down, staying close to Black Hart and avoiding eye contact with the Sheriff. Noah rarely spoke when he was cobbing for Black Hart. In the mountains, cobbing was another name for flunky, but Noah had no choice. Black Hart was his meal ticket. Noah flexed his hand, cramped from carrying Black Hart's heavy suit cases. He looked up and spoke. "You know Sheriff, I've lived in this town all my life and I've never missed voting in any election. And, I will certainly never vote for you again."

"Sorry to hear that, Noah. And, oh, by the way, Noah, just how many times did you sell your vote in those elections?" Sheriff Sizemore asked. But he hadn't come here to talk to Noah, and he dismissed him entirely. He turned to Black Hart. "I'm glad to see you've made the right decision, Black Hart," Sheriff Sizemore said.

"Is that what you call it?" Black Hart retorted. "I call it forced to leave town."

"Call it what you like. This is how it is going to be. You can make it easy, or you can make it hard. Suit yourself."

Black Hart had said all he wanted to say. He nodded to Noah to follow him. He walked over to the cashier's cage, reached inside his coat pocket and took out his wallet. He purchased a one-way ticket to Cincinnati. The cashier gave him his ticket and two tags for his luggage. Noah placed the tags on the two suitcases and they walked back outside.

It was after six o'clock, and all the passengers except Black Hart were aboard the bus. The driver placed Black Hart's luggage in the storage compartment. Then he turned and faced Black Hart. "Mister, we're running a little late. If you'll hurry and get aboard, we'll get started."

The driver climbed up the steps and into the bus. He took his seat and tapped his fingers impatiently on the big steering wheel.

Black Hart shook Noah's hand and patted him on the back. Then, just as he was about to board the bus, someone from the crowd yelled, "Speech! Give us a speech, Black Hart!"

Being a con artist and gambler, Black Hart understood all the tricks of manipulating a crowd. Years of quick decisions made at the poker table had made him a master of understanding people's emotions. He slowly turned, and for the first time, he took a good look at the crowd. He raised his hand into the air and waved. There was laughter and a smattering of applause as the gambler paused and waited for the right moment to speak.

"Ladies and gentlemen. As you know, I am being forced to leave the town I love and the place I was born thirty-two years ago. The reason for this is your Sheriff can't solve a crime that happened a few days ago. He needs a scapegoat, and he decided it would be me." Black Hart placed his right hand over his heart and patted it with sincerity. He leaned toward the crowd, his eyes asking for sympathy.

Someone in the crowd yelled out, "Yeah, Black Hart, we all know how honest you are!" The crowd erupted in laughter.

Black Hart raised his hand again for quiet. Then he continued.

"The Sheriff doesn't have a shred of evidence against me. I have always enjoyed making friendly wagers on ball games and horse races, so he's decided it's best for the town that I take the blame for this crime. Well, I have news for you, Sheriff. My leaving town won't stop sporting people from making wagers, and it won't stop whoever committed this terrible crime from committing another one."

Noah shot Black Hart a quick look and held up his watch for Bart to see. He pointed to the time. Inside the bus, the driver was looking frantic. He had a schedule to meet. He pulled the door handle, closing the door and opening it again, warning Black Hart that the bus would be leaving with or without him. But Black Hart scarcely noticed.

"Most all of you have known me all my life and know that I wouldn't so much as hurt a fly. Why, I would be the first one to come to a man's aid if I thought he needed my help."

The driver, having exhausted his patience, closed the bus door. The bus slowly moved through the crowd. Sheriff Sizemore's patience had also come to an end. His face was red, his steel-blue eyes blazing. He stepped in front of the bus and held up one hand.

Black Hart, engrossed in his speech, hardly noticed the bus. "Folks, we have an election coming up. I ask my friends and all the good people of Hazard to go out and vote against the Sheriff. I hope you will let him know that this is no way..."

Black Hart was cut short in the middle of his sentence as Sheriff Sizemore slapped a handcuff on one of Hart's wrists with one hand and dragged him by the collar of his coat with his other hand. The Sheriff's anger and strength overrode Black Hart's resistance. The passengers stared in disbelief as the Sheriff dragged Black Hart onto the bus, down the aisle and forced him into a seat. He then attached the other handcuff to the arm of the seat and locked it.

"I'm a citizen, and I don't deserve to be treated like a common criminal," Black Hart yelled. "Take these cuffs off me right this minute, or I'll jerk this arm off the seat of this bus!"

The Sheriff walked calmly to the front of the bus and gave the driver the key to the handcuffs. "When you get to your rest stop at Campton, you can take the cuffs off. Don't forget to return them to me on your next trip back."

Sheriff Sizemore stepped down from the bus. "Okay, people. Break it up. The show is over. Go back to doing whatever it is you were doing. There's been enough excitement for one day."

The Greyhound bus began to move, inching its way through the narrow streets of Hazard. As it slowly picked up speed, blue diesel smoke poured out the exhaust pipe. When the miles began to slip away, Black Hart continued to stare out the window. Lady Luck had not been kind to the gambler. As he watched the mountain scenery passing him by, he wondered what fate had in store for him in Cincinnati.

THIRTEEN

By February, Miles had almost forgotten he had ever worked for Black Hart, but today, for some reason, he and Cecil had walked by the Underworld Poolroom on their way home from school. Glancing down the stairs that led to the poolroom had made Miles think again about running bets for the gambler who never paid him. The rumor was that Black Hart had stayed a short time in Cincinnati, and then traveled down the Ohio River on the Delta Queen to New Orleans.

As Miles and Cecil walked on past the pool room, Miles stopped thinking about Black Hart almost immediately. Over the past several months something else had been occupying his thoughts. He had discovered he liked girls. He didn't understand what it was about them that made him blush when they smiled and said, "Hi, Miles." It was like they knew some deep secret that he didn't know, and they weren't about to let him know what it was.

It was Valentine's Day. Cecil and Miles had walked quietly for the most part as they went home. Cecil had stopped several times to take out one of the Valentine's cards he had gotten and read it to Miles. Now he asked, "How many Valentine cards did you get, Miles?"

"Oh, I don't know," Miles answered, suddenly embarrassed. "I didn't count them. Twenty-three or twenty-four."

"Is that all? I got thirty-two, and I even got one from Miss Turner!" Cecil gloated.

"Oh, come on, Cecil. Miss Turner gives all her students Valentines."

"Oh, I guess she does," Cecil admitted. "But I saw some of the ones she gave out, and none of them were as romantic as the one she gave me."

Miles stopped and stared at Cecil. "Cecil, you can take it from me. Miss Turner's only interest in you is in trying to pound some sense into that pea-sized brain of yours."

"Well, then why does she always ask me to dust the erasers and go to the cloakroom to get new chalk for the blackboards?" Cecil had turned red now.

"I don't know. Maybe she thinks it will keep you from daydreaming and staring at her all day."

"Well, when I get married, it'll be to someone who looks and acts just like Miss Turner!" Cecil said as he began to walk again.

"For the time being," Miles warned, "you had better forget about Miss Turner. You know her boyfriend is Randy Shepherd. He drives a coal truck, and from what I hear he's a guy you do not want to cross."

"Yeah, I've seen him, and I don't like him," Cecil said. "He's a big showoff. Sometimes he comes to school and picks up Miss Turner in that hot-rod car he has. He thinks he's the cat's meow."

Cecil turned onto the path that led up the hillside to his house. "See you tomorrow, Miles," he called out as he walked up the hill.

Miles yelled back, "Don't forget to listen to the radio tonight. The Lone Ranger comes on at eight."

"Wouldn't miss it!" Cecil yelled back without turning around.

As soon as Cecil disappeared, Miles pulled a valentine from his coat pocket, a special valentine, one he hadn't told Cecil about. It was the largest of all the valentines he had received. When he opened the card, a red heart fanned out, and it had two lollipops attached to it. Down at the bottom was a message written in small, neat letters. "Happy Valentine's Day, Miles! You will always be in my heart. Nancy Ann."

FOURTEEN

Miles would never forget the day he turned 14. It was the second day of June, 1941, a sad day for all baseball fans, but Particularly for Miles, whose life time dream was to become a big league baseball pitcher. On this day, Miles' hero, Henry Louis Gehrig, the famed first baseman for the New York Yankees, lost his battle to a rare and fatal type of paralysis.

Drucella, Evaline and Miles heard the news on their little Philco radio. The announcer broke in on the *Bob Hope Radio Show*. His voice trembled with sadness. "Ladies and gentlemen, it is with great regret that I must inform you of the Passing of the greatest baseball player and gentleman that I've ever had the pleasure to meet. Would you please join me in one minute of silence in honor of Lou Gehrig, the Iron Horse?"

When the minute was up, a recording of Lou Gehrig's voice echoed over the radio waves and traveled into the homes of millions of Americans.

> *Fans, for the Past two weeks you have been reading about a bad break I got. Yet today, I consider myself the luckiest man on the face of the earth.*

The announcer broke in:

> *Lou Gehrig, dead at the age of thirty-eight. We now return you to our regular program.*

Miles had seen Drucella cry only one other time. This was the day he saw tears roll softly down her cheeks. It was at the Memorial Service held outside the sealed off entrance that led to the area inside the Number Seven Mine where his father had died.

Drucella, who had been bred to repress any expression of emotion, got up from the table, placed her coffee cup in the sink, went to her bedroom and closed the door behind her. Evaline walked over to the window, pulled back the curtains and looked out toward the road and creek.

Bob Hope's program was still playing on the radio. To Miles, it didn't seem funny anymore. The comedian told a joke, and all the people in the audience laughed. Why were they laughing? Why were they happy when they should be sad? Didn't they know his hero, the great Lou Gehrig, had died? Miles turned off the radio and went to his room. His body ached and he felt pain, the same kind of pain, though not as great, as that he had felt when Drucella had told him his father would not be coming home again. Lou Gehrig's death was bringing it all back. It had been too dangerous to go back inside the mine and try to recover the miners' bodies. The mine was sealed off, and Jack Lot Mountain became their permanent burial site. Miles' body now ached again for his father. He thought of him inside the mountain.

Weeks passed and the pain over Lou Gehrig's death eventually began to subside. Miles, like Drucella and Evaline, tried not to think about their larger pain, the loss of Landon. They all looked for distractions.

That summer, Miles, Cecil and Wilbur camped out in the woods five times. They went swimming in the creek almost every day. They saw seven movies at the Virginia Theater where their classmate, Eugene, had gotten a part-time job. Dressed in his red-and-black "monkey suit," Eugene helped paying customers find their seats in the darkened theater with his flashlight.

After the movie started, Eugene would go to the dark corner of the theater and open the side door slightly. Miles, Cecil and Wilbur would quickly step inside just before Eugene closed the door. They all agreed their favorite movie that summer was *Gone with the Wind*. When Clark Gable delivered his final line, *Frankly, my dear, I don't give a damn,* they all stood up and applauded. They were so moved by the movie that they sat riveted to their seats while everyone else departed the theater. They listened to the haunting theme song until the screen went blank. As they stepped outside into the bright sunlight, Cecil said, "I don't think we'll ever see a movie as good as *Gone with the Wind* ever again."

Miles was excited when he got home that afternoon. He stood in the kitchen talking a-mile-a-minute as Drucella and Evaline fixed supper. He told Drucella and Evaline how brave and courageous Rhett Butler had been, how beautiful and spoiled Scarlett O'Hara was, and how she would do almost anything to get her way. He described the burning of Atlanta and how the new Technicolor film made it seem as though you were close enough to reach out and touch the flames.

"Okay, Miles, don't tell us the whole story! You'll ruin the movie for us." Evaline put her coffee down on the kitchen table.

"Us? You mean Ma might go see it?" Miles asked.

"Well, I don't see why not. She can go with me if she wants to," Evaline said.

"Lord a-Mercy, child!" exclaimed Drucella, turning from the stove, "I couldn't go to no picture show! Why, who on earth would take care of this place while I was gone?"

"Momma, this place will take care of itself. Now, it's settled. You and me are going to see *Gone with the Wind.*"

Drucella pulled up a corner of her apron and wiped her hands. "Well, I don't know. Why, I've only gone to two picture shows in my whole life." She stared blankly at the kitchen wall, lost in thought. "One was a war picture, *All Quiet on the Western Front.* I can't remember much about the other one."

That settled it for Evaline. She would take Drucella to see *Gone With the Wind.* "Momma, that was an old black-and-white movie. *Gone With The Wind* is in Technicolor. Now, we're going. Miles can stay here and watch the house."

"Oh, no I won't!" Miles protested. "I'm going with you. I want to be there when Ma sees Rhett and Scarlett escaping the burning of Atlanta."

The following morning, Drucella got up earlier than usual. She milked Brownie and opened another bale of hay for her. After she fed her chickens, she made a smaller fire than normal in the cook stove. By one o'clock, the fire was slowly dying.

"Momma, it's almost time to go. We don't want to be late and have to stand in line," Evaline warned, coming down the hall from her bedroom. She glanced at herself in the mirror in the hall and stopped to smooth down her dress and pat her hair one last time. She and Miles walked into the kitchen at about the same time.

"All right, I guess I'm ready," Drucella said as she handed Miles the heavy, iron skeleton key to lock the back and front doors.

Miles was staring so hard at Drucella it took him a moment to reach out and take the key. Drucella was wearing one of her prettiest dresses and high heels, she very rarely wore high heels and never during the week. She had her good pocket book tucked under her arm. Evaline smiled at Drucella. "Mama, you really look nice today."

Evaline had thought they would have plenty of time. But when they arrived, the line was down the block. "My goodness, would you look at that!" said Evaline. "Miles, here's two dollars. Get in line and get our tickets. Don't forget to give me my change. Momma and I will be looking in Carl's Shoe Store window."

Five minutes later, Miles stood beside the main theatre door holding three tickets and jingling fifty-nine cents of change in his pocket. He hoped that Evaline would just take the change and not count it. Across the street, he saw Evaline and Drucella admiring the styles in Carl's window. He caught their attention, held up the tickets and motioned for them. They had just crossed the street and Miles was giving them their tickets when Eugene walked up.

"Well, now," Drucella said. "Doesn't Eugene look nice in his red-and-black suit? His cap matches his suit, too!"

"You mean his monkey suit," mumbled Miles.

Eugene smiled, "Why, thank you, Mrs. Hudson." He greeted Evaline, then turned to Miles and winked. "I thought you saw this movie yesterday."

Miles smiled. "Yeah, I liked it so much I came back with Evaline and Ma."

"Well, there are a lot of good seats still left," Eugene said. "If you all will follow me, I'll get you seated."

As soon as they were seated, Evaline turned to Miles. "OK, Miles, I'll have my change now."

Miles put the change into Evaline's open hand. Before the last coin had settled onto her palm, Evaline knew exactly how much change she had coming. Looking at the change, she said, "Miles, I keep forgetting that you're no longer 11 years old."

Miles fidgeted and said, "I thought the lady might not realize how old I am, so I asked for a children's ticket, but she looked at me funny, and knew I was older, maybe because I have broad shoulders and am taller than most kids my age."

At that moment the movie began. The theme song filled the theater. The title appeared on the screen with the words slanted as though the wind were blowing them away. Miles felt the hair on the back of his neck standing up with excitement.

Miles knew that Drucella was enjoying the movie because although Drucella sat on the other side of Evaline and whispered her comments during the movie to Evaline, Miles heard her several times: "Well, I never!" . . . "Lord, have Mercy, how can someone so pretty be so mean!". . . "Mammy has more sense than all of them put together!". . . "Oh, what a lovable rascal!" And when she saw all the Southern belles in their long gowns dancing in the grand ballroom, he heard her distinctly: "If I had the pattern, I could make any one of those dresses!"

Evaline, the real movie fan of the family, was enjoying it too. Miles, having already seen the movie, glanced at Evaline and Drucella to see their expressions at key moments in the story. Drucella and Evaline gasped when they saw the hundreds of wounded and dead Confederate soldiers lying side by side on the streets of Atlanta. They grieved with Rhett when he lost his beautiful, young daughter, Bonnie, in a riding accident. And they looked in awe as Scarlett proclaimed, "I'll never go hungry again."

After the movie, Drucella took Miles and Evaline to the Fouts Drugstore. They all had chocolate sundaes, a treat Drucella paid for with her egg money. They didn't discuss the movie. They each savored it in their own way. Drucella did say one thing: "My goodness! Isn't Clark Gable the most handsome man you ever saw?"

As they walked the road into Jack Lot Hollow, Drucella realized that something had been missing in their family. She made a vow to herself that from now on, they would get out of the house more. In the future, they would do more things together.

As they rounded the last bend in the road and looked toward their house, they were startled. Gray smoke was pouring out of both of their chimneys. "Why, that can't be!" Drucella exclaimed. "Those fires were almost out. Someone is in our house!"

Miles and Evaline raced toward home. Miles reached the house first. He walked up to the front door and looked all around the property. No signs of anyone breaking in. He reached down to grasp the door handle when he heard someone cussing.

Miles stepped inside and slowly and quietly pulled the front door shut. He didn't want to make any noise and tip off the intruder. He slipped through the living room and stood just inside the kitchen door. A tall, thin man stood over Drucella's cook stove. He had a fork in his hand, and he was turning strips of bacon from one side to the other. Miles could see the fire was too hot for cooking. The hot grease popped and crackled while the bacon sizzled. The man hadn't seen Miles, and he continued to cuss the fire and popping grease. "Damn grease popping all over everything! Dammit to hell! I got this fire too hot," the man said to himself, quickly pulling his hand back.

"Who in blue blazes are you?" Miles demanded.

Startled, the man jumped and dropped the fork and a strip of bacon to the floor. He turned and faced Miles. "You sure scared the living hell out of me, Miles!"

"I'm glad I did. What are you doing frying bacon on our stove and in our kitchen?" Miles stopped, suddenly realizing that the stranger had called him by name. "And how did you know my name? Just who are you anyway?"

"Why, I'm Blue," the stranger answered, almost apologetically. "You don't remember me?" He smiled at Miles, but when Miles didn't show any sign of recognition, he continued. "Well, you were just a little fellow when you saw me last."

Blue was in his mid-thirties. He had a friendly face worn from years of hard travel and exposure to the elements. He wore faded buckled overalls. A yellow pencil stuck out from the front pocket.

While Blue and Miles had been staring at each other, Evaline had entered the house and now stood in the other kitchen doorway. She had picked up the iron poker by the fireplace when she came through the living room. She had it drawn back over her head, ready to strike. "Well, you're going to be black and blue if you don't tell us what you're doing in our house!"

"You must be Evaline," the stranger said, the smile on his face spreading. "My Lord, I knew you were going to be pretty when you growed up, but I never dreamed you'd be this pretty. I've been to Chicago, New York, damn near all over this country, and I ain't never seen a young lady more beautiful than you."

Evaline's face turned red. With her free hand, she pushed her hair back and straightened her dress. A slight grin came over her face, but she held on to the poker. Miles looked at Blue and then back to Evaline.

Just then, Drucella rushed in, out of breath. "I might have known it would be you," she said. Drucella had come through the living room as Evaline had done and could see the man's face clearly as he stood staring at Evaline. "No one in their right mind would be so ornery as to come into someone's house and just start cooking on their stove except Blue Knight." She pulled a chair out from under the table and sat down.

Miles and Evaline looked at Blue and then back to Drucella. Evaline lowered the poker.

"Blue Knight? That sounds like something out of King Arthur's court," said Miles. "I've been reading a book about King Arthur and the Knights of the Round Table."

The grease in the skillet popped onto Blue's finger and he wrung his hand to relieve the sting of the burn. "I once knew a feller who had been a king in one of them foreign countries. He abdicated his throne and moved to the good old USA. He was always asking me for advice. Well, one day when we were riding in his Rolls Royce, he..."

Drucella rolled her eyes and interrupted. "The first thing you all need to know about Mr. Blue Knight is he's my first cousin, and second and most important thing is he's the biggest liar God ever put on this green earth."

"C'mon now, Cella, don't go and tell them that. I might paint a picture a little rosier than it really is, but I don't lie."

Everyone looked at Blue. "Well, I don't lie that much," he said.

Her strength having returned, Drucella got up and took over the running of her kitchen. She made Blue a bacon sandwich and asked him all kinds of questions about her kinfolks while he ate. Drucella's mother and Blue's mother were sisters, but had seen each other only rarely over the past 10 years or so, usually when a family member had died. After answering Drucella's questions about his mother and other family members, Blue finally got around to asking the one question that had been on his mind ever since he jumped off the boxcar in the Hazard train yard. "Cella, I was kinda hoping you might let me stay with you all two or three days. It would only be until I can get my bearings and decide which direction I'll be traveling in."

Drucella studied Blue's face and then turned to Miles. "I'm thinking that would be up to Miles," she said. "He's become the man of our family. He would have to share his room with you. It's up to him."

"Oh, no, Cella, I wouldn't want to share his room," said Blue. "I've got my own bedroll with me, and I could sleep on the floor by the stove. I'm used to sleeping in boxcars and under bridges. I could keep the fire going all night, and the coffee would be piping hot when you all wake up."

Miles held his head up a little higher than usual. He got up from the table, picked up his coffee cup and walked over to the stove. He took his time as he poured more coffee into his cup. He felt proud of the new power Drucella had bestowed upon him. Everyone waited as he pretended to be in deep thought. At last he turned to Blue and broke the silence. "I guess it would be okay. You did say two or three days, didn't you, Blue?"

"I sure did," Blue answered. "Two or three days. Five at the most."

Later that night, after supper, Miles did his homework at the small desk in the dining room. He was just finishing and putting away his books, when Blue, who had been talking with Evaline and Drucella in the living room, came into the dining room to join him. Miles was glad to have an opportunity to talk with Blue, to hear more of his stories.

"Blue, where did you work last?" Miles asked.

"Now, let me see," Blue thought. "Yeah, that would have been Chicago. You see, my main trade is . . . well, I'm a steeplejack."

"A steeplejack? What's that?" Miles asked.

"That's a feller who puts up tall buildings. Some of them can be over a hundred stories high," Blue explained, his hand pointed to the ceiling and the heavens beyond. Miles knew this was another one of Blue's tall tales. He had seen pictures in his geography book of the tallest building in the world, the Empire State Building in New York City with over a hundred stories, but he'd never heard of any other building in New York, or Chicago, or anywhere else being a hundred stories high, but he had to give Blue credit, this sure was a good story.

Blue continued, "They call them skyscrapers in the big city. I reckon I was known as the best steeplejack in the whole city of Chicago."

"Wow! The whole city?"

"Well, now, there might have been one or two just as good as me, but I was a damn good steeplejack. Why, a good steeplejack can make himself fifty dollars a day in the big city."

"Man alive!" Miles shouted. "Fifty dollars a day! That sounds like a lot of money, Blue!"

"It sure is," Evaline agreed as she and Drucella came into the dining room to say good night to the men. "So what did you do with all that money? I mean, if you made all that money, why aren't you staying at the Palace Hotel?"

"Blue!" Drucella scolded. "For God's sake, quit telling all those lies. Don't you know you can go to hell for lying?"

"Cella, I swear it's the God's truth. I was a good steeplejack."

Miles knew there wasn't an ounce of truth in just about anything Blue said. But Miles had always loved a good story, and he was hungry for knowledge of the outside world beyond his beloved mountains. So what if Blue was lying? Hadn't the story about Rip Van Winkle sleeping for twenty years been a lie, too? The teacher had even made the class take a test to make sure everyone had read it. Why didn't Ma and Evaline realize that if Blue had been able to get a good education, with his creative imagination he would have been able to write stories just as good as Washington Irving?

Drucella and Evaline went to bed. Miles followed Blue into the kitchen and sat at the table as Blue unrolled his bedroll by the stove.

"Blue," asked Miles, "just how dangerous is it to be a steeplejack?"

It had been a long day and Blue was tired, but he was never too tired to go to his make-believe world … especially when he could take someone along with him.

"Dangerous?" Blue answered. "Are you kidding? Why, it's just as dangerous as coal mining. First thing you got to learn is never look down. You start looking down, and you can get into trouble real quick. One little mistake and it's all over. You can't let your guard down for one second when you're a hundred stories high."

"A '100 story' building?" Uh-oh, thought Miles, here we go again. "Did you ever come close to falling?" Miles asked.

"I not only came close to falling, I did fall!"

Blue watched Miles' face. Miles' eyes were wild with excitement. Blue was getting as much enjoyment out of telling his story as Miles was from hearing it.

"You fell? You fell off one of those skyscrapers? How high up were you when you fell?"

"Now, let me see," Blue started to talk, then paused as he rubbed his chin with his fingers. "I believe we had built that skyscraper up to about sixty stories high."

"What?" cried Miles in disbelief. "Sixty stories high, and you're still alive?"

Blue explained, "It was the damndest thing you ever saw in your life. We had just untied a bucket of bolts they had sent up to us when this greenhorn bumped into me. I fell down on that steel beam and rolled off the side. This old-timer by the name of Red Wilson, well, he sized up the situation real quick. As I went over the side, he grabbed the rope we had used to haul the bolts up and slung that rope at me with all his strength!"

Miles' mouth gaped open.

Blue went on. "It was almost impossible for me to catch that rope, but somehow I managed to get ahold of it. I hung on for dear life! When all the slack unwound out of that rope, I got a terrible jerk, but I hung on! Everyone said it was a miracle! You know, I think maybe it was. If that rope had been eight feet longer, I wouldn't be talking to you today."

"What about the fellow that bumped you? Did he ever apologize to you?"

"Oh yeah," Blue continued, loving that he had a captive audience. "That poor feller was more scared than I was! The boss man, Mike, came over and told me to take the rest of the day off with pay." He paused to study Miles' face. "I didn't do that, though. I told Mike I was going right back up on that skyscraper to finish out my day. You see, I knew if I didn't go back up on that skyscraper, I would be ruined as a steeplejack forever. If a steeplejack ever loses his nerve, he's got to get down off that skyscraper before he kills himself or one of his buddies."

"What about the fellow who bumped you? Did he go back?"

"No," answered Blue. "He never did. Mike sent him to the office to get his pay. They told him he wasn't cut out to be a steeplejack. It takes a certain breed of man to be a steeplejack. Some people aren't cut out for dangerous jobs like that." He sat in a kitchen chair and smiled as he began unlacing his boots.

Miles continued his inquisition. "Do you know what ever happened to him?"

"I heard he got a job working in a drugstore. They said he was a soda jerk. Only climbing he did after that was on a four-foot stepladder when he got something down from a shelf in the store!"

Miles went to bed, marveling at Blue's stories. The next morning, Blue had fresh coffee waiting for the family on the cook stove. And Blue continued to sleep in the kitchen, kept the fire going, and always had coffee ready each morning.

"Momma! Blue sure knows how to tell tall tales, but he never learned how to count. Do you know he's been here over a week?" Evaline complained. Through the kitchen window, she watched Blue and Miles finishing chores. She could hear Blue's voice, which seemed to get louder and louder as his story became more exciting.

"I know he has, honey, and he can stay until hell freezes over before we tell him to go. I gave Miles the honor of being the head of the family. It'll be his job to tell Blue when it's time for him to go," answered Drucella.

"Oh, Momma, Miles is so carried away by all those lies Blue tells that he'll never tell him he's got to go!"

"Evaline, we don't want to forget Blue's done a lot of work while he's been here. He's probably saved us fifty dollars or more. Don't you worry about Miles. He has Hudson blood running in his veins. He'll know when it's time for Blue to go."

Drucella knew that even though he lied non-stop, there wasn't a lazy bone in Blue's body. He was always on the lookout for something to do around the house. When Drucella said they might have to buy a new refrigerator because their Kelvinator kept shutting off and spoiling their food, Blue assured her he could fix it. He got up early one morning and walked to town. When he returned, he pulled the refrigerator away from the wall and installed a new cord. He plugged it back into the socket, and the refrigerator motor once again came to life.

It was during a thunderstorm they discovered the roof over the living room was leaking. A wet ring formed on the ceiling, and water began dripping down onto the pine floor. Drucella looked up to the ceiling and frowned as she placed a pan under the leak. "My goodness, I don't know what we're going to do! We can't afford a new roof."

"Now, Cella, there ain't no sense in you worrying about that leak. I'll take care of it as soon as the rain stops and the roof dries off."

"Are you sure you can fix it?" Drucella asked.

"Lord, yes," Blue assured her. "I can fix that little leak. Why, I've fixed leaky roofs all over the country!"

When the sun popped out, Blue climbed up on the roof to survey the damage. Drucella called up from the ground below, "Blue, you be careful! Don't go falling off the roof!"

"Cella," he hollered down, "don't you know telling a steeplejack not to fall off a one-story roof is like telling a fish to be careful in shallow water?" He inspected the roof, lifting a few shingles up and checking underneath. "Cella, it looks like your roof is still in pretty good shape. I would say it has about three or four years left in it. Now that leak is coming from around your chimney. What it needs is new flashing put around it."

"Just how much would new flashing cost?" asked Cella.

"Not one copper," said Blue. "I'll cut up those empty Maxwell House Coffee cans stored under your cabinet for my metal. I'll buy a can of Black Mammy, and I guarantee it will stop that leak."

Blue thrived on praise. Whenever he completed one of his repairs, Drucella lavished him with compliments, and he sat at the kitchen table like a little boy, his eyes sparkling, as Drucella prepared his favorite dessert—fried peach pies. He sipped his coffee and told his tall tales as he watched Drucella go about her cooking. Drucella and Evaline hardly paid any attention to all Blue's stories, although Miles still hung on his every word. Every now and then Drucella looked up from her cooking. "For God's sake, Blue, quit telling all those lies to these children!"

Blue always responded defensively, "I swear it's the truth! It happened just like I said it did!"

Miles knew he was somewhat like Blue. Whenever Mrs. Hargrove gave a lecture in class, Miles' imagination ran wild. He struggled to pay attention to the lecture as his mind took him down the Nile River to some lost forbidden city. Sometimes, he just stared out the window when Mrs. Hargrove stopped in the middle of a sentence. "Miles, get off that window ledge and come back into the classroom right this minute. Don't you know we're on the second floor, and if you fall you'll hurt yourself?" The entire class would break into laughter as Miles quickly picked up his pencil and pretended to be taking notes.

Two days ago, Mrs. Hargrove asked her class to write a short story no more than three pages long. This morning, Miles had noticed Mrs. Hargrove looking over her desk at him several times. Miles wondered just what kind of trouble he was in now.

Finally, Mrs. Hargrove stood up from her desk.

"Class, I have read all your stories, and I'm pleased to say they are all quite good. One of my favorites is 'The Mule Who Stole Corn' by Miles Hudson. Miles, would you come up front and read your story to the class?"

Although he wasn't quite sure he liked being the center of attention, Miles held his head high as he walked to the front of the room. He did not look at Wilbur or Eugene, afraid that they might laugh at him. Mrs. Hargrove smiled and handed him his story. He felt a strange power as the room became deathly quiet. Miles soon forgot any nervousness as he began to read. The class laughed out loud when he read the part about how Mr. Napier's mule, Mert, had learned to open his stall door and slip outside the barn to eat his fill of corn. And they laughed even louder when he got to the part how before daylight, Mert always returned to his stall and pulled the door shut with his head.

When Miles finished, there was loud applause. But he thought, real men don't write stories. You would never see Roy Rogers or Gene Autry writing a story. Besides, when would they have the time? They are always too busy chasing down cattle rustlers, or saving the ranch owned by a beautiful girl. Yet he remembered how once he had picked up a copy of *Life* magazine in the Fouts Drugstore. Inside was an article about a writer named Ernest Hemingway. The article said he had houses in Cuba and Key West. There were pictures of him hunting big game in Africa. Maybe writing stories wasn't such a sissy thing after all.

Now, Miles and Blue were chopping wood in the barnyard when a flock of wild geese flew over the barn.

"That's a bad sign," Blue said, letting the axe rest on the chopping block for a moment. "When you see geese going south this early in the year, you better get ready for a bad winter. Sorta reminds me of the time I went to Miami for the winter."

Without thinking, Miles laughed out loud. Blue was surprised by Miles' laughter. He turned and gave him a long, hard look. Then he smiled and they both laughed together. They knew they were both hopeless adventurers who only wanted their lives to be more exciting than they were. Blue also knew the time had come for him to be on his way.

That night, as Miles climbed into his bed, he had a deep sense of sadness. Blue hadn't said anything about leaving, but Miles knew he would be gone when he awoke in the morning.

He fell asleep worrying about what might happen to Blue as he traveled the country. The following morning, the fire was burning, the coffee was hot and Blue was gone. A note lay on the kitchen table.

Dear Cella, Evaline and my dear friend Miles,
I've always had a hard time saying goodbye, and I think this one would have been the hardest one of all. Thanks for all the kindness you gave me. I hope I brought a little sunshine into your life.

FIFTEEN

A fter being a steady couple for almost two years, Charlie's infatuation with the beautiful Evaline had not dwindled, and they loved being together. One of their favorite meeting places was the lunch counter at the Five and Dime where they sat side by side for lunch and conversation. They especially enjoyed overhearing the local gossip and the various opinions as to the best movies at the local theater.

Charlie and Evaline enjoyed good movies, and rarely missed one. Evaline especially looked forward to the ride to town in Charlie's pick-up. Following the movie, Evaline also looked forward to their trip to Fouts' Drug Store where Charlie never failed to buy her a copy of the latest edition of *Photo-Play* magazine and where, at the soda fountain, they would enjoy Charlie's favorite drink, the "purple cow," a half glass of Coca-Cola with a large scoop of vanilla ice cream on top, served in a Coca-Cola glass with a straw and a long-handled spoon.

Their evenings together were generally at Evaline's house, and when the weather permitted, just sitting in the swing on the front porch talking late into the evening about how the Wills' saw mill was doing and the increase in business since the war had begun in Europe, or about the dream house Evaline hoped to live in someday. Sometimes they didn't talk at all, and just listened to a lonesome whippoorwill calling out its name.

Charlie was a caring person, and he had become a good listener. He knew Evaline had been forced to grow up fast after her father's death, and she now craved the lost attention Landon had once given her. Charlie never failed to remember to comment on how nice Evaline looked, and often told her she looked like the movie star, Linda Darnell.

"Oh, Charlie! You know I don't look a bit like Linda Darnell," was Evaline's usual response, but Charlie thought there was considerable resemblance. Like Miss Darnell, Evaline had dark eyes, jet-black hair and lots of spunk. Charlie was pleased to note that Evaline had begun to part her hair to one side, as did Miss Darnell, and hoped the combination of his sincere compliments, as well as his caring attention and patience, would be the road map to Evaline's heart.

One night, after seeing *How Green Was My Valley*, they sat side by side in a corner booth in Fouts' Drug Store. They were sipping their purple cows, when Charlie nervously took out of his shirt pocket a small box wrapped in white paper with a pink bow on top.

"Would you like to see what's in this box?"

"Is it a present for me?" Evaline asked with a smile.

"Well, I guess you could say that." He placed the box in Evaline's hand.

She quickly put her spoon on her napkin and began tearing away the white paper. When she got down to the small, black, hinged box, she paused for a moment and stared at it. "Oh, my Lord! Is this what I think it is?" She flipped open the lid. "Is this an engagement ring?"

"It sure is!" Charlie beamed. "And it cost me a bundle, too. One thing's for damn sure, they don't give diamond engagement rings away."

"Charlie, it's beautiful! How much did it cost?" Evaline asked excitedly pulling the ring out of its cushioned slot. She stared at the beautiful yellow gold ring with a solitary diamond.

"I'm glad you're sitting down because I don't have any smelling salts with me. Why, this rock cost me three hundred and seventy-five dollars at Frank's Jewelry Store. It had been marked five hundred dollars, but Mr. Frank gave me a hundred-and-twenty-five-dollars off," Charlie answered proudly.

"Let's go home!" Evaline had tucked the ring safely back into its slot and held the open box in her hand. "I can't wait to show Momma and Miles my diamond ring!"

"Now, wait just a darn minute! You haven't given me time to ask you to marry me yet. We got to do this the right way, or it won't be worth a tinker's damn."

"Well, what are you standing around waiting for? Why don't you go ahead and ask me then?"

Charlie took a second or two to compose himself.

Evaline could tell Charlie had been practicing for this moment. He looked into her eyes, and slipped the ring on her finger. He gulped hard. "Evaline, will you marry me and be my wife?"

Evaline raised her hand up to her face and looked admiringly at the diamond ring that encased her finger. "Yes, I'll marry you, silly. Do you think I would be so dumb to turn down a diamond ring like this?" she laughed. Then she put her arms around him and pulled him close. "What took you so long to ask me, Charlie Wills?"

"Great Scott! I can't believe I asked you to marry me, and you said yes!"

When they reached the Hudson house, Evaline was out of Charlie's pickup before it came to a full stop. She ran across the swinging bridge and hurried up the front-porch steps. "Momma, Momma! Where are you?" she called.

"We're in the kitchen. Something wrong?"

The rush in Evaline's footsteps and the high-pitched excitement in her voice had surprised Drucella and Miles. Both turned expectantly toward the door.

"No! Everything is perfect!" Evaline flew into the kitchen and hugged Drucella tightly. "Everything is just the way I want it." Evaline let go and held out her hand. "Look, Momma, I'm engaged! Charlie asked me to marry him. What do you think of my ring?"

"Oh, my Lord! I wasn't expecting anything like this," said Drucella. "Why, I'm completely befuddled. I don't know what to think. It's an awfully pretty ring, but are you and Charlie sure you all are ready to get married?"

"We're sure, Momma. I'm 19, and Charlie's 21. We're as ready as we're ever going to be. You're happy for us, aren't you?"

She studied Evaline's face, flushed with excitement. "Yes, I'm happy for you!" Then she heard Charlie's footsteps in the hall and turned to face him. "Why, I would be right proud to call Charlie Wills my son-in-law."

Charlie walked over to Drucella and gave her a hug. "Why thank you, Drucella."

Evaline turned to Miles, who was sitting at the kitchen table. "Well, how about you, Miles? Aren't you going to say anything? Aren't you excited for me?" She went over to ruffle his hair.

"Sure, I'm excited," Miles answered, leaning back in his chair to avoid Evaline's reach. He folded his arms across his chest. "But I knew about this over a week ago. You see, Charlie had to get my permission to ask you. You know, me being the head of the house and all."

"Well, excuse me, Mr. Head-Of-The-House and all, but how did a blabbermouth like you keep a secret for a whole week?" Evaline laughed.

"It wasn't easy, but Charlie said if I didn't tell you or Ma, he would give me a dollar!"

"Miles, you would do anything for a dollar! I can see the headlines in the Hazard Herald now, *Local Boy Sells His Soul For One Dollar,*" Evaline teased.

Everyone laughed except Miles. Even Drucella thought it was funny and laughed as much as Evaline and Charlie. But Miles' face turned red, and he hurriedly walked out the back door and into the barnyard. He picked up his axe and began splitting firewood as fast as he could. He knew everyone thought he was angry and embarrassed because they had laughed at what he might do for a dollar, but that wasn't it. The truth was he hadn't given it much thought when Charlie told him he would like to ask Evaline to marry him. There had always been the chance that Evaline would turn Charlie down. He had always liked Charlie, but now that he thought about it, he hated the thought of Evaline's leaving home and starting a life away from them.

Evaline watched Miles from the kitchen window. "Momma, should I go out there and talk to him?"

"Lord no, child. He'll be all right. He's just at that age when his feelings can be hurt over the least little thing. Don't worry about him. He'll forget all about it in a little while. Now, just when do you and Charlie plan on having this wedding?" Drucella indicated that they should all sit down.

"We're thinking about late March, or early April. Somewhere around greenup time." Evaline looked at Charlie. He smiled and nodded. She turned to Drucella. "Would that give us enough time to get everything ready?"

"Lord, yes. We won't need to start making any plans until after New Year's. It's going to be lots of fun looking at pictures of wedding gowns and deciding which you like best! Just think, I finally get to make your wedding gown! I've been thinking about this for a long time!"

SIXTEEN

Sunday, December 7, 1941
Hazard, Kentucky

Miles and his family enjoyed living in the sleepy little town of Hazard, nestled in the foothills of the southern Appalachian Mountains, where weeping willow trees lined the banks of the North Fork of the Kentucky River that flowed through the core of the small town. The peaceful river, the streams, and the hills that encircled the town had always given its residents a feeling of seclusion from the outside world. On December 7, 1941, that secluded world was shattered.

It had been like any other Sunday. Charlie drove the Hudson family to church. Evaline and Drucella squeezed into the front seat with Charlie. Miles climbed into the back of the pickup truck, and they drove out of the hollow to the Jack Lot Baptist Church.

Brother Carlson preached on greed and selfishness. The morning sun shone through the stained-glass windows, and its rays warmed the church. Brother Carlson had preached for fifteen minutes when Miles began to nod. Miles opened his eyes and sat up straight as Brother Carlson's voice heightened.

"Brothers and sisters, you know the devil needs tools to work his meanness, and two of his favorite tools are greed and selfishness. You can store up all the wealth and riches in the world, but in the Lord's eyes, you'll be nothing more than a pauper. You see, wealth and riches don't mean a single, solitary thing to the Lord. The Lord's not impressed with how much wealth and riches you have. Help me out somebody, somebody say Amen!"

"Amen!"

"Thank you, Sister."

"The Lord's not impressed with that new, shiny automobile. Somebody say Amen!"

"Amen!"

"Thank you, Brother."

"Now, I'm going to tell you what **does** impress the Lord. If you're going to impress the Lord, you've got to give to the poor. You've got to give part of your earnings to the church to impress the Lord. Let me hear an Amen! Don't store up your treasures here on earth and end up reaping the fires of hell. Store up your treasures in heaven and you'll have everlasting life. Now, Brother Miller will pass the collection plate."

Miles intended to give a quarter as his offering, but after Brother Carlson's hellfire sermon, he dropped two quarters into the collection plate.

"Now, brothers and sisters, before we close our service today, I want every man, woman and child to bow their heads," Brother Carlson said. "Lord, we've come to your house today to worship you and give thanks for all your blessings. We want to pray that you help the people of England in their struggle to protect their country from the evil tyrants of the world. We pray that you guide President Roosevelt and give him strength to lead our country through the uncertain times that surely lie ahead. We ask all these things in your name. Amen."

After church, Charlie dropped the Hudsons off at the swinging bridge and promised Evaline he would return later that evening.

At three o'clock, the church bells began ringing at the Jack Lot Baptist Church. They rang nonstop for a half hour. Drucella, Evaline and Miles stood on the front porch and looked out toward the mouth of the hollow. They tried to fathom what could be so dire to cause someone to ring the bells for so long, three hours after the service.

"Maybe the church is on fire?" Miles guessed.

"No," Drucella said. "If it were, we would see smoke rising above the hillside."

"I can see Charlie's truck coming up the road," Evaline shouted.

Miles peered over Evaline's shoulder. "Yeah, and he's driving really fast," Miles said, stepping off the porch and out into the yard.

"Well, the church is definitely not on fire. If it were, Charlie would have stopped to help put it out," Evaline said.

Charlie's truck rolled to a stop, and he leaped out the door and ran across the swinging bridge. "Have you heard? Have you heard? The Japs attacked Pearl Harbor?"

"Pearl Harbor? Where's Pearl Harbor?" asked Evaline.

"It's a naval base in the Pacific. In Hawaii," he answered over his shoulder. Charlie was crossing the porch and heading inside, going straight for the radio.

Charlie was already tuning in the news as the Hudsons followed him inside and gathered around the radio. For some reason Miles had that uneasy feeling in his stomach, like being called to the Principals office and not knowing what you've done. Evaline took Charlie's arm and held on tightly as if by holding him, she could keep him, keep all of them, out of war. Charlie put his hand in Evaline's and gave it a quick squeeze, but kept his attention on the radio. "Who do these Japs think they are? Don't they know they're fooling with the greatest country in the world?" he said as he finally got the radio tuned in.

Everyone listened quietly to the first details of the attack on Pearl Harbor.

"Well, it looks like the fat's in the fire now," Charlie said. "I don't see any way out now that those sneaky little bastards have attacked our naval base. I guess I had better start getting ready to go to war."

"What? You can't go to war! We're getting married in March!" shouted Evaline. She took him firmly by the shoulders and forced him to turn from the radio and face her.

Charlie met her gaze. "Well, I'm afraid Uncle Sam won't be too concerned if we get married, or not. I would bet I won't be in Kentucky four weeks from today."

Evaline's temper began to rise. Her face turned red and her dark eyes filled with anger. "Damn those Japs! I hate every one of them. They not only bombed our naval base, they ruined my wedding! I wish they were all dead!"

Miles didn't want Evaline to be upset. "Charlie won't be gone long," he told her. "Our country will wipe them out." He looked to Charlie for confirmation, but Charlie smiled weakly and shrugged his shoulders.

"Oh, Miles, you don't know what you're talking about!" Evaline turned and stormed down the hallway to her bedroom.

That night, as she tossed and turned while trying to go to sleep, Evaline began to formulate in her mind a plan that did not mean waiting until March to get married to Charlie Wills, the man she loved, who would soon leave her, and possibly never return.

SEVENTEEN

T here had not been much traffic in Anderson's store that morning. It was Thursday, usually the slowest day of the week, and the day that all the workers cleaned the store from one end to the other under Doris' supervision. Doris' husband, Jack, was at his post behind the meat counter, trimming the fat from the T-bone steaks that had arrived earlier that day. Whether he was trimming steaks, or checking his meat inventory, Jack had learned over the years to find things to do, particularly on store cleaning day, to curb Doris' temper.

Even Mr. Britches was trying to stay out of the way. His long tail had been stepped on more than once this morning. Each time it happened Mr. Britches gave out a loud meow and jumped up into Doris' lap for protection. As Doris patted Mr. Britches' head and rubbed his stomach, she kept a stern look on her face to let the workers know she meant business.

As work activities continued, Doris noticed that Evaline, always a fast worker, worked even faster today, and Hernando, also a fast worker, had given Evaline a dirty look, no doubt, thought Doris, because Hernando felt Evaline was trying to make everyone else look bad.

Eventually Doris' curiosity got the best of her. "Evaline, you're working like a woman possessed. Why don't you take a break? Let's go outside and let you catch your breath."

As Doris and Evaline started toward the door, Hernando followed, but he stopped dead in his tracks when Doris said,

"Hernando! We're taking a break, not you! Go back to your cleaning for now."

"I'm sorry, Doris," said Evaline, tears streaming down her face, "I should have told you this morning, but Charlie and I didn't want anyone to know, or to try to change our mind, but we're planning to run off and get married, just across the state line, in Wise, Virginia. The War has changed everything, Doris, and we don't want to wait. You're my best friend. Do you think we're doing the right thing?"

Doris didn't hesitate to respond. "Yes, the War does change everything, but even if it didn't, in life, you've got to reach out and take a big chunk of it, and squeeze that big chunk of life until it oozes through your fingers. Now, what do you need to do to get started?"

"I knew I could count on you, Doris," said Evaline.

"Well" said Doris, "to ensure you have lots of good luck, you'll need to wear 'something old, something new, something borrowed, and something blue', and a penny in your shoe."

"So!" said Evaline excitedly, "do you mind my leaving early today to get married?"

"Yes, you can leave early today," said Doris, "take all the time off you need, and you'll get paid as if you were here working your regular shift. That's mine and Jack's wedding present to you and Charlie. By the way, where are the clothes you're taking with you?"

"I packed my suitcase last night," said Evaline, "and hid it behind the large bushes next to the swinging bridge. Charlie came by last night, and picked it up. It's in his pick-up, and I'm all ready to go."

"Evaline, do you really think that old pick-up will make it to Wise, Virginia without breaking down? If it broke down, it would ruin your wedding plans."

"I never thought about that," said Evaline, with a concerned look on her face. "Anyway, Doris, I don't know if I will ever be able to thank you enough for what you're doing for us."

Later that day, Doris asked Evaline to walk with her up the sidewalk leading to her house. As they were walking, Doris said, "Evaline, as you know, Jack and I have a Pontiac that we keep in our garage. We don't drive it very much because we have just about everything we need here in the store. The car's in good shape, but a mechanic told us we were doing our car more harm by letting it set in the garage than if we drove it on a regular basis. So, you would be doing us a favor if you and Charlie drove our car on your honeymoon."

Evaline was speechless. Never would she have imagined that Doris would make such a generous offer. When she was finally able to speak, she said, in tears, "Yes, Doris, we would be pleased to take the Pontiac on our honeymoon."

Doris was watching for Miles, and knew he would be coming by later that afternoon to walk Evaline home. When Miles arrived, Doris motioned for him to come back behind the counter.

"Miles," Doris whispered, "Evaline and Charlie left earlier today to go get married. Evaline wanted you to tell Drucella, as well as Charlie's mom and dad, that they are certain that they should not wait to get married."

Miles was stunned, but he recovered. "When did they leave? I've got to stop them. Ma is gonna skin her alive. She was supposed to wait, and Ma was going to make her wedding dress." He turned for the door.

Doris yanked him by the collar. "Whoa, there. This isn't your business. You leave them alone."

"I guess you're right. I wonder where they are now."

EIGHTEEN

C harlie was as excited about driving the Pontiac as he was about getting married. "Evaline, I hope someday we can have a car like this Pontiac."

As they continued to drive through the beautiful mountains, Charlie became lost in his thoughts and was less-and-less concerned about going into the War.

After a while, Charlie noticed a small creek that ran beside the road, and pulled off.

"This is a perfect place for our picnic," said Charlie. "You get the blanket, and I'll get the basket. Hold my hand, and we'll slide down the hill together."

Charlie sat down on a rock, slipped off his shoes and socks, placed his feet in the cool stream, and said, "If married life is going to be like this all the time, I'm going to be very happy."

After they finished their picnic lunch of fried chicken and potato salad, Charlie patted his hands on his stomach and said, "Wow, I think I'm going to love married life."

The happy couple drove the Pontiac to Wise, Virginia, and arrived just in time to get a license, and find a justice-of-the-peace who performed the ceremony, then declared they were "man and wife," and congratulated "Mr. and Mrs. Charlie Wills."

Evaline then gave Charlie a kiss, poked him in the ribs, and whispered, "Charlie, pay the man!"

The following day they took the two-lane, winding road from Wise, Virginia, to Gatlinburg, Tennessee. As they pulled into the small town, they stopped at a motel, checked in, and then asked the desk clerk to recommend a good restaurant.

"Howard's is the place you want to eat," the desk clerk said excitedly. "He not only has a great restaurant, he is also a nice guy."

They drove the short distance, parked the Pontiac, and went inside. The hostess took two menus, and led them to a table near the window.

"This is the nicest restaurant we've ever been in," said Evaline. "This is like being in a movie. Now Charlie, I know you'll watch your manners."

As they were finishing their meal, Howard came to their table, introduced himself, and said, "Now, you know, I can almost spot the young, newly married couples when they first come into my restaurant. Seems they're always a little nervous, maybe afraid they'll do something wrong, but once they begin to relax, they end up enjoying a great dinner, and having a very good time."

Evaline and Charlie liked Howard, who put them at ease right away. He said he didn't have a piece of wedding cake to offer them, but he had some delicious smaller cakes he'd like to provide for dessert, with his compliments and which they eagerly accepted.

As they were leaving, Howard came back to their table, thanked them for coming in, and wished them his very best for a safe trip home and a long and happy life.

Evaline gave Howard a big smile, hugged him, and said, "Howard, I don't know whether we'll ever be back here again, but one thing's for sure, we'll never forget you!"

After two exciting days of sightseeing in Gatlinburg and in the surrounding Smokies, Evaline and Charlie drove back to Hazard and returned the Pontiac to Doris and Jack Anderson. Later that evening they were on the way to spend the night at Evaline's and were listening to the radio in Charlie's pick-up truck. *Silent Night* was interrupted with a news flash.

"The Naval Secretary has reported that the official count of lives lost in the surprise attack by the Japanese air raid at Pearl Harbor on December 7 is as follows. Ninety-one officers and 2,638 enlisted men are known dead. In addition, the Battleship Arizona and five other war ships were destroyed in the attack."

Evaline turned the radio off. "I feel like I'm losing you." She encased Charlie's hand in both of hers and looked at him.

"Oh, everything is going to work out all right. You'll be okay," Charlie said. He slipped his hand away so he could put his arm around her and hold her close.

"I'm not as strong as everyone thinks I am."

"Well, our big problem right now is slipping into your room without your Ma or Miles waking up."

"It doesn't matter if they wake up or not, if we're married, and I have the certificate in my purse to prove it!" Evaline scooted aside so Charlie could open the truck door.

Charlie laughed. "That's easy for you to say! You don't have to face the head of the house like I do!"

"I think the head of the house is getting a little too big for his britches," Evaline laughed, too.

Evaline reached down into the floorboard of the truck and picked up a paper bag. "We don't want to forget the Roy Rogers alarm clock we bought him."

Evaline unlocked the front door, and they tiptoed through the house to Evaline's room.

The next morning, Charlie awoke to the smell of coffee perking and bacon sizzling. "Evaline," Charlie whispered. "Do you think your Ma knows I slept in your bed last night?"

"Yeah, she knows you're here. Nothing goes on around here that she doesn't find out about!"

"Do you think we should get up now?" Charlie asked.

But before Evaline could answer, there was a tapping on the door. "Who is it?" Evaline asked.

"It's me," Miles answered. "You two better get up and face the music. Ma's not one bit tickled over you all running off and getting married."

Evaline and Charlie got dressed and walked into the kitchen holding hands. Drucella, who was standing at the cookstove preparing breakfast, threw a quick glance at them over her shoulder. Miles was standing by the kitchen table.

"Okay," Miles said. "Are you two ready to face the jury? Do you have anything to say before I pass sentence on you?"

"Oh Miles, be serious for once in your life," Evaline scolded. She faced Drucella's stern, straight back. She had known Drucella would be disappointed, but she hadn't thought she would be cold. "Momma, I know we let you down, but we decided we had to get married now." She looked to Charlie for support before continuing. "We just didn't want to wait now that the country is at war."

"I have to admit I'm a little disappointed," Drucella said, her back still to them. "But I know I'm being selfish. Why, I've made wedding gowns for just about every family in the county. I always dreamed that one day I would make one for my own little girl," she finally turned to face them, "but if you're happy, that's all that matters."

"We are happy," Evaline said, "and we're going to make the most out of the time we've got before Charlie has to go to war."

Drucella nodded toward the kitchen table already set with four plates. "We're glad to have Charlie be a part of our family."

"Charlie, Mr. Farmer at the hotel told me you may not have to go to war," said Miles, as everyone sat down for breakfast. "He said because of your Pa's sawmill business, you could probably get deferred. He said the country is going to need coal and lumber to help fight the war."

"Well Miles, that's one thing I will never do. This is one thing I won't try and get out of," replied Charlie. "I would do almost anything to stay home and take care of my wife, but when my country calls me, I'll be ready to go and protect it."

"I'm thinking I'll go down and sign up and go serve my country too. I don't want to be left out. Momma, would that be alright with you?" Miles asked.

"Miles, be serious. They're not going to take anyone your age," Evaline snapped at him. "War is serious, not some big adventure."

Then Charlie added more gently, "Miles, your time is not right now. We hope you never have to go."

NINETEEN

T he news of the Japanese attack on Pearl Harbor had shocked and saddened the people of Hazard. Their shock quickly turned to outrage and anger. The following morning, a long line of volunteers wanting to enlist had formed outside the recruiting office. The oldest volunteer was a seventy-year-old veteran of the First World War. Harve Slone had honorably served his country twenty-three years earlier and was now in line to volunteer to serve again. That morning, he had driven his truck the 30 miles from Pippa Passes where he taught American History at Caney College.

The youngest volunteer was a fifteen-year-old boy who had gotten up before daylight to hitch a ride from the small community of Kingdom Come. Shade Hawley stood in front of Harve Slone in the long line that stretched out the door and down the sidewalk past Powell-Hackney Dry Goods and Fabrics. His unruly blond hair hung down over his forehead, and he kept pushing it back out of his eyes.

"Son, if they take you in the Army, you won't have to worry about keeping that hair out of your eyes. They'll give you a crew cut real fast," Harve joked.

"Yeah, I know, my Pa was in the service before I was born, and he told me all about it. Why, he said they would give me brand-spanking new clothes and, well, I'm not sure I believe it or not, but he said they'll give you two pair of new shoes. I don't rightly know why they would do that. A fellow could only wear one pair of shoes at a time. Why, I'd be tickled to death to just have one pair of new shoes. These old ones I got on are hand-me-downs, and every time it rains my socks get wet!"

"Well, now," said Harve focusing his steel-gray eyes, on the young man, "I hope you're not joining the service just so you can get some new clothes."

"No, sir, that's not it. That's not it at all! You see, I got an uncle who's been serving on the Arizona at Pearl Harbor. We don't know if he got killed, or not. Only word we've heard so far is what they say on the radio. My Pa won't admit it, but I think he's dead. That's the reason I want to sign up. I want to go and fight those Japs who ambushed our soldiers."

Harve leaned heavily on his homemade hickory cane. He felt a sharp pain in his right leg and hip, and he wished he had a place to hold onto for support with his free hand. The pain intensified, and he placed his hand on Shade's shoulder for a moment and then quickly withdrew it, but not before Shade turned and saw the pain in the old man's face.

"That's all right, mister," Shade said. "Any time you feel tired, you're welcome to lean on me."

Harve, standing 6'1" and broad shouldered when he wasn't leaning on his cane, was neatly dressed in a flannel shirt and blue jeans. He stared again at the young boy standing in front of him. Harve wondered what could be the real reason this young boy was standing in line hoping to go off to war. The young boy's unruly hair gave the impression that it had been caught up in a whirlwind. His clothes were threadbare and had no doubt been purchased at a rummage sale. The boy became uncomfortable as Harve looked him up one side and down the other. Shade turned back and forth nervously, and kept brushing his hair away from his face as the line moved steadily toward the door.

"Do you think you could spare a cigarette, mister? I smoked my last one over two hours ago, and standing in this line is giving me the heebie-jeebies."

"I sure can," Harve said, and he reached inside his shirt pocket and pulled out an unopened pack. He tore the wrappings from the top of the pack and smacked the bottom against the palm of his hand. Two cigarettes popped up from the corner of the pack.

"Lucky Strikes! Wow!" exclaimed Shade. "I haven't smoked a Lucky Strike since I don't know when!"

Harve struck a wooden match with the nail of his thumb and extended it to the boy to light his cigarette.

"Man, there's nothing like a Lucky Strike!" the boy said after blowing a smoke ring into the air. "You know, they say cigarettes are going to be hard to come by now that the war has started. Truth be said, they have always been hard for me to come by!"

"What did you say your name was, young man?" Harve asked.

"I didn't say, but it's Shade. Shade Hawley. I'm from up the road a piece. Up around Kingdom Come."

"You don't say! Well, I'm Harve Slone from Pippa Passes. I teach history at the college."

"Huh, I would never have dreamed you was a teacher. You don't look like a teacher to me."

"Well, I can't help what I look like," Harve said as they stepped inside the door. Harve bent down and tilted his cane against the coat rack. "You know, Shade, I may need to take you up on your offer to lean on you a bit. I won't have a Chinaman's chance of getting in the service if they see me leaning on a cane."

"If you don't mind me asking, Harve, just how old are you?"

"Now, that's really funny, Shade. I was just about to ask you the same question!"

Shade shook his head and looked at Harve before he spoke. "At first I was a mind to lie about my age and tell them I was eighteen. But what the hell, I know they wouldn't fall for that, so I decided to go ahead and tell them the truth." Shade paused for a moment as he looked down at the linoleum floor. "I'll be sixteen in a little over two months from now," he said.

"Good Lord, Shade! I hate to tell you this, but I stand a better chance of getting in the service than you do! The government's not about to take anyone who's under eighteen. The one thing they don't want to do is get this country's mommas on the warpath. You're doing the right thing by not lying about your age." Harve studied Shade's face where the disappointment was evident. "Now, I'm not saying you don't look big enough to be eighteen, but when that recruiting sergeant looks you in the face, he's going to know better. Why, I'm taken aback to think your momma would agree to let you join the service at your age."

"I have never really had a momma. She died giving me birth. There's just me and my Pa, and a few kinfolk. My Pa and me, well, we don't get along too good. He's got a way of drinking a little too much shine and when he does, he can get real mean. He says it was me who caused him to lose his wife, and he hardly ever lets me forget it."

Harve now knew why this young boy had gotten up before daylight to volunteer to go off to war. Facing the war probably seemed more inviting than what he was enduring at home. The line moved toward the large, wooden desk where two recruiting sergeants were interviewing the volunteers.

"By the way, Harve, you never did tell me how old you are."

"Oh, that's right. I never did, did I? Well, I'll be seventy-one when my birthday rolls around this coming January. You see, I've already crossed that big pond once to go and fight the Germans in the last war."

"I don't mean to be nosy or anything, but wouldn't it be better to keep on teaching school and let us young folks go and fight this war?"

"The way I see it, Shade, I don't have a hell of a lot of time left. My wife passed away four years ago, and to tell you the truth, after teaching school for over twenty years, I'm just plain bored to death with it." Harve Paused as one of the men sitting at the desk got up. Shade took a deep breath. He would be next. But the sergeant at the desk went back to his paperwork. Harve continued his story to pass the time. "Oh, I know if they take me, they won't let me do any serious fighting, but I could show our boys how to shoot and take care of their rifles. I could tell them what to expect on the battlefield and how to take care of themselves. I'm not one to brag, but I got my fair share of Germans in the last war. Why, I can knock the eye out of a hawk over a hundred feet away. I guess that's the only thing that's not gone bad on me is my eyes. Seems like about all I ever do is teach history and go squirrel hunting. Oh, I might drive over here to Hazard every two or three weeks and go to a good Western picture show."

"Next please! Who's next? Are you next in line, young man?" one of the sergeants asked.

"Yes sir! I sure am!" Shade said as he sat down in the chair across from the recruiter.

Harve moved up behind Shade's chair and put his hands on the back of the chair for support.

The sergeant looked into the boy's young face and then glanced at the other recruiter sitting beside him. The other sergeant quickly looked down at the papers on his desk and began writing. "Now, young man, just what can the Army do for you today?"

"Sir, I want to join up with the Army and go fight for my country."

"What's your name and how old are you?"

"My name is Shade Hawley, and I'll be 16 years old on my next birthday."

The sergeant smiled at Shade and at Harve standing behind him. "Well, now, Shade, the first thing I want to do is shake your hand and thank you for wanting to join the Army. I'm Sergeant Robert Lee Moran from the great State of Virginia." The sergeant extended his hand across the desk and shook Shade's hand. "Now that we know each other, Shade, I've got to tell you that you've got to be 18 before you can join the Army."

"Yes sir, I know my age is against me, but I was hoping you could overlook my age. You see, my Pa wrote a letter granting me his permission to join the Army." Shade quickly removed the letter from his back pocket and passed it toward the sergeant. The sergeant held up his hand to refuse the letter, but seeing everyone staring at him and the young man, he accepted it. As he unfolded the crumpled piece of notebook paper, the room became quiet. All eyes were now on the sergeant, and everyone waited to see what the decision would be. After looking at the letter, the sergeant spoke softly. "Shade, do you mind if I read your letter out loud?"

"No sir, I don't mind at all."

The sergeant cleared his throat.

> *To Whom It May Concern:*
> *My name is Oliver Hawley, and I take pen in hand*
> *on this December 8, 1941, to write this letter for my*

boy, Shade. This boy takes more after his Ma than he takes after me, and that's a good thing. He came into this world early and we never made it to the midwife's house. His Ma died in the shade of a sycamore tree giving him birth, and that's why I named him Shade. He's a stubborn, headstrong boy, and I've never seen him back down from any kind of a fight. To my way of thinking, he would make a good soldier and do his country proud. I hereby give my permission for this boy to join the Army and go fight the Japs, Germans or whoever else might take up arms against this country.

Army Veteran of the Last War
Oliver Hawley

Harve knew disappointment awaited Shade. He patted him on his shoulder, and like everyone else in the room, waited for the sergeant's decision.

"Shade, I want you to know I would be honored to fight by your side anywhere, anytime, but my hands are tied. We have rules and I've got to obey them. There's nothing I can do."

Shade was disappointed and embarrassed. His head dropped and he looked down at the floor. He was ready to turn and run out of the recruiting office when Harve placed his hand on the back of Shade's shoulder. "It's all right, son, there will be another time."

"He's right, Shade," the sergeant said. "The way I see it, this war is going to last at least five years. Go back home and finish high school, and then come back when you're 18. Yes, indeed, this country's going to need brave, young men like you if we're going to win this war. Be sure to get that degree because you look like officer material to me."

As Shade turned away, he could only manage a faint, "Yes, sir."

Harve took his pack of Lucky Strikes from his pocket and passed them to Shade. "Now, don't you go running off. Wait for me outside because I'm going to buy us a plate lunch at the Five and Dime."

Outside, Shade lit his cigarette and leaned against the concrete wall beside the recruiting office. He was still smoking his cigarette when Harve stepped outside the door. "Are they going to take you?" he asked.

"No, son, they don't need men my age anymore. They say I can be more help to my country by staying here and teaching history. Why, I all but got down on my hands and knees and begged them to let me join, but nothing I said did any good."

Shade, still feeling like an outcast, flicked his cigarette butt into the street.

"You got no call to feel bad," Harve said. "Like the sergeant said, wait a couple of years, and they'll sign you up in a heartbeat."

"I know, but I had my head set on going now. Two years seems like a long time to wait."

"It will go by quicker than you think. Just wait until you get to be my age, and two years will go by before you can turn around. Just be happy you'll be able to go in two years. All the waiting in the world won't help me. I guess I had my time, and it's selfish of me to want to have it again."

"I'm really sorry they didn't take you, Harve. I would have given anything if we both could have signed up and gone together."

"Well, no use in us moping around here like two sick kittens. Let's head on down to the Five and Dime before it gets crowded, and I'll buy you that plate lunch I promised."

After eating big helpings of meatloaf and mashed potatoes, Harve and Shade walked up and down the aisles and inspected the entire store's merchandise, a long candy counter with weighing scales, toys and children's games, cookware and sundries. Shade was astonished by the large aquarium used for selling goldfish. He watched in amazement as the goldfish swam in and out of the replica of a small ship sunk in the white sand. "I've never seen anything like this before in my life! I believe I could stay here all day and watch these pretty fish swim. I'd give anything if my Pa could see this!"

"Well, some day when you join the Army, you're going to see things you never dreamed of seeing," replied Harve. "Now, why don't you watch these fish swim while I pick up a couple of things?"

A few minutes later as they walked outside the Five and Dime, Shade reached out to shake Harve's hand. "I guess I had better try to hitch a ride back to Kingdom Come. It's sure been a pleasure meeting you, Harve, and I want to thank you for the plate lunch you bought me."

"You're more than welcome. I only wish we were traveling in the same direction so I could give you a ride."

"Don't worry about that. I won't have any problems. The first ride I caught brought me all the way to Vicco this morning. Only took me three rides to make it to Hazard."

Harve hesitated. He stared at Shade. "You know ever since I met you there's one thing that's been bothering me."

Shade gave him a puzzled look. "What's that?"

"It's your hair. You know you would be a good-looking young man if you had a decent haircut. Who cuts your hair?"

"My Pa cuts it, but I guess he doesn't cut it too good."

"I'd like to take you to Shelton's barber shop and let you get your hair cut before you go back home."

"I couldn't do that right now. I've only got 20 cents with me, and I know a haircut would cost more than that."

"I think I can manage to pay the 50 cents they charge to cut a head of hair."

"I can't let you do that, Harve. You've done too much for me already. I'm beginning to feel like a real first-class bum. I smoked your cigarettes, and you bought my dinner. I got to stop somewhere." He smiled, but shook his head.

Harve put his hand inside the brown paper bag that held his purchases from the Five and Dime. He took out a small pad and quickly wrote an I.O.U. "Now, if you will sign this I.O.U. for 50 cents, everything will be squared away."

Shade took the pencil and slowly signed his name.

"You know, Shade, it's funny how a red-and-white barber pole always reminds me of a stick of peppermint candy," Harve said as they entered the barber shop.

"You fellows needing a haircut this afternoon?" Virgil asked as he got up from his barber chair, automatically brushing off his white shirt.

"I just got one a week ago, but I think this young man could use one," Harve said.

Virgil folded his newspaper and smacked it against the seat of the chair as if he was dusting away any hair left by the last customer. "Okay, son, hop right up here and have a seat. I'll see if I can straighten that hair up a tad."

Virgil took his comb and tried to part Shade's hair. "Ouch!" Shade yelled as he jerked his head away from the comb.

"I sure hope you didn't pay anyone for gapping up your hair this way," Virgil said.

"No, my Pa cut it."

"Your Pa? Well, he really gapped it up pretty good, but where it's growed out some, I think I can straighten it up." Virgil glanced over at Harve who was already seated and leafing through a magazine. "Now I'm going to lean you back in this chair so I can wash your hair."

"I didn't know you would need to wash my hair," Shade said. "Will it cost extra for you to do that?"

"Why, yes it will," Virgil replied. "It costs 50 cents for a haircut, and 25 cents for me to wash it. You hair's in such a mess that there's no way I can cut it if I don't wash it first."

"I only borrowed 50 cents. I didn't know you would need to wash it," he said trying to get up.

Harve looked up from his magazine, but before he could speak, Virgil said, "Now, don't go getting your shorts in an uproar, young man. Since I don't have anyone waiting, I'll give you the works for 50 cents."

There hadn't been a customer in his shop all day, and Virgil was delighted to have a head of hair to cut as well as someone to talk with, so he was taking his time cutting the young man's hair. Virgil was quick to give his opinion on any subject a customer might want to discuss, and he didn't mind letting anyone know how he felt about the war, Kentucky basketball or the weather. Today he was talking non-stop about Pearl Harbor as he worked on Shade's hair.

Shade's back was facing the mirror, and Virgil made sure not to turn the chair where Shade could see the transformation that was taking place. Shade could only wait for Harve to look up from his magazine and then study his facial expressions for a sign of what was taking place.

After about 30 minutes--Shade thought he had surely been in the chair a couple of hours--Virgil finally turned the chair around to face the mirror. "How does that haircut suit you, young man?" Virgil asked with a grin.

Shade stared in total bewilderment at the reflection looking back at him. The boy with the crew cut was clean and sharp-looking. He looked like the recruit Shade longed to be. He scarcely could believe what he was seeing. "Is that really me?" he asked. "I can't believe that's really me."

"Well, it is," Harve said getting up and standing behind him. "You look like a whole new person."

Harve gave Virgil a dollar and told him to keep the change.

"Thank you very much, and whatever you do, don't try cutting this young man's hair again. Bring him back to my shop, and I'll be happy to cut it for him."

"Oh, you don't understand," Harve said, "I'm not this boy's Pa. I'm his friend." He saw the surprise on Virgil's face. "That's right, we only met this morning and we became fast friends."

"In fact, I would say best friends," Shade said abruptly.

As they walked down the sidewalk, Shade kept touching his hair and looking in all the plate-glass windows to make sure his new haircut hadn't disappeared. Harve stopped in front of a red Model "A" pickup truck with black fenders. He took out his key and unlocked the door.

"Jeepers! Is this your Model A truck?" Shade asked.

"Yeah, it belongs to me. I bought it new 10 years ago, and it still runs like a scalded dog."

"Wow! You don't see many of these still around anymore," Shade said. He rubbed his hand over the hood of the pickup. He could almost see his reflection in the paint.

"Maybe you could come over to Pippa Passes sometime, and I could give you a driving lesson."

"Yeah, maybe I could. I'd like that, and I could pay off my I.O.U."

"That would be fine, mighty fine. Just call the college and let me know you're coming." Harve extended his hand. "Good luck, Shade. Take care of yourself, now."

"Before I go, I need to ask you a question."

"Okay, Shade, go ahead."

"You know when I got turned down at the recruiting office today?"

"Yeah, I sure do. I think I will remember that for a good while." Harve leaned on his cane.

"You know, I keep thinking about what that sergeant said about me looking like officer material. Do you think he just said that because he thought I was pining real bad? Do you think he really meant what he said?" Shade stood tall and waited.

"Yeah, he meant what he said," replied Harve. "When a man's been in the Army long enough to make sergeant, you can bet he's not going to pull any punches."

"Do you know what made him think I could make an officer?"

"Yeah, I know what he saw in you. You see, he saw things in you that you probably would never see in yourself."

"Like what?"

Harve looked steadily at him. He saw a healthy young man, not quite 16, but determined to get into the army. "Well, I think he saw bravery. Someone who would take charge in a bad situation and stand by his fellow soldier."

"Do you think I could really do that?" He asked.

"I not only think you could do it, I know when the time comes, you will."

Shade put his hands in his pockets. The two men looked at each other, both knowing this friendship was something special. Shade nodded to Harve, turned and began to walk.

Harve got into his truck. He sat and watched as the boy walked on down the street. Shade stopped halfway down the block for one last look at Harve, he waved and then turned back around and continued walking. "You know, Harve," Shade said out loud, "I think I'll get started back in school."

TWENTY

The letters to the young men always began the same way: "Greetings from the President of the United States …"

It had been several weeks since Pearl Harbor, and Charlie's "Greetings" letter had not arrived. Yet, even though he would not be in the Service as quickly as he thought, he had no doubt the letter would arrive any day, and he wanted to make sure that Evaline would be okay.

At Charlie's insistence, Evaline had moved into the Wills' house. When Charlie left for the service, she would be there with Everett and Anna Mae Wills, Charlie's Parents, and with Adam, Charlie's younger brother. Staying with the Wills, Evaline would be much closer to her job at Doris's store. Doris had given Evaline time off so that the newlyweds could spend as much time as possible together before Charlie left for the service.

Every day, it seemed one or more of Charlie's friends received their notice to report for induction. After waiting several more weeks for his Greeting, and wanting to be ready when called, Charlie went to the induction station, which had been set up near the Five and Dime, and took his physical. Healthy and strong, at six foot one and 170 pounds, he passed the exam with flying colors, and was sent home for two weeks to get his affairs in order.

As the two weeks neared an end, Charlie and Evaline nervously awaited the mailman. Evaline could always tell by the expression on the mailman's face if they had survived another day before Charlie received his notice to report for duty.

The day Charlie received his orders, Evaline noticed the mailman walked a little slower than normal, and there wasn't a trace of a smile on his face. When Charlie and Everett came home for dinner, their noon meal that day, Charlie tore open the envelope as Evaline clung to his arm. Anna Mae had cooked pork chops, Charlie's favorite, after she saw the envelope Evaline took from the mailman. Sitting at the table, Evaline squeezed Charlie's hand under the table. Anna Mae and Everett ate quietly as if this were just another day. As upset as the family was, they also felt relief that Charlie had finally received his orders. "You know I won't be able to ever come back home until I leave home," Charlie told them.

Charlie's orders required him to report to the Hazard Bus Station on April 6 to take a special bus to Cincinnati. According to the letter, he would be required to take an oath to defend his country against all enemies, both foreign and domestic, after which he would be sent to basic training.

On the Monday morning Charlie was scheduled to leave for the service, Anna Mae prepared a big breakfast for the family. Everett ate quietly, staring steadily at his plate. While eating breakfast, Anna Mae and Evaline laughed and talked about how handsome they thought Charlie would look in his Army uniform. They made Charlie promise to send a picture of himself in his uniform as soon as he could. The family was careful to talk only of pleasant things, like the house Charlie and Evaline planned to build when he returned home. The one thing they dared not talk about, although it was on everyone's mind, was that this could be the last time they would ever see Charlie.

A steady rain had settled in on Sunday night. Charlie had done his best to talk Evaline out of going to the Bus Station with him. He preferred to say his goodbyes to the women at home, but Evaline would have none of it. She wanted every precious second she could have with Charlie.

"Evaline, for heaven's sake!" Charlie said. "Look outside! It's raining cats and dogs. Now there's not one bit of use in the world in you going to the Bus Station on a day like today. I think it would be best to say our goodbyes right here at home."

"Well, Charlie Wills," Evaline replied, "you can think what you want to think, but I've been planning on seeing you off at the station, and that's exactly what I'm going to do."

Charlie rolled his eyes, shook his head and walked away. He knew Evaline's mind was made up, and there was no way anyone could change it. Evaline turned to face Anna Mae. "Could I please borrow your umbrella?" she asked.

"You sure can," Anna Mae replied. "There's one in the closet by the front door. You're more than welcome to it."

Everett took his watch from his side pocket and held it back from his eyes to be sure he was reading the Roman numerals correctly. "My goodness gracious! It's already six-thirty! We're going to have to get started if we're going to get you to the Bus Station before seven."

"Charlie, I'm going to wake your brother," Anna Mae said. "I know he would want to say goodbye before you go."

"No, Ma. Don't wake Adam," Charlie said. "With all this rain, he won't be able to work at the sawmill today, so he can sleep in for a change, and besides, we already said goodbye."

Anna Mae's tired eyes looked into Charlie's face. The dreaded time had arrived. There would be no great outburst of emotion. That would not be the way of these proud descendants of pioneer stock.

She and her family had been bred to face any and all situations without willful sorrow.

Anna Mae remembered how Charlie had hugged his teddy bear when he was only one; she remembered the little boy who climbed up into her lap with his book of stories for her to read. Today, she was losing him. Still looking at Charlie, she spoke to her husband and new daughter-in-law. "Everett, would you and Evaline mind waiting in the truck? I want to have a minute with my boy before he leaves."

Everett and Evaline walked out quietly. Anna Mae took Charlie's hand in hers and gave it a tight squeeze. "You've always been a good son to your Pa and me. Now you go and do what's got to be done, and we'll be waiting here for you when you come back home."

Charlie pulled her close and gave her a hug. Then he leaned down and lightly kissed her on the forehead. "I love you, Ma."

"I know, son. I know you do," she said. She smiled and slowly pulled away from Charlie trying not to let him see the tears in her eyes. Charlie picked up his small zip-up bag that contained his toothbrush, razor and a change of clothes. He stepped out the door. He stood in the yard in a trance and took one last look at the small farm. The rain ran down his face and soaked through his clothes. He was lost in his thoughts until he heard Evaline calling his name.

"Charlie! Charlie Wills! What on earth are you doing?" she screamed at him from the truck where she and Everett sat waiting. "Do you want to catch your death of cold and die before you step one foot on that bus?"

Charlie ran to the truck and slipped into the seat next to Evaline. Anna Mae watched from the window. Charlie's eyes were moist. Everett and Evaline looked straight ahead, and Charlie stared off into space as the rain continued to pepper the windshield. Evaline tried hard to remember all the things she wanted to tell him before he boarded the bus.

At the Bus Station, a small crowd with umbrellas and raincoats had gathered under the canopy to await the arrival of the bus. Everett parked the truck across the street from the station and took another look at his watch. "Well, Charlie, it looks like you got about ten more minutes before the bus will be getting here. I won't be crossing the street with you, son. I'll say goodbye here." He held out his hand to Charlie. "You remember how you've been raised, and whatever you do, be sure you do it honorably."

"I will, Pa. I won't let you down. Why, I'll be back home before you hardly have time to know I'm gone," Charlie replied.

"You be careful, son. Your Ma and me, we're going to be waiting here for you."

"I know you will. Goodbye, Pa."

"Goodbye son. May God be with you."

The two men turned away from each other so neither could see the other's tears.

Charlie and Evaline hurried across the street under the yellow umbrella. As Charlie shook the water from the umbrella, Evaline looked at the young recruits waiting under the Bus Station's canopy. She thought most of them looked as though they'd had too much to drink and gotten very little sleep the night before. Their faces were full of false bravado.

"Charlie, I brought some things for you to take with you, so we'll need to hurry before the bus gets here." Evaline was fumbling in her purse.

"I'm sure I've already got everything I'm going to need," Charlie said, "toothbrush, razor and a change of clothes. That's all the letter said to bring."

"Charlie, I'm not talking about that stupid letter the Army sent you." Evaline pulled a chain with a Saint Christopher medal from her purse and slipped it over his head leaving her arms around his neck. "Wear this around your neck, Charlie, and don't ever take it off. It's supposed to keep you safe."

"Evaline, we're Baptist, not Catholic," Charlie said.

"I know, Charlie, but a lot of people believe in Saint Christopher. Right now, we need all the help we can get!"

Her arms still wrapped around his neck, Evaline leaned in and kissed Charlie.

One of the more rowdy recruits jeered, "Hey honey, I'm going away, too. Don't I deserve one of your kisses?"

"Yeah, me too!" another recruit called out. "Would someone please give me a pencil so I can get this babe's address? I'd like to write her a long love letter," he laughed.

Charlie's face turned red, and he shook his head in anger. "See, I told you. We should have said our goodbyes at home."

"Oh, don't pay them any attention. They're just jealous," Evaline said. She kept her arms around him.

A loud cheer erupted from the crowd as the troop bus pulled up alongside the curb. A short, heavyset sergeant in his thirties stepped down from the bus. "Okay, you bunch of freeloaders," he said. "Line up and give me your name and number as you board. Come on! Come on! Hurry up! The war will be over before I get you goldbrickers to Cincinnati."

"Hey Sarge, we ain't sworn in yet," a freckle-faced youth called out. "Is it too late for us to change our minds and go back home?"

When most all the recruits were now on the bus, Charlie and another young man were still saying their farewells. Evaline realized their last minutes together had now turned into precious seconds.

From her coat pocket, she hurriedly took a picture of herself that she'd had made by a local photographer. She held it out to Charlie. "Charlie, paste this inside the top of your helmet. Then when the danger is over and you take your helmet off, the first one you see will be me."

"Okay, lover boy," the sergeant shouted from the door of the bus, "are you coming with us, or should I tell President Roosevelt you decided to sit this war out and maybe you'll catch the next one?"

Before Evaline could comprehend what was taking place, Charlie had kissed her a final time and was racing through the rain toward the bus.

"Well, ain't that nice!" the sergeant said as Charlie boarded. "You decided to honor us with your presence. I was beginning to think you were going to be the first person ever to be court-martialed before he even joined the service."

As Charlie found a seat by the window, the recruits whistled and called out, "Hubba Hubba."

Charlie stared out the bus window at Evaline standing in the street under the yellow umbrella.

Eli, who had been taking everything in from the doorway of the Taylor Hotel, across the street from the Bus Station, thought the sergeant was being too hard on Charlie. He had known Charlie and his family for years and felt insulted on Charlie's behalf. His anger began to boil. Eli reached down to the floor and gathered Whiskers up in his arms. "Come on, Whiskers, we're going to tell that sergeant a thing or two before that bus leaves."

Eli made a mad dash out the door and through the rain toward the bus. Holding Whiskers under one arm, and waving the other over his head, he shouted, "Dagnabit, Sergeant! You might as well get off Charlie Wills' back right now because he's going to make one of the best damn soldiers this country has ever seen!"

The sergeant was taken aback as he watched Eli and Whiskers getting soaked in the pouring rain.

"Charlie Wills, you be sure to shoot one of them Japs for Whiskers and me!" Eli shouted as the bus pulled away from the curb.

At the sight of Eli and Whiskers' two-man brigade, the recruits on the bus broke out into hysterical laughter. Evaline, feeling sad and melancholy, did her best not to laugh, but she couldn't help herself. She took one look at Charlie in the bus window, and they both burst out laughing together.

Charlie pushed his window down and leaned outside the bus. Rain pelted his face. "The first shell I fire at the enemy is going to be for Whiskers and you, Eli!" he yelled out as the bus picked up speed. Charlie was still smiling and waving as the bus turned the corner. "I love you, Evaline," he called back, and then the bus was gone.

Everett crossed the street and stood beside Evaline. "Hellfire! We ought to send Whiskers and Eli over there. Why, they'd have this war done and over within a couple of months," he laughed. This time, Eli laughed, too.

Aboard the bus, the excitement was over, and most of the recruits began settling in. During the long ride to Cincinnati, they would try to catch up on the sleep they had missed the night before. Charlie was still angry toward the recruits for jeering at Evaline and spoke only when necessary to the young men around him.

The rain was still coming down as the bus made its way toward the city limits. It was the type of day when Charlie would have enjoyed staying inside and reading one of Jesse Stuart's novels by the fireplace. Charlie watched from the window as the scenery passed by. He saw a man chasing after his umbrella after the wind had blown it out of his hands and down the street. Charlie thought, "I wish that was all I had to worry about. He will catch his umbrella and go home tonight, but I may never see my home or Evaline again."

The bus hadn't even gotten out of the city limits and Charlie was already homesick. He was joining the great exodus of young people from the small towns, valleys and hollows, in the eastern Kentucky Mountains, destined to join thousands of others like themselves from all parts of the country to make up one of the greatest fighting forces the world had ever seen.

Charlie took the Bible that Brother Carlson had given him from his coat pocket. He thought back about what Brother Carlson had told him when he presented him the Bible in church. "Charlie, God has a plan, and He has picked you to be a part of His plan. You see, Charlie, what most people don't understand is God doesn't make mistakes. God's plan is already laid out, and He alone knows who will come back, and who will go to live with Him in His heavenly home. Now, when you're troubled, and you don't understand, randomly open your Bible and read. God will give you the answer you seek."

Charlie opened his Bible and read the first line his eyes fell upon:

I will lift up mine eyes unto the hills from whence cometh my strength.

TWENTY ONE

Miles found his goose-feather pillow at the foot of his bed and hurriedly covered his head with it. Now the shrill ringing of his Roy Rogers alarm clock didn't sound nearly as loud. He waited until the alarm completely ran down before he removed his head from under his pillow. He got up and went to the bathroom.

"Good Lord, where did all these pimples come from?" he muttered studying his face in the mirror. Brother Carlson had said the Lord works in mysterious ways, but it just didn't seem fair that the minute God let you start liking girls, He would suddenly change your voice and give you a whole new bunch of pimples, to boot! Miles was almost certain any girl, at the sight of him, would feel like throwing up.

Miles tiptoed into the kitchen and raised the dishcloth that covered his plate to see what his Ma had set aside for his breakfast - a biscuit and two strips of bacon. He parted the biscuit and placed the bacon inside to form a cold sandwich. At least the coffee was hot. No need to complain. Complaining would be unpatriotic since some of the country's fighting men on the battlefields probably wouldn't be having any breakfast at all. He ate breakfast quietly, now and then glancing at Drucella's door. Now, if only his luck continued to hold, he would be out the back door before she realized he was gone.

After he finished, he scraped his plate and put his dishes in the sink. He opened the screen door. The squeaking reminded him that he had never gotten around to oiling its hinges. He froze in his tracks.

"Miles, is that you?" Drucella called out. She appeared from around the corner. "Have you had breakfast? Now, just where on earth do you think you're running off to this early?"

"For Christ's Sake, Ma! I can't answer but one question at a time."

"You know I don't like for you to use Christ's name to express yourself," Drucella said sharply. "Now, don't let me hear anything like that come out of your mouth again."

Miles sighed, still holding the screen door open. He hoped he would be able to get away quickly. "All right, and if you must know, the Three Musketeers are going to the top of the mountain today to hunt zang. Mr. Herd said a man checked into the Taylor Hotel, and he's paying 55 cents a pound for ginseng. One thing's for sure, the Musketeers are going to cabbage on some of that city slicker's cash."

"Well, you had better keep a keen eye out for snakes," Drucella said. She looked at the dishes stacked neatly in the sink and seemed satisfied with his plans. "And be sure you're home before the sun goes down behind the mountain."

"The Three Musketeers" was the name Cecil, Wilbur and Miles had started calling themselves. The Musketeers did intend to go zang hunting, but not this Saturday morning. Miles hated lying to Drucella, but he knew his mother wouldn't approve of their planned adventure. Plans for this Saturday had been made over a week ago when Cecil had first told them about the man who had built a house in the shape of a giant goose. The Musketeers had decided to hitchhike the ten miles to the small community on the other side of Walkertown to see the Goose House. Drucella had forbidden Miles to ever hitchhike.

"Cecil, I hope you're telling us the truth, and not leading us on a wild goose chase," Wilbur laughed as the Musketeers began the ten-minute walk that would take them from the 100-year-old oak tree, their gathering spot, to the highway.

"What I'm telling you is just what my Pa told me, and I'll have you know my Pa don't lie."

"You know, Cecil, it's a shame you don't take more after your Pa." Wilbur gave Cecil a friendly poke in the ribs. Cecil tossed his head back and laughed.

"Well, you can bet your sweet ass on one thing," Miles warned. He stopped for a moment, bent down and retied the shoelace that had been dragging in the dirt. "If we get caught hitchhiking to Walkertown, we're all three going to be up the creek without a paddle."

"Yeah, but a house that looks like a goose——I can't wait to see that!" Wilbur grinned. The other guys nodded their excitement.

"You know, wouldn't it be funny if a hunter from the flat country had too much to drink and stumbled out of the woods upon a giant goose house?" Cecil said. "I bet he would throw his bottle away and never take another drink as long as he lived!"

Miles laughed. "Yeah, he would probably wet his pants and run for cover!"

Soon the boys passed Mr. Herd's turkey farm. Wilbur picked up a rock and threw it at the broken board in the fence the Musketeers used for target practice whenever they passed. His aim was off today. The rock sailed over the board and judging from the noise the turkeys began to make, the Musketeers figured that the rock must have landed in a group of turkeys. The Musketeers took off toward the highway before Mr. Herd could come out and investigate.

At the highway, the Musketeers stood on the side of the road with their thumbs waving in the wind. A black sedan whooshed by. "Thanks a lot, mister! It's not like you got a whole carload of people," Wilbur yelled out to the lone driver. With all the Musketeers' newfound teenage energy, they found it was almost impossible to stand in one spot for any length of time. They playfully pushed and shoved each other back and forth as they waited to thumb down the next car.

"Can you imagine how fast Miss Turner could get a ride if she was hitchhiking?" Cecil asked. "All she would have to do is pull her skirt up past her knees, and cars would be slamming on their brakes and running into ditches and trees."

"Why, it would be the damndest pileup anyone ever saw in their life!" Miles laughed.

The Musketeers' heads went up at the same time. A car was coming. A Ford station wagon with a young lady driver. Wilbur tucked in his shirt, pulled his shoulders back and put on his Sunday smile before he stuck out his thumb.

"Wipe that silly smile off your face," Miles said. If she sees you, she sure as hell won't stop." The young lady looked straight ahead as she passed them. Disappointment crossed all their faces. They began walking again.

Suddenly, the station wagon's brakes squealed, and the car came to an abrupt stop. They stared in disbelief. Then, the race was on.

"I get to ride shotgun," Wilbur called out as they all ran toward the waiting station wagon.

"Not if I get there first, you don't," Cecil shouted back over his shoulder.

But Miles, as usual, was ahead of the pack. As he reached out to open the front door, the pretty lady pressed her foot down on the gas pedal, and the station wagon lunged forward leaving the Musketeers choking in a cloud of exhaust fumes.

"We love you, too, Tokyo Rose!" Wilbur shouted bitterly.

"Yeah, and we don't accept rides from Nazi spies!" Miles called out to the disappearing station wagon.

An hour later, after being passed up by several cars and trucks, the Musketeers were having second thoughts about hitchhiking a ride to Walkertown. "We may as well call the dogs, and piss on the fire," Cecil said gruffly. "If we get to Walkertown today, it looks like we're going to have to hoof it."

"Yeah, we've done wasted the biggest part of our Saturday morning, and we haven't even come close to getting a ride," said Miles. "I say we thumb one more car and if we don't get a ride, then we go to the Virginia Theatre and see if Eugene will slip us in the side door."

"I'm all for that," said Cecil. "I heard there's a war picture playing that's starring John Wayne, and the cartoon is the *Three Stooges*." Cecil grinned.

Then they heard a chug-chug-chug off in the distance.

"Hey, I think I hear our last car coming now," Wilbur shouted.

"Sounds more like a motor bike than a car to me," Cecil commented.

A little red truck about half the size of a pickup appeared on the horizon.

"Holy cow! What in tarnation is that thing coming up the road?" Miles shielded his eyes from the sun as he peered down the road at the on-coming truck. "It looks like one of those midget pickup trucks."

"I've heard of those midget trucks, but I never thought I'd ever see one of them in the mountains," Wilbur replied.

"They call them Austin Bantams," Cecil offered. He had never seen an Austin Bantam himself, but he had heard Austin Begley talking about a tiny truck one day in the barber shop. Austin Begley had been to Cincinnati to see the car, and Cecil remembered that the man and the car's name were the same.

"I don't care what they call them. I wouldn't be caught dead riding in that tin cup. Quick guys! Get your thumbs down before he sees us and stops," Miles shouted.

The Austin Bantam, a truck no larger than most dining room tables, slowly came to a stop beside the Musketeers. A small man, Miles figured even shorter than Mickey Rooney, leaned over to one side and rolled the passenger window down. "You boys needing a ride?" he asked in a high-pitched voice.

"Well, I'm not really sure. We were just about ready to go back to town when you stopped," Miles stammered, wondering if the Musketeers could all get into the truck.

"Well, if you think I've got all day to sit in the middle of the road while you're making up your minds, you got another think coming," said the man irritably. "Now, I'm going as far as Dwarf. If you want a ride, hop in the back."

The Musketeers shrugged and then crowded into the bed of the small pickup. It putt-putted on down the highway,

"This reminds me of the *Wizard of Oz*," Cecil whispered. He didn't think the driver could hear him, but he wasn't taking any chances.

"Yeah, we're off to see the goose house. The wonderful goose house with the Munchkin from Dwarf," Miles laughed.

"Be quiet! He might hear us and put us out on the side of the road," said Cecil. "It's embarrassing enough just riding in this tin cup, much less getting set out on the side of the road by a Munchkin."

They crossed the bridge over the North Fork of the Kentucky River and puttered up the hill that ran by Riverside Cemetery. The boys fell quiet as they passed the gravestones.

"I just felt a cold chill like someone just stepped on my grave," Wilbur said with a shiver.

"I felt it, too. It made the hair on the back of my neck stick out." Cecil looked to Miles waiting for his response, but Miles seemed unaffected.

"Have you guys gone completely nuts?" said Miles. "I didn't feel a thing. I think you guys are letting your imaginations run away with you."

"Well, I know what I felt," said Wilbur. "I just hope we don't end up having to walk by this graveyard after dark." Wilbur shuddered again.

The Austin Bantam climbed to the top of the hill where the road leveled out and continued north on Kentucky 15. For the first time that morning, the clouds parted. The boys welcomed the warm rays of the sun. They rounded a curve in the road, and there it was in all its glory, glowing in the bright sunlight.

The Goose House looked as though it were nesting in the warm sun, and its head appeared to be at least forty feet above the ground. Its orange bill was pointed toward the highway as though it might rise up any moment and walk across the road, taking trees and telephone poles with it.

Miles lightly tapped on the truck's rear cab window and asked the driver to stop. The Musketeers jumped over the tailgate and onto the road. Miles walked to the driver's window. "Thanks mister, we really appreciate the ride," he said, but the driver already had the truck in gear. He waved out the window as he left.

"Well, upon my word and honor, I ain't never seen anything to beat this in my entire life," Cecil managed to sputter.

Miles was equally impressed. "Yeah, I wish I had thought to bring Evaline's camera. I would give anything to have a picture of this goose house."

Mr. Stacey, owner of the "Goose House" was proud of his house, a novelty anywhere, but certainly here in the mountains. The property was not only Mr. Stacey's home, but his business as well. Two red gas pumps with glass globes that lit up at night sat in front of the house. Not far from the gas pumps was another, smaller goose-shaped structure with a window in its side, a refreshment stand where customers could buy a frozen custard or a hotdog for a dime.

The house had made Mr. Stacey an overnight celebrity. He seemed to enjoy his popularity when crowds of curiosity seekers followed him around the house. Today, Mr. Stacey had just begun a tour when the boys arrived. Seeing the excited, curiosity on their faces, he invited them to join the young couple who had stopped for gas and marveled at the strange house.

Mr. Stacey told the story of how he had found a dead goose in the woods and had gotten his idea to build the house. He explained in detail how he had carefully constructed the house to just the right scale in proportion to the size of a real goose. Mr. Stacey lived in the top of the Goose House, and he showed them a few of those rooms. The boys asked about the rumor that he had a safe built inside the goose's bill where he kept his money and valuables. He would not confirm or deny the rumor. He would only say, "Oh sure, and the goose house has wings so it can fly away at night and return early in the morning before anyone wakes up."

The visitors, having spent an hour touring the Goose House, bought hot dogs, and prepared to get on their way. They asked if the boys needed a ride, but the Musketeers wanted to spend more time with Mr. Stacey; and as it turned out, the visitors were not going their way anyway.

Miles knew that he and the Musketeers would have no problems getting home. Someone was always stopping for gas. Sure enough, a tall man in a '39 Plymouth stopped about twenty minutes later. Miles waited until he saw the man preparing to leave and then asked, "Say, mister, any chance we could get a ride back to Hazard with you?"

The man looked the boys over for a moment or two. "Well, I guess so." He stared particularly hard at Miles. "Sure. I'll give you a ride."

On the road, with the boys sitting side-by-side in the back seat, the driver introduced himself. "Well now, I'm Ulysses Walters. And who are you boys?" Ulysses stared at the boys in his rearview mirror as one by one they introduced themselves. He stared particularly hard at Miles, the last to introduce himself.

"We sure want to thank you for giving us a ride, Mr. Walters," Miles added after he had given his name. They rode in silence for a while. Miles wished they were in the back of the pickup truck so they could talk with each other without the driver hearing.

"You know, boys," Mr. Walters began, glancing at Miles in his mirror, "I read an article in the *Louisville Courier Journal* about these young boys who were hitchhiking in Arizona and flagged down the wrong person. They were warning people about the dangers of hitchhiking. What happened to those boys in Arizona wasn't very pretty." Mr. Walter's eyes met Miles' in the mirror. Miles was uncomfortable now. "Miles Hudson, I know your momma, and I knew your dad, and I don't want to have to go to your house and tell your Ma that you boys have been hitchhiking."

They were Passing Riverside Cemetery again. Mr. Walters glanced toward the boys on the back seat. Wilbur and Cecil, who were sitting beside Miles, seemed more frightened by his story, and the threat to notify their parents, than Miles did. They looked pale and had strange looks on their faces. Mr. Walters thought he had achieved the desired result. He concluded, "So you guys are going to promise me that you will never hitch-hike again?"

"Sure, Mr. Walters." Miles breathed a quiet sign of relief. The man knew his Ma. That's why he had been staring at Miles.

Miles turned to wink at Cecil and Wilbur, but he couldn't get their attention. They looked straight ahead, not speaking. Each was wondering if the other had just felt a chill go up his spine.

TWENTY-TWO

"It is well that war is so terrible, lest we grow too fond of it."
Robert E. Lee, December 13, 1862

Charlie was at last on his way. Even though the fighting was several thousand miles away, most everyone he knew was trying to make a contribution to the war effort.

The scrap metal drives seemed to be never ending, and on many days dump truck after dump truck added metal to the ever growing pile of scrap metal in front of the Court House. Charlie was impressed that much of the metal had been collected by young children and teen agers going door-to-door. On special occasions the Hazard High School Band played patriotic songs, as the trucks dumped their loads, and the crowd cheered.

For Charlie, and the other recruits, the bus ride to Cincinnati was uneventful and passed quickly. Charlie dozed and thought about Evaline, the war, and how he couldn't wait to make the Japs pay for Pearl Harbor.

Next morning in Cincinnati, Charlie boarded a different bus and noticed they were traveling into the sun, and east, from Cincinnati, instead of west to some location that would get him on his way to the Pacific. Later that day, he learned why. They were traveling to Maryland for basic training at Fort Meade, and that meant he would not be fighting in the Pacific, but in the Atlantic.

Basic training at Fort Meade was not easy for Charlie, but because of his size and strength, not as difficult as for some of his buddies. The training seemed to be never ending, and Charlie observed new recruits coming in almost daily. They must be planning something special for us, thought Charlie, otherwise they'd have shipped us out of here long ago.

On October 24, 1942, following a 5-hour bus ride, and not sure where they were going, Charlie and hundreds of other recruits arrived at Newport News, Virginia, boarded a large military ship, and began a 3,800-mile trip across the Atlantic Ocean.

No idea where we're going, thought Charlie, but definitely not to the Pacific. He later found out - they were not going to fight the Japanese, or the Germans, but the French.

On November 8, after a transatlantic voyage of 15 days, Charlie's ship, and others from the U.S., having sailed further than any other American amphibious invasion force in history, became Part of Operation Torch, the name given to the Allied invasion of north Africa, under the command of Lt. General Dwight D. Eisenhower.

And it was on this same date, November 8, that Charlie went to war as one of more than 60,000 men, mostly Americans, and with only minimal basic training experience, who had been transported to north Africa from ports in the United States and England.

As directed by General Eisenhower, Allied forces would launch simultaneous invasions into Casablanca, Oran, and Algiers. Charlie's unit was under the command of General George S. Patton, who would lead the Casablanca invasion. Other generals had been assigned to direct landings into Oran and Algeria.

Since an estimated 50,000 French troops were waiting for the invasion to be launched into Casablanca, it was decided by Patton to launch invasions near Casablanca, rather than in Casablanca. One of those locations was Mehdia, about 75 miles north of Casablanca, and Charlie's unit was part of several thousand troops charged with securing control of the Port-Lyautey airfield near Mehdia, and airfields were desperately needed as the closest friendly airports were located over a thousand miles away.

The invasion began just before dawn, and Charlie's landing craft was one of the few that survived the offshore heavy fire from French cannons, as well as the very rough Atlantic surf which capsized dozens of landing craft that never reached the shore. He and his fellow soldiers, virtually none of whom had any real battle experience, having just arrived from the 3,800 mile transatlantic voyage, went directly from basic training to extremely fierce fighting with the French forces, who were determined not to surrender the airfield to the Americans.

At first Charlie was just scared, as he'd never really thought about dying, and he was shaking, so hard he could hardly hold his rifle, much less fire it, but then he heard a voice, a very familiar voice.

"Hey, Hazard boy, I thought you hillbillies were tough!"

It was his drill sergeant, whose voice now was not threatening, or intimidating, as it had been at Fort Meade, it was loud, but comforting. Before Charlie could respond, he heard it again.

"We're all scared. It's okay, but only way we're ever going to survive this, is to kick some ass. Are you in, or not?"

Charlie was even more scared now. He wanted to answer but now could only think about the beautiful Evaline, his family, her family, and especially Miles, who he knew eventually would also be fighting for his country, and trying to save his own life.

And then it happened, Charlie's fear suddenly turned to anger. He decided he would indeed fight to the death for his country, and he hoped and prayed he'd have even a slim chance of going home alive.

"I'M IN!" shouted Charlie. "And what about you, sergeant? You want to stay here and keep talking, or go help me kick some ass?"

The fighting was nonstop from the early morning of November 8 through the morning of November 10 with little or no gain by the Americans, but then a new drive began, this time with tanks and Navy dive bombers, and by nightfall the airfield had been secured.

Charlie, for the first time in nearly three days started to relax, just as one of the officers shouted, "Remember men, as we've told you many times, watch where you're stepping, this place is covered with land mines."

Good advice, thought Charlie, as he slowly took another step, and heard a strange click just as his foot touched the ground.

TWENTY-THREE

"**H**e's awake! Someone get Dr. Mills. Hurry! Someone get Dr. Mills immediately."

Charlie waited. Then he heard the other voice, the voice he dreaded hearing, a soldier's voice screaming: "Where's my leg! My leg's gone! Oh God in Heaven, my leg's gone! I want my leg! Where is the rest of me? Where is my doctor? Where is my leg?"

Charlie had already been at Walter Reed for four weeks, and the screams never failed to bring back painful memories. The talk came first, all the different voices. Charlie was scared. Why could he not wake up? He tried to open his eyes, but his eyelids were too heavy. Like a rising window shade his eyes slowly opened. He wanted to move his head, but it hurt too much. There was a strong smell of ether, and then he realized he was in a hospital room. The image of the people gradually became clearer.

Then he saw a nurse dressed in a white uniform, with a white cap on the back of her head. He saw a tall doctor, also dressed in white, with a stethoscope wrapped around his neck. The doctor wanted to take his temperature, but Charlie pushed him away. Charlie couldn't talk; his mouth was too dry. He pointed to the water pitcher and back to his mouth. The nurse poured a glass of water and placed a glass tube in it. She raised Charlie's head, and he sipped the water. The water tasted cool and good. The tall doctor gave Charlie a shot, and the nurse gave him a pad and pencil. "How long have I been here?" The nurse held up three fingers. Charlie nodded. The tall doctor put his hand on Charlie's shoulder.

"Charlie, we're going to take good care of you. Now get some sleep, and we'll talk again in the morning."

Charlie was exhausted. He closed his eyes and fell asleep. The following morning Charlie was more rested. His head and neck no longer hurt. He could take a drink of water whenever he wished. When the day nurse walked into the room she was surprised.

"Well, would you look at you, looking all around the room? Why, you couldn't do that yesterday. You're doing much better."

"When do you think I'll be able to get out of my bed?"

"Maybe today. Let's see what your chart says. Why, yes, this afternoon. Now how does that sound?"

Charlie smiled as he pulled the cover away from his body. He looked down. Then he screamed.

"Where's my leg? Where's my doctor? Why in the hell was I the last one to find out about my leg?"

Dr. Mills was very sympathetic with Charlie's anger and claimed full responsibility for Charlie's not being aware that his leg had been amputated.

"Charlie, we're very overworked at this hospital, and sometimes things slip by. This was one of those things."

After Dr. Mills answered all of Charlie's questions, he gave strict orders Charlie was not to be disturbed.

Charlie finally settled down, resigning himself to the reality of his missing leg. Then the melancholy set in. He wanted to shut everyone out. When the nurse came in, Charlie turned to face the corner of the room and pulled the cover up over his head. But the nurse was firm with Charlie. She refused to let Charlie shut himself off from the world. She carefully pulled Charlie's cover from his face.

He looked up at her and she said, "Mr. Wills you can't get better by facing the wall. You've got to face the problem."

Slowly, Charlie regained his composure and began to think about all the different emotions other patients were experiencing. Some soldiers had lost both legs, one or both arms, their eyesight, and even worse, their abilities to reason, to think clearly, to be thankful they were still alive.

Time passed slowly in the hospital, and Charlie's recovery was taking much longer than seemed to be required for other amputees. Dr. Mills told him his slower recovery was because he had both leg and hip injuries. Dr. Mills told him to just be patient, try to make the best of it, and to remember even more time would be required for his adjustment to an artificial leg.

In time, Charlie got over wanting to be alone, and made friends with two other soldiers, both from eastern Kentucky. Plug Amburgey was from Whitesburg, and Oscar Fields, was from Jenkins. Plug had also lost a leg, and Oscar had lost his ability to reason. The three became good friends, often playing gin rummy for hours on end at a penny a point. Having no idea whether it would work, Charlie and Plug, hoping to help Oscar come to terms with his mental problems, assigned him the task of keeping a ledger with totals calculated after each round to show who owed who and how much. Oscar eagerly accepted the assignment, and while no one actually checked his figures, he did a good job.

Early during the week when Plug and Charlie were scheduled to be released, the three sat playing gin rummy. Plug suggested that he and Charlie help Oscar write a letter home. Charlie stared silently at his cards. "You help him, Oscar," Charlie finally managed. Plug didn't want to push Charlie, but he couldn't help thinking that writing home more often would help Charlie, too. "It's not the easiest thing to do," Plug said quietly, "but I want them to know I'm not dead. Now, go on Charlie. It's your play."

Charlie was finally dismissed in June. He felt good and had mastered walking on his crutches with only minor discomfort. He had refused an artificial leg, just said he'd like to think about it. Plug had been released several days before Charlie, and Oscar was to stay longer for further evaluation. In the usual good-bye ritual, nurses, doctors, and patients who had become friends, lined the hall near the doorway to shake hands with Charlie and wish him well as he left. When Charlie reached Oscar, he extended his hand and said the same thing Plug said to both Oscar and Charlie just a few days earlier: "Stay in touch. I'll write you as soon as I get home."

But as he said it, Charlie wondered if he was wrong in not mentioning his lost leg in his letters to Evaline. He just couldn't bring himself to think of how this would affect her. He had some thinking to do before he reached Jack Lot Hollow.

TWENTY-FOUR

A wakened by the blast of the train's whistle, Charlie sat upright in his seat and watched the gray smoke disappear outside his window.

"Next stop, the Queen City, Cincinnati," the conductor shouted, making his way down the aisle.

As the train slowly wove its way into Cincinnati, Charlie was astonished to see all the bright lights still glowing in the tall buildings at two o'clock in the morning. Charlie had dark circles under his eyes, and his cheeks were hollow. For the first time since leaving the Walter Reed Military Hospital, he felt as though he was really going home. On the other side of the Ohio River lay his beloved Kentucky, and a hundred-and-seventy-five miles to the southeast were the mountains, and his wife, the wife he had been dreaming of for more than two years. And now he wasn't sure he was ready.

The train jerked and slowly came to a stop at the terminal. Struggling to lift his suitcase from the rack above the seat, Charlie lost his balance and found himself falling back into the aisle. His face turned crimson as he made a futile effort to pull himself up from the floor.

"Here, solider, let me give you a hand," a portly man said, helping Charlie up into a standing position. "I'll carry that suitcase for you," the man insisted. He reached for the suitcase, but Charlie blocked him.

"No, thank you, sir, I can take care of it myself," Charlie replied, his voice firm.

"Oh, I don't mind. It's no trouble." The man reached again for the suitcase. "Why, it's the least I can do for someone who has sacrificed so much for our country."

"If it's all the same to you, sir, I'd rather do it myself." Charlie said, reaching for his crutch to steady himself.

"Well, excuse me for living," the man replied. He turned and reached for his own suitcase. "I didn't mean to offend you. I was only trying to be helpful."

Charlie wondered if it would ever stop. Had fate sentenced him to a never-ending line of people who would always want to do everything for him? Didn't they know they were killing him with kindness? Maybe it would all change once he was home and out of uniform.

"No offense taken," Charlie said. He placed his wooden crutch under his arm and dragged his suitcase down the aisle.

The portly man waited until he was sure the soldier was out of hearing distance. He turned to the lady behind him. "I don't know why he's got his tail feathers all ruffled up. You know there's a whole bunch of our fighting men who won't be coming home at all. Why, you'd think a man who'd lost his right leg would be more than happy to have an American citizen offer to carry his suitcase for him."

A woman dressed completely in black had been watching the interaction from her seat across the aisle. She turned away and looked out the window, and then looked back at the portly man. "I just think he's a proud man, and he doesn't want to be treated as though he was an invalid," she replied quietly.

"Maybe so, but I think he ought to be grateful that people offer to help him." The lady in black started to comment, then decided against it. The man looked puzzled as he studied the lady's face for a moment.

"Did you start to say something, ma'am?" he asked.

"Why, yes I did. I was going to ask you if you had ever served in the Armed Forces."

"Well, no, I haven't," the man admitted, his face reddening a bit. "Ma'am, I'll have you know I was deferred from the service. You see, I had an accident that kept me out of the war."

"Oh, really, may I ask what kind of accident you had?"

Beads of sweat popped out on the man's forehead. He was obviously embarrassed. "It's something I'm not proud of," he said uncomfortably. "You see, I was chopping firewood when my axe slipped, and I ended up cutting off my trigger finger."

"How very unfortunate," the lady said. She got up and walked down the aisle.

In the coffee shop, Charlie set his suitcase down by the stool. By using the counter and his crutch as a brace, he managed to pull himself up onto the stool. The overhead fan slowly turned while the radio behind the counter continued to play popular war songs.

Charlie took a deep breath and glanced quickly at the blackboard menu on the wall. If he were going to be on the train bound for home, he only had time for a cup of coffee. The waitress, clad in a white cap and apron, tried not to notice that the solider had one of his trouser legs pinned neatly below his waist.

"Hi, sweetie, could we fix you some breakfast this morning?" she asked.

"No, I guess not," Charlie replied. "My train leaves in ten minutes. I'll just have a cup of coffee."

"Okay, sweetie, one cup of java coming up." She placed a saucer and a cup on the counter and began to pour him a cup of coffee. "Going home?"

"Yeah, that's right."

The short order cook tapped the small bell on the pass-through from the grill to let the waitress know three orders of bacon and eggs were ready to be served. The waitress easily balanced the plates, one on the inside of her left arm, the other two in the palms of her hands. As she placed the plates on the tables, she was amazed to find herself stealing glances back at the tall, rugged-looking solider. He wasn't a handsome man. His face looked worn, and crow's feet had formed around the corners of his eyes, but there was something about the way he talked and carried himself on his one leg.

"Why don't I warm your coffee for you, sweetie?" The waitress came back around the counter and stood holding the coffee pot in front of Charlie.

"Yeah, that would be fine," Charlie said.

"Well, I'll just bet all the pretty girls back home are going to be real glad to see a handsome man like you. Now, don't you go misbehaving when you get back, sweetie."

Charlie smiled at her.

"No danger in that," Charlie said. He held the St. Christopher medal up to his face, remembering how Evaline placed it around his neck to protect him. "I'm a married man."

"Married? Well, you don't say! I'll just bet that little wife of yours is going to be real proud to have you back home."

"I certainly hope so," Charlie said. He reached down into his pocket, seeing his pant leg neatly tucked and pinned below the knee.

He withdrew a handful of change and put more than enough on the counter to cover the cost of his coffee. "I certainly hope so," he repeated.

"Oh, no, you don't need to do that," the waitress said, seeing the mound of change on the counter. "I wasn't going to charge you."

"Well, then, why don't you put all that change in your apron and keep it for a tip."

"Thank you, sweetie."

Charlie took his last swig of coffee, adjusted his crutches and headed for the door where another, younger soldier stood watching. As Charlie neared the door, the soldier held it open for him.

"Thank you, brother," Charlie said as he passed through the door and onto the platforms.

The train whistle blew, and Charlie hurriedly made his way to Track No. 5. A smile came over his face when he saw the big steam engine with the four coaches attached. This would be his last train change. He was finally boarding the train that would carry him all the way home.

The thought of being only four hours away from Evaline sent a wave of excitement throughout his body. His suitcase now felt light as a feather. It seemed as if his entire body were floating up the train's steps and down the aisle of the coach.

"Need some help with your luggage, soldier boy?" the black porter asked.

Charlie, now in a much better mood, smiled at the porter. "No, thank you," he said, easily tossing his suitcase into the rack above his seat.

The train jerked and Charlie put his hand on the back of the seat to steady himself. As they slowly pulled away from the terminal and the big steam engine picked up speed, Charlie settled back into his seat, lit a cigarette and watched the telephone poles go racing past his window. Not many people traveling this early in the morning, he thought, looking around the dimly lit coach.

A sailor who had been sleeping in the seat across from Charlie was now awake, and he took a drink from a bottle inside a brown paper bag. Charlie's eyes opened wide, and he gasped as the sailor lowered the paper bag from his face. The sailor's ghastly skin looked like hot candle wax melted over his entire face. His eyes peered out through two small slits, and he hardly had a nose at all. His flaming red hair quickly gave away his Scot-Irish heritage. When he spoke it was in a thick Appalachian drawl, one of the most beautiful accents in America, and only found in the most remote areas of the southern Appalachian Mountains.

"Say, thar, soldier boy, could I interest ya in a good drink of Kentucky whiskey?" his voiced growled.

Charlie, still reeling from the shock of seeing his face, stammered and managed a polite, "No, thank you."

"Well, then, soldier boy, if ya not interested in a good drink of whiskey, jus' maybe ya be interested in makin' a little trade." The sailor sounded like a carnival barker in a sideshow. "Step right up, ladies and gents, yeah, ya too, young feller, step right up here, and I'm gonna tell ya what I'm gonna do. I'm gonna trade ya one of mah legs for a new face." Charlie wanted to turn away, to stop staring, but he couldn't. "No, wait, I'll even do better than that. I'll trade ya both mah legs and a bottle of Old Grand Dad for one face," the sailor sobbed.

The sailor and Charlie could only stare at one another. The silence was deafening. After what seemed like an eternity, Charlie broke the silence, "Now, just what kind of whiskey did you say you had in that paper bag?"

"I got good Kentucky whiskey, the best whiskey ya gonna find on this whole planet," the sailor said proudly, cradling the bottle in his arms.

"Well now, I reckon a good drink of Old Grand Dad would take a lot of the rough spots out of the ride back home," Charlie said, and he reached across the aisle for the brown paper bag. The sailor's upper lip curled in what Charlie assumed was a smile. Charlie accepted the whiskey the sailor handed to him and took a long swig. He passed the bottle from his right hand to his left hand, and reached out his right hand to the sailor. "Charlie Wills."

The sailor clasped it. "Luke Wilder."

Charlie took another drink and handed the bottle back to Luke.

The train continued on its journey, crossing over high bridges and traveling through dark tunnels. The engineer blew the whistle, and with each passing mile the brown paper bag got lighter.

A warm glow consumed Luke Wilder's body as he began to divulge some of his most harbored secrets to Charlie.

"Why, I don't reckon I was ever more than thirty miles away from Hell Fer Sartin Creek until the Japs bombed Pearl Harbor. I was a real heller. Folks 'round home said I was as wild as a Comanche. Weren't 'bout nothin' I wouldn't do, git drunk, run after bad women and lay out in them ginnie barns until midnight. Worked in the coal mines and made a little dab of money, but come Saturday night, I was always ready to plow up the countryside." Luke's lip curled into his disfigured smile. He was remembering better times. "I never went home 'til I had spent ever' penny of mah pay!'

Charlie had the bottle now. He took another swig from the bottle and handed it to the sailor. Luke went on.

"Now, that all came to a screechin' halt once mah Ma got sick and tired of mah wild ways. Told me if I didn't stop mah drinkin' and git right with the Lord, she would put me out of the house and disown me. Now mah goin' to church turned out to be a pretty good thing. Ya see, that's where I first saw Alifair. Hit was a cloudy Sunday mornin' and the sun hadn't showed hits face all day. Well, now, all at once a single spray of sunlight showed through the stained-glass window, and all those bright colors were reflectin' off Fair's face and hair. Why, hit was the damndest thing ya saw in ya life. With all them colors shinin' on Fair's face and hair, she looked jus' like an angel."

Luke stared out the window for a moment, then looked back at Charlie. His upper lip was curled again, but now, as he remembered seeing Fair for the first time, his face really was smiling.

"Everyone was lookin' in awe and wonderment at what the Lord was tryin' to say, but I knew He was tellin' me I needed to git married to that girl. Now, there was one hitch to us gettin' married. Ya see, I couldn't ask Fair to marry me if I couldn't talk to her. Her Pa knowed 'bout mah wild ways, and he said he'd jus' be damned if his only daughter was gonna marry up with a no-good vagrant like me." Luke juggled the whiskey bottle he was holding in his left hand, and held up his right hand. "Upon my word and honor, if I didn't make a point of bein' in that church ever' time the doors opened. I got me a job at the sawmill. Why, I even got up in church and preached 'bout the devil and the hold he had on me, made Ma real proud."

"I reckon, sooner or later, I would have given up on that girl 'cept whenever Fair caught her Pa not lookin' she would always give me a big smile. Ya could pretty much say we was stuck on each other. Hit took me nigh on to two months before I could even sit on her front porch with her. Her Pa finally mellowed out a bit and went ahead and gave his okay for us to git married and set up housekeeping."

"Well, now everythin' went along pretty good until the Japs bombed Pearl Harbor." He took another swig and handed the almost empty bottle across the aisle. "I went ahead and signed up with the Navy. Didn't want to go to the Army and have to lay out on the cold ground in the sleet and snow. Ya see, I knowed in the Navy I would git a clean bed and three hot meals a day."

Luke paused briefly, cleared his throat, took another drink from the bottle, and continued. "Well now, I got assigned to a freighter in the North Atlantic. We were carryin' cargo of ever' sort ya could think of, food, timber, ammunition, tanks. You name hit, and we was probably carryin' hit. We was part of a big convoy, fifty vessels of ever' sort of ship ya could think of, thar was oil tankers and even fishin' boats. Yes, sir, fifty ships and 1,500 men all ready to deliver war supplies to those men who would be able to use them to blast the livin' hell out of them Krauts."

"Now they had been talk about enemy subs bein' in the waters, and sure enough, they were a layin' in wait fer us. Ships were flashin' their lights all around us, and the night was as black as a witch's heart. I was at mah station in the engine room when a 'tin-fish' came a crashin' into the side of our ship. Black smoke, fire and hot steam seemed to be everywhere."

"Now we knew we only had 'bout three minutes to git the hell off that tub. We knew we might be lucky enough to escape the first torpedo, but the chances of escaping' the next one would be slim or none. I can't say I remember a whole lot 'bout gittin' off that ship. Hit seemed like one minute I was in the engine room, and the next minute I was bobbin' up and down in the middle of the Atlantic Ocean!"

"Now, I didn't have an inklin' I was burned as bad as I was until I jumped into that cold ocean water. Mah face felt like hit was on fire! I don't think I could have ever stood all that pain. Only thing that saved me was a young doctor who ended up on our raft. He grabbed his doctor bag before he went over the side of the ship. Lucky for me, there was a bottle of ether in hit. Whenever mah pain got so bad I couldn't stand hit no more, he would put me back to sleep."

Luke fell silent for a moment. Charlie passed the bottle back to Luke. Luke just held it as he began to speak.

"They said we were adrift ten days before bein' picked up by one of our ships. I was sent back to the States where I ended up spendin' six weeks in one of them burn control centers. Ya see, the war had ended for me."

Luke wiped tears from his eyes. The two men were silent. There was nothing more to say. Somewhere between Ravenna and Pigeon Roost, Luke and Charlie finished off the bottle of Old Grand Dad and fell asleep.

Hours later, the porter lightly shook Charlie's arm. "Wake up, soldier boy, wake up now," the porter said. Charlie looked up from under the blanket the porter had draped over him. He had a splitting headache, and his mouth was as dry as cotton.

"You got kinfolk gonna meet you at the station?" the porter asked.

"No, no one will be there," Charlie replied. "I didn't write and let anyone know I was coming home."

"Now, why you go and do a thing like that for?" the porter asked. "Not one bit of your kinfolk gonna be at the station to meet you after all you done been through?"

"Well, you see," Charlie said, "I'm only part of the man I was when I left home. I just wasn't sure I would go home right now." Suddenly Charlie was embarrassed that he was telling the porter his troubles. "I thought I might get off the train in some small town and maybe buy me a fishing pole, maybe even buy a little tent. You know, just fish and camp out a while before I went home, might get me to thinking straight before I had to face my wife Evaline and all my kin." Charlie pulled the blanket tighter up around his shoulders.

"Just what on God's green earth are you talking about, boy?" the porter exclaimed. "You gotta straighten up. You're not going to have to face up to nobody. Your wife and kinfolks gonna be proud for what you went and done for this country. Now, you stop talking all that foolish talk right now. You straighten yourself up right this minute, you hear?"

"I don't know. I guess I just wasn't sure," Charlie said wiping the sleep from his eyes.

"It don't make one little iota," the porter said. "You're still a soldier in the United States Army, and you need to be proud of that." He yanked the blanket away and began to fold it. "Now, you go on back to the toilet and wash your face and comb your hair. I'm gonna fix you a glass of tomato juice with a twist of lemon in it. You gonna look like a soldier when you get off this train. Hurry up, now! The sun's coming up, and we're only five miles outside of Hazard."

In the seat across from Charlie, Luke opened his eyes sleepily, yawned and stretched. He checked the bottle for one last swig, but it was empty. He looked across the aisle for his new friend. The seat was empty, but Charlie's suitcase was still in the overhead rack. A minute later, he saw Charlie coming down the aisle. "I've got a splitting headache," he said, rubbing his forehead.

Charlie got his luggage down from the rack above his seat. He turned to face Luke. The face that had shocked him so badly when he first saw it didn't make him wince anymore. "Luke, we need to stay in touch with each other. I got a feeling that we both need all the help we can get, so if you ever need me, I'll probably be in Jack Lot Hollow. Or better yet, why don't you and your family come visit us sometime."

"Well, I don't know what I'm going to have to face up to when I get home. I hope everything will turn out all right, but we can't be absolutely sure." Luke's lip curled up and Charlie smiled back at him. "I'll get off the train in Jeff, and then I'm dreading hitchhiking on the road that leads to Hell Fer Sartin Creek."

Charlie had no promises to give Luke. Charlie wasn't even certain what he faced himself, but he was going home to find out. He and Luke shook hands. Then Charlie stepped down from the train, and just as he crossed the platform to find a taxi, he saw Luke wave.

TWENTY-FIVE

Sunday, June 6, 1943
Hazard, Kentucky

I t was one of those beautiful June mornings in the mountains. The sky was a powder blue, and the sun reflected off the puddles of water left by the early morning rain. The air was crisp and cool as it filtered through the pine trees that touched the sky. Charlie's heart was pounding with excitement as the taxicab turned onto the gravel road that led into Jack Lot Hollow. He unbuttoned his shirt collar and felt again the Saint Christopher medal Evaline had given him before he left for the War. "Thank you, Saint Christopher, for letting me make it back home alive, even if I did lose a leg doing it," Charlie said.

"What was that you said?" asked the taxi driver as he hit another bump in the road.

"Oh, nothing. Nothing at all. I was just thinking out loud."

"Well, the only time you gonna catch me talking to myself is when I want to talk to a smart person." The driver laughed heartily at his own joke.

Charlie gritted his teeth as the wheels of the taxicab bounced off another bump in the road. "Jesus Christ, Mister!" Charlie said. He grabbed the seat to keep from sliding into the door. "When was the last time you put shocks on your taxi?"

"Shocks? You kidding? You, of all people, should know you can't buy a set of shocks with us in a war and all."

"Maybe you can't, but you can at least try and miss some of these bumps in the road, or slow this damn thing down!" Charlie said sharply.

"Well, now," the driver leaned over the steering wheel and pulled his cap down a little further to block the sun, "I guess soldiers like you that's been overseas never give much thought about all the government rationing all of us people been going through in this country. Why, I suspect you probably been able to get just about anything you want overseas."

"Yeah, one thing I sure got was a leg blown clean off," Charlie snapped back. "Now, how would you like to go overseas and get that?"

The driver never answered. He kept one eye on the road, and the other eye on the solider in his rearview mirror. A dog jumped up from the side of the road, and the driver swerved and did his best to hit it. "Came close to getting that one," he said.

"You sure did," Charlie said. "Sounds like you're a natural-born killer to me. You know, you might ought to sign up for the service and go overseas. Then you could kill Germans and leave poor, helpless dogs alone. Only problem is, those Germans are gonna shoot back at you."

Again, the driver never answered.

Charlie's excitement grew as they rounded the bend and passed the coal tipple. Charlie buttoned his coat, adjusted his tie, and smoothed his hair. The taxi came to a stop beside the swinging bridge.

"That'll be one dollar and a half," the driver said gruffly.

"Jesus Christ! A dollar and a half?" said Charlie. He fished in his pocket for the fare. "Why, before I left home you could go anywhere in the whole county for seventy-five cents," he mumbled.

"Well, mister, like I told you, it's all this government rationing that's going on. Besides, I got a family I got to feed."

Charlie grudgingly handed the driver a two-dollar bill and impatiently waited for his change. Now that he was actually home, he couldn't wait to see Evaline.

"Well, my goodness gracious alive," said the driver, "a two-dollar bill. I haven't seen one of these in a good while. Now, let me see, I know I've got some change here somewhere. It'll just take me a minute or two to find it." He fumbled through his pockets. "Mister, it looks like I plumb run out of change. You sure you ain't got a dollar and two quarters on you?"

"Just keep the damn change! Maybe you could save it up toward a new set of shocks before you jar somebody's eyeteeth out." Charlie already had the door open and was struggling with his crutch and suitcase.

"Well, mister, I'll tell you what I could do for you," said the driver. "Why don't I carry that suitcase of yours across that swinging bridge? It'll make it a lot easier for you with you just having one leg and all."

"I can carry my own suitcase," Charlie said defiantly, getting out of the car, slamming the door, and hobbling toward the swinging bridge.

The clean smell of cedar wood burning in the cook stove was in the air as Charlie stepped onto the back porch. The aroma of bacon and buttermilk biscuits was sharp, and he could hear the coffee pot perking on the stove.

Charlie heard Evaline's voice, calm and sweet. He reveled in her mountain accent. It had been two years since he had heard it. "Momma, should I go ahead and take the biscuits out of the oven now?" she asked.

"Take another look at them, and if they're a light brown on top, they'll be ready to come out," Drucella said.

Evaline looked out the screen door, straight at Charlie, but she didn't see him. Charlie suddenly felt as if he were an intruder, and his face turned red. His eyes were glued on Evaline, and he watched her every move. Her dark hair was shining, her cheeks a rosy red. She wore a black sweater over her white blouse. The skirt she was wearing was red-and-black plaid. She looked even more beautiful than Charlie remembered.

He swallowed hard and bit his lower lip. A tear trickled down his face. He spoke softly. "Evaline."

Evaline quickly looked up from the stove and back to the screen door. She saw the outline of a soldier, and for a brief moment she couldn't tell who he was. Her mind slowly became aware of what her eyes were seeing.

She dropped the pan of buttermilk biscuits on the table. She ran to the screen door and threw it open. Evaline caught her breath, and tears filled her eyes. She embraced Charlie.

"Oh, thank you, Lord! Thank you Lord for answering my prayers." Suddenly she pushed away from him. "Oh no, Charlie, oh no! What did they do to my Charlie?" But before he could answer, Evaline was hugging Charlie again.

Drucella came out to the porch and draped her arms around both of them. "You know, Charlie, the Lord works in mysterious ways. He took your leg, but He got you back home with Evaline and us, so let's just be thankful the War's coming to an end, and you're safely back home."

"It's good to be home," said Charlie. "How's Miles?"

"He's doing really good in school," said Drucella, "just turned 16 last Wednesday, growing like a weed, and interested in girls."

"Sounds like me at that age," said Charlie, "I'm really looking forward to seeing him."

Evaline's mountain spirit was strong, and she had learned to accept the things she knew couldn't be changed. Charlie hadn't been home for more than an hour, and Evaline devised a plan for his recovery. She made light of Charlie's missing leg. "One thing you can count on is we're going to win the three-legged race at the next July 4th picnic," she laughed.

"Yeah, but I sure don't want to enter the ass-kicking contest," Charlie shot back.

He and Evaline had breakfast and then went for a walk along the creek's edge. Evaline was amazed that Charlie kept the same pace on his crutches as he would have if he still had both his legs. They listened to the hum of the soft breeze rustling through the cornfield and the rippling waters hurrying over the sandstone rocks in their rush to the sea. This was the music of the mountains. The music Charlie had missed without realizing it.

"How long do you think it will take for us to get our house built?" Evaline asked looking at the land beside the creek that Everett gave them as a wedding present, a perfect spot for their house.

"Oh, I'm not sure. Probably a lot longer now that I've got just one leg."

Evaline put her hands on her hips. "You had better not try and get out of building me my house, Charlie Wills. You got no excuse to not build me my house. Your Pa made you a part owner in his sawmill and gave us the land to build on. You got no excuses. Do you understand what I'm telling you, Charlie Wills? Do you?"

"Yeah, I understand what you're telling me," Charlie laughed. "I reckon I do understand." Evaline smiled and rushed over to put her arms around him.

Charlie buried his face in Evaline's hair, happy to be home with her, and happy that Evaline hadn't changed. It wasn't only her beauty that had attracted him to Evaline. It was also her spunk and her ability to stand up for herself in the face of difficulties.

In the days to come, after they moved back in with Anna Mae and Everett, Evaline was very sympathetic and patient with Charlie when his dreams carried him back to the battlefields and the hell of war. The one thing she would not do was let Charlie feel sorry for himself, and quit. He might be minus one leg, but he was still Charlie. The same Charlie who once found a robin redbreast with a broken wing and carried it home in his coat pocket. The same Charlie who picked wildflowers on the mountainside and brought them to her in a fruit jar. He only had one leg, but in Evaline's eyes, Charlie was still the best damn man in the mountains, as far as she was concerned.

While Charlie was away, Evaline thought often about her future, as well as about her and Charlie's future, of owning a business, having a better life, and how she might help support her widowed mother. She was also concerned about Charlie's working at the sawmill with only one leg.

Now that Charlie had been home for a few weeks, and was becoming more and more like the Charlie he used to be, Evaline was eager to share with him a conversation she'd initiated with Doris about the Andersons' future plans for their store, and what their plans might mean for her and Charlie's future. Seeing she definitely had Charlie's attention, Evaline told him she'd approached Doris several weeks before, with a very serious question.

Charlie leaned forward in his chair as Evaline told him of her conversation with Doris, and that she had chosen a day when Doris had been concerned about her arthritis.

"I told Doris that I knew she loved the mountains, but the mountains were not where she and Jack needed to be. I suggested they could sell their store and move to Arizona, to a drier climate. I also told her I thought it would be good for her arthritis, and thought maybe I had been too forward, but Doris didn't seem to notice.

"Doris agreed and acknowledged Jack's age. She said they'd save some money and had been thinking for some time, but hadn't decided when."

Evaline said, "Doris then smiled, reached for her hand and said I had been a godsend for her and Jack, the daughter they never had. She also said she would like nothing better than for us to have the store."

"I told her that you had always wanted to have your own business and that we didn't have much money, but if she'd trust us, we'd never let her down."

"Doris said she did trust us, but business was business, and she'd have a contract drawn up right away and put their store in our names. So, all I had to do was to talk with you, and nothing would suit her more than for us to have the store."

Charlie, having been home only a few weeks, and now thinking about the possibility of owning their own business, sat by the fire gazing at Evaline, thinking what a great helpmate she was, and how much her love meant to him.

Evaline smiled, as she looked up from the handwork she was doing, and caught him looking at her.

As they talked, Charlie was amazed at Evaline's inner strength. Strong like these mountains, he thought. He held her close, glad to be home.

TWENTY-SIX

t was 8 o'clock in the evening when the old reliable Greyhound bus pulled up under the awning that led into the Hazard Bus Station. Its air brakes hissed as the driver cut off the engine.

"Folks, be sure to get all your belongings, and thanks again for riding Greyhound," said the driver. "Now if you will line up outside, you can pick up your luggage."

A tall, thin, distinguished looking gentleman collected his two suitcases and crossed the street to the Taylor Hotel. He noted the hotel hadn't changed much, except it did have a new neon sign flashing over its door. The lobby looked the same right down to the lit up pinball machine under the stairs. He continued to look around, and then he spotted Eli's cat, Whiskers, sleeping on the hotel desk.

"Well, I'll be damned! Is that you, Whiskers? I see you still got your same old job catching mice and sleeping."

Whiskers stood up, arched his back and stretched, then jumped off the hotel desk and crossed the room to the sofa.

The man hadn't noticed the brown blanket stretched over the leather sofa until Whiskers jumped up on it, and a head popped up.

"Whiskers, go away! Can't you see I'm trying to sleep?"

Eli slowly sat up on the sofa and rubbed his eyes, then squinted and looked at the man. "Am I seeing things? Are you who I think you are? No, it can't be! You're supposed to be dead. Are you a spirit, or a ghost?"

"Eli, stop all the babbling. I've been traveling all day, and I'm tired. Now, get your sorry ass off the sofa and get me checked into my room at the top of the stairs."

Eli turned and looked at Whiskers. "Black Hart? Why Whiskers and me heard you got shot in a poker game in New Orleans, and we also heard you got killed at the blackjack table. By the way, Black Hart, just where did you get killed?"

Black Hart glared at Eli. "Eli, I know you're the biggest gossip in town. So, before the news is out all over town, I'm going to tell you one time, and one time only, the true story of what happened."

Eli was all ears, and to make sure Black Hart would not be disturbed, Eli picked up Whiskers, sat on the sofa, and listened.

Black Hart began. "Well Lady Luck had been on my side for quite a while. As a matter of fact, I had become pretty famous and was considered by many to be the best poker player in New Orleans."

He continued with even more enthusiasm. "I was invited to all the best parties in the city, and one day this invitation came from the Mayor of New Orleans. He said I had been selected to play poker with five other players who the Mayor said were considered to be some of the best poker players in the world, and one of these players was coming from Paris, France."

Eli's eyes widened as he listened.

Black Hart paused, shrugged his shoulders and sighed. "The problem was the qualifying fee was $2,000, and I had only $1,500, in my bank account, but a banker friend offered to put up the other $500. I accepted, and we were in the game."

"This would be my big chance. This would show everyone I was not a flash in the pan, and I would have respect. I even talked the best tailor in New Orleans into fitting me with a fine suit for the game." He flicked a piece of lint off the expensive suit he was wearing now.

"In case the game went for a long time, I packed extra clothes into a suit case. Like a boxer, I trained hard, got my rest, and ate the right foods. I was excited, and I was determined. In short, I was ready."

"Just before the game was to begin, the Mayor introduced us to those in the audience. We all shook hands, the Mayor gave a short speech, and the game began. The crowd was polite, but watched carefully, trying to read the expressions on each player's face. When a player left the game, they gave polite applause."

"I decided I'd play my regular game," said Hart. "Why should it fail me now? It had carried me from the coalfields of Kentucky all the way to New Orleans, so I decided I would stay with what brought me. My bank roll was up, then down, but so was everyone else's."

"After about six hours, people began to fold, then they were out. After eight hours, it was down to the Frenchman and me. He did his best to rattle me, but it didn't work. I knew when I had a good hand, so I'd go to my bag of tricks, and use all my poker skills as necessary to stay in the game. He tried to bluff me, but the $2,000, he started with was running low. Realizing he was trying to buy the game, I knew it was going to be all or nothing, so I stayed with him right to the end."

"When we showed our cards," said Black Hart, "he had a King, and an Ace in the hole. I had an Ace showing, and an Ace in the hole. I had felt all along two Aces would win the game. I was right, and I won the game, and the money." Black Hart rubbed his hands in glee, savoring the memory. Then he cleared his throat and continued.

"We had heard the Frenchman had a bad temper, and couldn't stand to lose, and we had heard right. When the game ended, he vented his anger, and said, 'As they say in America, you are a cheating son-of-a-bitch." Black Hart laughed.

"I decided to let it go," said Black Hart. "I had won all the money. I didn't have anything to be angry about, and I walked away. I was trying hard to be a gentleman, but the Frenchman had other ideas."

"Anyway, I took the elevator to the hotel lobby, and just as I stepped out of the elevator, he was there, waiting for me. He said he was challenging me to a duel, and before I realized what was happening, he slapped me in the face, and said, 'You're not only a cheating son-of-a-bitch, you're also a cowardly son-of-a-bitch."

"The only thing I could think of to say was 'I think you should go home, and get some rest. This was only a card game.' I had hardly finished speaking when he reached into his coat pocket, and pulled out a gun. I had no choice but to move fast, so I put my hand as fast as I could in my inside pocket, just under the left lapel of my coat, pulled out my derringer and fired, just barely missing the Frenchman's heart." He heard Eli gasp.

"It was later ruled that I acted in self-defense, and I was free to go. The Frenchman stayed in the hospital a couple months, and was deported not too long after his release."

Here, Black Hart took a long pause, buffed his nails on his lapel, and inspected them. Eli started to get up, and Whiskers jumped to the floor. But Black Hart wasn't quite finished. He motioned for Eli to stay seated.

"The morning after the game, I went to the bank and made a deposit of $12,000, of which $2000 was to cover my qualifying fee, and the $10,000 I had won from the Frenchman and the other players. Shortly thereafter, I repaid my banker friend the loan of $500, plus an additional $200 interest. He told me, 'I knew you had it in you, which is why I knew it wasn't much of a risk, so the next time you need a stake, call on me.'" Black Hart smiled and picked up his suitcases.

"Now Eli," said Black Hart, "can you remember all that?"

"Sure. Sure, Black Hart," said Eli finally getting up.

"I'm going to be around for a few days, but right now I'm tired from my travels, so if you'll give me the key, I'll just head up to the room." He had crossed the floor with his suitcases and signed his name in the guest registry on the desk.

"Suit yourself," Eli said and handed him the key.

Black Hart slept late the next morning. Eli wasn't in the lobby when Black Hart left. Black Hart decided to make the Hazard bank his first stop for the day.

When Black Hart walked into the bank, everyone looked up. As everyone stared at him, he walked up to the only available teller. "Well, have you heard the news?" the teller asked.

"What news? Has Eli been spreading gossip again?"

"No," the teller said, looking surprised. "You really haven't heard the news?"

"No," said Black Hart, "what news?"

"You're going to love this," said the teller.

Black Hart was confused, but eager to hear more.

"Sheriff Sizemore," said the teller eagerly, "went before the Grand Jury and testified that Noah Brewer confessed to the assault on the Hudson girl that happened four years ago."

Black Hart was overwhelmed. He hugged everyone he saw, then walked across the street to Sheriff Sizemore's office, and hugged the deputy who greeted him.

Sheriff Sizemore came out of his office. "Black Hart, I owe you an apology, and if you don't want to shake my hand, I will certainly understand."

"Sheriff, I will be glad to shake your hand," said Black Hart. "You did the right thing by running me out of Hazard, and it was one of the best things to ever happen to me."

Sheriff Sizemore smiled. "Black Hart, I can see you've become a real gentleman, and if you want to stay in Hazard, and you don't break any laws, it's fine with me."

"Thank you, Sheriff, but I think I've found my new home in New Orleans."

TWENTY-SEVEN

"**M**a, just what would you think if I told you I was gonna go ahead and join the Army?" Miles tossed the question out as casually as possible as he crossed through the living room on his way to the kitchen. He had just come in after opening a new bale of hay for Brownie, his last afternoon chore. Cecil, Wilbur, and he were going to meet at the oak tree later to talk about their new favorite topic, girls. It was a normal, quiet afternoon. Although Miles was pretty sure he already knew Drucella's reaction, this seemed like a good time to say aloud what he had been thinking about for months.

"I guess I would think you would be disobeying me," Drucella said without looking up from her sewing machine. "You know, I've been hoping and praying this war is going to be over with before you're old enough to go. Anyway, I don't think the service will take anyone who isn't 18."

"Ma, you just don't understand." Miles stopped to watch Drucella at the sewing machine. She was having trouble with the overalls she was mending for him. Her reaction was just as he expected—she was definitely against it, but she wasn't taking him seriously. "You see, if I don't hurry up and get into this war, I'm going to miss out on the greatest crusade of the century."

"Well," Drucella snapped, "you're not 18, so forget about it. And, I know you've been talking with Charlie about the War."

"The only thing Charlie told me was fighting for your country is a decision each person has to make for himself, and I've made my decision. Don't you see, Ma?" Miles persisted, "I could go right now. I heard talk they're having a tough time signing up new recruits to make their quota." Drucella stopped her sewing machine, but Miles continued. "They say if you're six feet tall and you lie about your age, they usually just look the other way. I'm going to go ahead and tell them I'm 18 and be done with it."

"Oh, I see you're not only going to disobey me, but you're going to be a liar, to boot." Drucella looked at her son. She didn't want this to be a serious discussion. "Now, just how do you think the Lord's going to feel about that?"

Miles walked decisively over to the door.

"Ma, I don't think the Lord's got time to worry about me telling a little white lie when the whole world is fighting a war," he replied, his back to her. He turned back to face her before he put his hand on the door. "Can't you see, Ma? I just got to get in this war before it's too late. It's something I just got to do."

"You're brave and headstrong," Drucella said, "just like your father. Your father would have gone to war, too." Drucella smiled a bit, a pained smile, and looked deep into a corner of the ceiling. "Where are you Landon?" she asked quietly. "I need your help right now."

Miles opened the door and walked out, hurrying to meet Cecil and Wilbur. He didn't look back.

During the next week, Miles didn't mention his thoughts to Drucella again, but getting into the war was constantly on his mind. The urge to join up was especially strong each time Miles sat in Mr. Watson's Current Events class and listened to war news on the radio. Mr. Watson encouraged active student participation in discussions about the war, and plotted the course of the war on the big map of Europe that hung on the front wall of the classroom.

After Mr. Watson turned off the radio one day, Miles jumped out of his seat. Using the index finger of his left hand he made a mustache across his upper lip. He extended his right arm, Palm down, as he had seen in newspaper pictures, and shouted, "Heil Hitler!" The other students laughed. Mr. Watson, smiled, but he didn't really laugh. That surprised Miles.

"OK," said Mr. Watson, "we've had our little laugh." Miles sat down as the class settled down. "How many of you heard Winston Churchill's speech on the radio yesterday?"

Miles was serious now. He had heard the speech on the little Philco Radio at home. He raised his hand. Mr. Watson called on Miles for comment. Miles stood again and told the class what he remembered about the speech. He ended with his favorite Part. "I loved the Part where Churchill said 'There will always be an England'." But as Miles sat down, he wondered if the England Churchill spoke so lovingly about would always exist. Miles wanted to see it now. He wanted to join the war, join the adventure. He longed to get away from home, grow up and make his own decisions. And so, he made his first big decision right then. He would go to the recruiting station and sign up that afternoon.

After school, as he neared the hickory tree with the knothole, Miles began looking for a rock. When he reached his usual throwing spot, he took his stance, aimed and threw. He was surprised when the rock bounced off the tree. He was sure he had hit the hole. Miles walked up to the tree, and standing next to it for the first time, could see that the bark around the edge of the knothole was chipped and marred where his misses over the years had scarred the tree. Probably not that important, anyway, thought Miles, as my dream to become a major league baseball player is not going to happen.

Down at the station, the Army recruiter grinned at Miles as he shook his hand. "Well now, son, it's going to be a great educational experience for you," he said. "The only advice I can give you, young man, is keep your head down, your eyes open, and don't volunteer for nothing."

A week later, Miles said his goodbyes to Drucella, Evaline and Charlie. He had the same feelings he had felt so many times since his father's death. But now, it was Charlie standing with them, the four of them standing alone against the world. Drucella kept her emotions contained while she studied the features of Miles' face. Then it was a quick hug and kiss on the forehead, and Evaline's voice trailing after him, "You be sure you write us as soon as you get settled."

TWENTY-EIGHT

Miles walked the road that led out of Jack Lot Hollow. It was a Saturday morning in October. Miles' great adventure had begun, and he felt intoxicated to be on his way. He passed the meeting places of the Musketeers, familiar landmarks such as the old coal tipple where each game of the fox and hounds began, then the huge oak tree that was supposed to be over one-hundred-and-fifty-years-old. He couldn't be sure when, if ever, he would ever see these things again, but those were kids' meeting places. He had new places to see. He had made his decision.

When Miles arrived at the Bus Station, he was surprised to hear a three-piece band consisting of a trumpet, trombone and clarinet playing *"Over There."* Most of the other recruits had already said their last goodbyes and were on the bus. A few had gotten back in line for a second helping of coffee and doughnuts. The biscuits and a couple of strips of bacon that Drucella had fixed for Miles this morning had fueled his walk to the Bus Station, but with all the excitement of this new adventure, Miles realized he was hungry and got in line. He picked up two doughnuts.

Miles watched as mothers and girlfriends clung to their loved ones before they boarded the bus. Suddenly, he realized he was the only recruit who didn't have anyone there to see him off, and a wave of loneliness washed over him.

Then Miles caught sight of a familiar smile in the autumn sunlight. Nancy Ann looked up in surprise as Miles' eyes met hers.

Her shiny brown hair was in a ponytail tied with a red ribbon, and she wore a matching red cardigan over her white starched dress. The coffeepot Nancy Ann was holding almost slipped out of her hands, and a stream of coffee poured from the spout onto the pavement. The recruit in front of Nancy Ann quickly jumped back out of the way with his empty cup still in his hand.

With a half-smile on her face, Nancy Ann stared at Miles. Her mother took the coffee pot from her hands and began filling the other recruits' cups. Nancy Ann slowly walked toward Miles. When she reached him, she took both of Miles' hands in hers and pulled him close. "Miles Hudson, just what in the world do you think you're doing here? You know you're not old enough to join up. Why, you're only a junior in high school."

"Yeah, I know, but not so loud, Nancy Ann!" he whispered. "This was just something I had to do."

"You mean, you were just gonna leave without saying goodbye to any of your friends from school?"

"Yeah, I guess I was," Miles stammered. "I thought it would be the best way."

Nancy Ann's face was flushed. Her temper flared. "Well, it's not the best way, you dope," she said angrily. "Just what if you had gone off to war, and I would have never seen you again? I can't imagine all the thoughts that would have gone through my head, never knowing why you didn't say goodbye to me."

"I'm real sorry about that, Nancy Ann," Miles said, looking down at the pavement.

"Well, you should be. Now, before you get on that bus and go off to war, I'm going to give you a goodbye kiss, and I don't mean a little peck on the cheek either."

"You mean right here in front of everyone?" Miles blushed.

"That's exactly what I mean, right here in front of God, and everyone else who might be looking." Nancy Ann sounded just like Evaline when her mind was made up. "We've been dragging our feet too long. It's time we admit how we feel about each other. Now is that gonna be all right with you, or not?"

"Yeah, I think I would like that a whole lot." Miles looked for a trash can for his half-eaten doughnut.

Nancy Ann took the doughnut from Miles' hand and put it on the table. Then she laid a whopper of a kiss on Miles. He thought his heart would stop. The other recruits yelled and whistled. The kiss left Miles a little dizzy, and he didn't know what to say, so he simply grinned, snatched his bag and headed to the bus.

"You be sure and write me at least once a day," Nancy Ann called out as Miles hurriedly boarded the bus.

"Would ya like to have my seat by the window so ya can wave goodbye to ya girlfriend?" a blond-haired recruit asked Miles.

"Gee, thanks, Mister, that's mighty nice of you," Miles replied.

"No problem, no problem at all," the recruit grinned.

Nancy Ann and her mother waved until the bus was out of sight.

At last they were on their way. Miles relaxed and turned to the blond youth who had given up his window seat. "My name's Miles Hudson, what's yours?"

"Well, I'm right proud to know you, Mr. Miles Hudson. My name's Shade, Shade Hawley, and I'm from up the road a piece, up around Kingdom Come. I can't wait to git my training over with, and git in this war. Ya see, I'm gonna make one of the best damn soldiers this country's ever seen."

Miles thought about many things as the bus made its way through the mountains, his family, the War, and whether he'd make it back. Most of his thoughts, however, were about Evaline and Drucella, and whether they would be okay. Then he quickly reminded himself this should be among the least of his worries, as Charlie had promised he would be taking very good care of them.

TWENTY-NINE

M iles did not arrive at Fort Jackson, South Carolina, at nine o'clock Monday morning as scheduled. By then, the savage snowstorm that was sweeping the East Coast had closed roads and delayed trains as much as six-to-eight hours. He watched as the snowflakes continued to fall outside the train's window, and he was reminded of the pillow fights he and Evaline had when he was small. The train pushed on through the deep snow and arrived at Fort Jackson in the early afternoon.

Miles and the other recruits lined up at the supply counter and were issued clothing and toilet articles before they were assigned to one of the many barracks on the base. His barracks looked as though they had been haphazardly nailed together in the middle of the night. Each of the two-story buildings had lines of bunks, only a few feet apart. Miles discovered that the bathroom, with its shower heads, sinks and toilets, were much better than the outhouse he had left behind.

The barracks to which Miles had been assigned were his new home for his basic training. There was little time to get acquainted with his new neighbors who occupied the bunks on either side of his. The men barely had time to put away their new clothes and make up their bunks before they were marched outdoors into the snow and near-zero temperatures. Each was issued a shovel and put to work helping to rid the walks and streets of wet snow.

When the lights went out in the barracks at nine-thirty, all the practical jokers came out of the woodwork and competed to see who could get the most laughs. One soldier imitated the meowing of a cat, another the mooing of a cow, and then there was the famous whistle-snorer. Who are these clowns? Miles wondered. Are they afraid and trying to act like Sgt. York or something? Miles tossed in his bunk, wishing for quiet so he could get some rest. Once everyone finally settled down and the barracks fell quiet, each man was left alone in the dark with his fears and hopes of what the war and the uncertain future might hold for him.

Wake-up call came at five-thirty, and roll call followed fifteen minutes later. By six o'clock, bunks had been made, and everyone was showered, shaved and dressed, and having breakfast in the mess hall.

From the start, dissension arose between the men from the North and those from the South. Northerners were resentful over having to train in the South. They made it plain that they didn't like the way the Southern food was prepared. They laughed and made fun of the Southerners who had to have their bowls of grits each morning. They unmercifully teased and laughed at the mountain men's accents and their love of biscuits and gravy.

The men from the South teased right back, calling the Northerners "city slickers" and "carpetbaggers" who would eat anything that swam or crawled in the ocean. Although most of it was good-natured teasing, a few recruits, some from the North and some from the South, carried the teasing a bit too far and their tones were always too bitter. Whenever those guys got going, Miles thought it was as if the Civil War were being fought all over again.

It all came to a head one morning in the mess hall. Earlier that morning, when everyone marched into the mess hall, they were surprised to find large bowls of biscuits and gravy sitting in the middle of the long wooden tables. The Southerners were delighted. They hurriedly got their trays, went through the line, and took their seats. The Northerners grumbled out insulting remarks about the South and being forced to eat biscuits and gravy.

Miles was one of the last men to arrive for breakfast. After going through the line, he stood with his tray looking for an empty seat. He could see only one place open. He was left with no choice. He would have to take a seat at a table occupied by the angry men from the North. Miles walked over to the table and noticed that at least there were plenty of biscuits and a full bowl of gravy left on this table. Miles took a deep breath and tried to ease onto the end of the bench, but the northerners made it difficult. They made it clear that if Miles wanted a seat, he would have to sit in the middle of the bench, across from their ring leader, a guy named Hardin.

Rodney Hardin, a stout, heavyset young man from New Jersey, enjoyed taunting the Southern men the most. He started the ribbing. "Okay, you dumb hillbillies sop up your gravy and biscuits before they get cold, but don't forget who kicked your asses in the Civil War," he laughed.

Miles could have cared less who had won the Civil War, but it always made his blood boil when Rodney called the men from the South "hayseeds" or "dumb hillbillies." Miles had not said anything up to this point; he had not participated in any of the name-calling. But he had already decided that everyone had put up with Rodney long enough. His father, Landon, had always said the best time to put a fire out is before it gets a big start. Miles' eyes became a deeper shade of gray as he stared across the bowl of gravy and into Rodney's face.

"Just what do you think you're looking at, hayseed?" Rodney shouted. He wasn't teasing. He was angry and mean.

Ordinarily, Miles would have let the remark go and begin eating, but not today. Miles knew this was the time to put a stop to Rodney. "If I'm looking at you, I'm looking at nothing," Miles snapped back.

"You got some kind of beef with what I'm saying about your precious biscuits and gravy?" Rodney sneered.

"What I'm really trying to do, Rodney, is figure you out. I guess what you're trying to tell us is you don't like biscuits and gravy."

"Hell no, hillbilly, I don't like your biscuits and gravy, and I sure as hell don't like you!"

"Well, now, Rodney, have you ever tried eating biscuits and gravy?" Miles asked. He had looked at Rodney's cleaned plate without a trace of gravy on it.

"Hell, no hillbilly, I wouldn't eat that slop if I was on a deserted island and I was starving to death!" Rodney shouted. He swept his hand across the table knocking his plate to the floor. His buddies at the table snickered and wondered if Miles, usually quiet, would take the challenge.

"If you've never tried them, then how do you know you don't like them?" Miles asked. He reached across the table, grabbed Rodney by the hair, and dunked his face into the bowl of hot gravy.

Rodney's screams and obscenities could be heard from one end of the compound to the other. Everyone watched in shock as Miles flew over the top of the gravy bowl and caught Rodney with a right hook to the jaw. Surprised by Miles' quickness and strength, Rodney fell back onto the floor with Miles on top of him.

All the men in the mess hall were on their feet now, surrounding the fighters, giving them room to brawl, and cheering them on. Miles heard the whistles and the shuffling of feet around them when the MP's arrived, but he and Rodney continued to roll around on the plank floor swinging their fists at each other until two MP's pulled them apart.

"Outside! Everyone outside!" one MP yelled. He jerked Miles off Rodney and yanked Miles upright. The other MP got Rodney to his feet.

The MP holding Miles seemed to be the one in charge. He looked at Rodney's blood-red face. "Get this man to the infirmary. Those might be 2nd-degree burns on his face. I'm taking this one to the guardhouse."

The MP handcuffed Miles and hauled him away. Miles stretched out on the hard bunk without a mattress or pillow and read all the graffiti that had been written on the walls by former prisoners. Miles felt no remorse. The way he saw it, Rodney had insulted him and his family's way of life, but worse than that Rodney was simply a bully.

Rodney was not the first bully Miles had known. He had dealt with his kind before. In the coal-mining town of Hazard there had been no shortage of bullies. Walter Herald and Harry Price were always hiding in the alley by the Family Theater, ready to pounce on the weak and unsuspecting.

Miles had taken great pride in bloodying Walter's nose and breaking Harry's glasses when the two bullies had tried to take his lunch money. Word had quickly spread among all the school's bullies that Miles would fight back. In the mountains of southeastern Kentucky, it was still an eye for an eye.

No matter the consequence for dunking Rodney's face in the bowl of hot gravy, Miles knew he had done what he had to do, and he was at peace with himself.

The commander came to see Miles. He scowled and pointed his finger, threatening to have Miles drummed out of the service. Miles was told he was a hothead and didn't deserve to wear a uniform. But once all the shouting and insulting remarks had stopped, Miles was surprised that his sentence was only seven days of hard labor.

During the day Miles was required to work a full ten hours. In the morning, he was given a pick and shovel and put outside in the cold to dig ditches. In the afternoon he was brought inside, given a toothbrush and made to clean the latrines. After dinner he scrubbed pots and pans in the mess hall before being locked up for the night back in the guardhouse.

"Sir, I don't know why you let Hudson off as easily as you did," Corporal Moore said to the commander in his office.

The commander went over to a large globe by the window.

"Corporal, believe me," the commander replied, "if this country wasn't at war this very minute, I would have thrown the book at Hudson. To be perfectly honest with you, we're not winning this war right now. In fact, we're getting our butts kicked all over the globe."

The commander spun the globe and watched as it circled around and around.

"You see, Corporal, the top brass are always looking for men like Hudson because in the heat of battle, some men are going to turn tail and run. The one thing you can count on is it won't be someone like Hudson. When he sees his buddies dropping all around him like flies, he won't get sick and throw up. He'll get mad as hell and, by God, Corporal, he'll stand his ground. The enemy will have to kill him because his kind won't give an inch. Corporal, it's men like Hudson who are going to turn the tide for us in this war."

THIRTY

Word about "The Gravy Bowl Incident," as it became known, quickly spread from one barracks to the other. The story became more exciting each time it was told. One version said Miles was a direct descendant of Randall McCoy, the head of the McCoy clan, the one who led the fight against Devil Anse Hatfield in Kentucky's bloodiest feud. All versions of the story went on to say that Miles was a cold-blooded killer from the mountains of Eastern Kentucky, and any Germans unlucky enough to come into contact with him wouldn't stand much of a chance.

Rodney's buddies from the North continued to be bitter over the commander's decision to transfer Rodney Hardin to a new training camp, while Miles was allowed to continue his training at Fort Jackson. They insisted that Miles' sentence of serving just seven days in the guardhouse had been only a light slap on the hand. Miles overheard two Northerners saying he was a lunatic who should be drummed out of the service forever.

The Southerners had a different opinion. To them, Miles was a hero. They were proud that one of their own had stood up for them. They even went so far as to search out a recruit who had been a tinsmith in civilian life. They secretly took up a collection of fifteen dollars and engaged the tinsmith to hammer out a copper medal in the shape of a gravy bowl.

One evening, as the men were finishing their meal in the mess hall, two Southerners stood up and came to attention. Royce Reed, a recruit from Atlanta, shouted out, "About face!" Then, the two men marched over to the table where Miles was sitting. Royce hovered over Miles and called, "Attention!" Miles, startled and surprised, removed his napkin from his lap, stood up and came to attention. Everyone watched to see what was going to happen next.

Tom Daugherty, from Mount Dora, Florida, held his shoulders back and his head high, and read the words written on the homemade paper-bag certificate:

> *For courage shown above and beyond the call of duty, we proudly present to Private Miles Hudson, the distinguished Gravy Bowl Medal.*

Royce took a step forward and pinned the medal to Miles' shirt pocket. The two men saluted Miles and quickly marched back to their chairs.

The Southerners laughed and applauded while the Northerners booed and called out obscenities.

The last two weeks of basic training were made up of grueling physical tests to measure each man's ability to survive in the heat of battle. The most dreaded tests were the obstacle course and the twenty-five-mile hike with full packs.

The final 25-mile hike was no problem for Miles, with his Cherokee blood, blinding speed, and strength. On the hike, he was the fox again, uncatchable, just as he had been in all those games with Cecil and Wilbur. Miles was the first to complete the hike and in record time. For this feat, he earned the nickname "Speed."

Tom Daugherty, another Southerner, was the last man to finish the 25-mile hike. As he staggered across the finish line, he was greeted with playful catcalls of, "Better late than never," "Come on Daugherty, get the lead out," and, "Yeah, slowpoke, hurry up and get in the truck; we want to get back to the barracks before the sun comes up!"

Tom, embarrassed and angry, swallowed down the last drop of water in his canteen. The empty canteen slipped away from his hands and fell to the ground. A cloud of dust formed around his boot as he kicked the canteen into the air. He looked hard and long at the men in the two waiting trucks. He angrily turned his back to them and began hiking the 25-miles back down the road that led to the barracks. The chatter of the men stopped, and they looked at each other in disbelief.

"Tom's not only slow, he's completely nuts!" Artie Linder, a recruit from New Jersey, shouted.

"Yeah, he's slow as hell and he's nuts, but he sure has a lot of tough bark on him," Carl Hale commented. Carl was from Altoona, Pennsylvania.

"But for the Grace of God, there go I," Miles said, leaping off the back of the truck and following Tom down the dirt road.

"Well, if that stubborn Irishman can make a 50-mile hike, so can I," Royce Reed said, grabbing his backpack up again. He jumped from the truck and ran after the two men.

Tom heard the men coming up behind him. He turned to face them. "I don't need you son-a-bitches. I'm gonna do this my way."

Miles shrugged. "We know Tom, but we're all in this together. We're all behind you." Miles turned to the truck and motioned for all the men to follow. And they did. Some of the men were laughing, some grumbling, as everyone in Company B got out of the truck and followed Tom down the dirt road.

"Jesus Christ, has this war made fools out of everyone in it?" the truck driver shouted as he started the engine and drove back toward the barracks.

For the first time, the Northerners and the Southerners were bonding. All at once, it didn't matter how Tom talked or where he was from. He was one of them. He was family, and they all knew families stick together.

Miles and Tom walked together at the head of the pack. Miles kept up the pace, encouraging Tom and anyone else who got tired. When the finish line came into view, Miles lagged back. The other men followed his lead. They stopped to tie their boots or to take a drink of water from their canteens. They were making sure that Tom would be the first man to finish the hike.

The men of Company B completed the 50-mile hike in twenty-two hours without a single man dropping out. For this feat, Company B received a special merit from General Martin.

A Letter to Drucella

Dear Ma,

My basic training is almost over, and believe me, it hasn't been easy. At first, I didn't know if my body would be able to take all the punishment from doing all of the things our drill sergeant expected us to do.

After the first two weeks, my red sunburn turned into a light brown tan, and the softness in my muscles went away. I now feel better than I have ever felt in my life, and I know I'm ready to face whatever awaits me on the battlefield. Does my room look like it did when I left home? Are my records and comic books still on the shelf above my bed? Please don't change my room. I would like to come home and see it the way it was when I left home.

Do you ever see Nancy Ann? If you do, does she ever ask about me? I think about you and Evaline most all the time. I would gladly give all I have if I could once more sit on our front porch with you and Evaline and listen to the lonesome whippoorwill calling out its name.

Love always,
Miles

THIRTY-ONE

N ever in his wildest dreams had Miles imagined he would ever see New York City. He remembered all those times he had sat in the dark Virginia Theater and marveled at images of the greatest city in the world on the screen. Now, as the train known as the New York Central inched its way into the big city, Miles moved from one side of the train to the other, constantly changing seats, trying to see everything. His throat felt dry from all the excitement, and he made several trips down the aisle to the water cooler at the end of the car.

"Grand Central Station!" the conductor called out as he hurried down the aisle of the coach.

The enormity of Grand Central Station took Miles by surprise. He could only gape at the interior of the largest building he had ever seen. The ceiling looked as though it were over one hundred feet high with large windows that let the sun stream down into the building like giant spotlights.

This is a city inside a building, Miles thought. He walked past a barber shop much larger than the one in Hazard, a restaurant, and several specialty shops. At the newsstand, Miles glanced at the headlines in several of the newspapers calling attention to the actions of the Allied Forces in Sicily. He walked a bit further and stopped in front of a flower shop where a man was buying a bouquet and talking excitedly about his girlfriend who would be arriving soon.

As Miles stood outside the flower shop listening and marveling, he glanced at the plate glass window and saw a reflection of people across the way, and wondered if his eyes were playing tricks on him. No, his eyes weren't playing tricks, he thought as he watched in amazement as people were hurriedly stepping on some sort of moving steps that seemed to float them upward, he assumed to the next floor of the building.

Miles walked across the floor and approached the stairs cautiously. He could hear the clicking of the stairs as they moved. After watching several people step onto the stairs, he felt brave enough to give it a try. He clutched the moving rail with his right hand and carefully stepped onto the escalator. He watched his feet as the step he was standing on moved closer to the second floor. Before the step disappeared, he knew he would have to leap clear of the machine or his foot might be sucked under with the disappearing step. So before his step flattened, he made an awkward leap onto the floor. His head was spinning, and he felt sick to his stomach as he sat down on a long wooden bench.

Miles guessed there must be over a thousand people inside Grand Central. They all seemed to know exactly where they were going as the loudspeaker called out arriving and departing trains. A pretty young lady placed her suitcase on the bench beside Miles. She smiled, and then she began to laugh.

"Was that the first time you ever rode on an escalator?" she asked.

"An escalator? Why, no, it isn't!" He blushed. "I mean, well, I guess it is," Miles stammered.

"I thought so," she teased. "You looked like you were scared half to death. Now, just what's your name and where are you from? Podunk Junction?"

Miles looked at the girl. She sure was pretty. She had brown hair with hints of red. Her face was open and friendly. He wanted to know her name.

"Now, you wait one minute, young lady," Miles said. "Just hold your horses. What business you got asking me all these questions? In the service they tell us, 'Loose lips sink ships,' but if you must know," he paused and smiled at her, "My name is Miles Hudson, and I'm from Hazard, Kentucky."

"Hazard?" the girl said, plopping herself down on the bench with her suitcase between them. "I've heard stories about Hazard! Is it really as tough a town as people say?"

"Nobody in Hazard is going to bother anyone unless you bother them first," Miles replied. "Now, you tell me your name. Where are you from? Boston or Philadelphia? But you don't talk like a city slicker."

"Lord, no! My name is Holly Harris, and I'm just a plain little country girl from West Virginia who's come to the Big Apple to become famous!"

"And how in Heaven's name do you plan to do that?" Miles said.

Holly took a deep breath, rolled her eyes and spoke in a firm voice. "My good man, I'll have you know I have this one quality they call talent. Why, I won the West Virginia State Drama Contest for my reading of Emily in Our Town."

"Holly, I don't remember reading anything like that in school," Miles said, realizing he had put his foot in his mouth. Now she knew for sure that her education was much better than his. Holly decided to let him off the hook and didn't say anything. But she still wanted him to know she did have talent.

"Well," Holly said. "Why don't I do the last few lines of my reading for you?"

"Sure, go ahead. I would love to hear what won that state contest for you," Miles said. His face was still warm from his embarrassment.

Holly stood up and took stage about three feet in front of him. She took a deep breath, positioned her body, and composed her face. Then she lowered her head for only a moment. When she lifted her head and began to speak, she was suddenly someone else.

Miles listened transfixed. Other people stopped to listen, too. When Holly lowered her head again to signal the ending of her piece, Miles stood and began the applause. Holly's face glowed, a mixture of pride and embarrassment. Not knowing what else to do, she bowed to the crowd as they began to disperse.

"Wow," Miles said. "I can see why those judges picked your reading to win that contest! How many shows have you appeared in since you've been in New York?"

"Lord have mercy, none yet!" Holly laughed as she moved back to the bench. "I've only been in New York for a month-and-a-half. Just what is it you think you do when you come to New York? You don't get off the train and walk into the first theater you see and get the leading role in a Broadway play!"

"Oh, I see," said Miles. "Lightning hasn't struck yet."

A smile hovered on Holly's lips as she watched the people hurrying in and out of Grand Central Station.

"No, lightning hasn't struck yet. But it will. You'll see," she said. She picked up her suitcase. Miles reached to take her case, but Holly shook her head and Miles complied.

"Well, what are you doing in Grand Central Station with your suitcase? Are you giving up and going back home?" Miles asked.

"Hell, no! I haven't given up. I just got back from Beckley, West Virginia." Holly turned to leave. She seemed to expect him to walk along with her, so Miles picked up his own suitcase. Holly continued as they walked. "I went home to see my Pa. He's not been doing too good. They say he's got lung disease from working in the coal mines all his life. He wanted me to come home for a few days."

"Didn't your mother try to fatten you up while you were home?" Miles smiled. "You look like a good strong wind would blow you clean away."

"Is that so?" Holly retorted. "Well, maybe someone should have taken the time to tell you about escalators when you were home. You looked like you were going to have a heart attack when you jumped off that escalator."

"Yeah, I guess I was pretty scared," Miles laughed. They were almost to the street now. "You know, I've only got one night to spend in New York before I board the Queen Mary for England. I was wondering if you would let me buy you supper?" Miles paused for a reaction. She turned to him with just a hint of a smile, enough for Miles to continue. "And maybe we could take in a good picture show?"

"No, I don't think so," Holly said still grinning. "Anyway, I'm not dressed to go out for dinner. Besides, what would I do with my suitcase?"

Miles had stopped walking. He was looking at the rush of traffic, a street filled with cars and a sidewalk crowded with people. He had to think quickly. "I could flag down one of those yellow taxicabs. We could go to your place and then come back to Times Square." Miles hoped that was the right thing to say.

"I don't know," Holly mused. "Why, I just met you, and I don't know anything about you at all."

"Not a lot to know about me," said Miles. "I'm just a fish out of water trying to enjoy myself while I still have the time." He smoothed his uniform a bit and switched his case over to his left hand.

Holly paused. She gave Miles the once-over from head to toe. "All right! It looks like you talked me into it," Holly said. "I've had a lot on my mind lately. I guess it's about time I had a night on the town. Anyway, I hate to think what might happen to you in this town without me to show you around."

At the Italian restaurant Holly picked for them, a violinist played soft music, and light from a candle flickered on the red-and-white checkered tablecloth. They ordered wine, a garden salad, and spaghetti and meatballs with cream sauce. While they waited for their meal, they ate Italian bread with butter and toasted each other's hopes and dreams with red wine. They never made it to Radio City Music Hall, but they did go to the Astor Theatre in Times Square, a plush movie theater with thick red carpet and a gold-plated staircase that led up to the balcony. They saw a war picture, *Since You Went Away,* starring Robert Walker, Jennifer Jones and Guy Madison. When "THE END" appeared on the screen, tears welled up in Holly's eyes and ran down her cheeks.

"I don't think it was right for Robert Walker to die and leave Jennifer Jones a widow," she lamented. "It just ruined the entire picture for me."

"Well, you can't let it bother you," Miles said. "It's only a picture show. Now, why don't we cross the street and have a cup of coffee in that café?"

It was one o'clock in the morning when Miles flagged down a taxi to take them back to Holly's apartment.

"How about some red wine?" Holly asked in a stage whisper once the taxi ride was underway.

"You mean, while we're riding?"

Holly put her finger to her lips. "Sure, why not? I stole two wine glasses and slipped the bottle of wine into my purse!" She pulled two glasses out of her purse and held them up triumphantly.

"You know you're a nutcase, don't you?"

"Yeah, I know," she laughed. She pulled the wine bottle out and handed it to Miles.

"You're pretty," Miles said. He pulled the cork out of the bottle and poured wine into the glasses Holly held. Then he recorked the bottle and slipped it back into Holly's purse.

Holly handed Miles one of the glasses. "Do you really think so? I always thought I was just a plain Jane. Not much to look at. Just another girl."

"Not really. You've got a great face, and I enjoy looking at it!"

"That's very kind of you to say. Now move over here by me." Miles slid across the seat and put his free arm around Holly's shoulder. "Isn't that the cat's meow?" Holly asked as she snuggled in.

"It most certainly is." Miles smiled.

The cab driver stole another glance at the two in his rearview mirror.

Inside Holly's apartment, Holly handed Miles a pillow and blanket and showed him the couch with a reluctant smile. But hours later, Miles still had not fallen asleep. His mind raced with fear and excitement over what lay ahead for him across the ocean. The flashing light from the neon sign outside Holly's window pierced through the Venetian blinds and struck Miles squarely in the eyes. He covered them with the palm of his hand and rolled over to the other side of the worn-out sofa. Miles figured it must be about five o'clock now, too late to try to go back to sleep. The honking of the cab drivers' horns had already begun. He would have given five dollars for a cup of black coffee and two aspirins.

Careful not to make any noise that would waken Holly, Miles got up. In the bathroom, he gingerly removed the underwear hanging over Holly's shower curtain, turned on the shower and let the spray of cool water refresh his body.

A half hour later, Miles slipped down the stairs and out the door into the light rain and yellow lights of the city. As the cab pulled away from the curb, he thought he heard a girl's voice calling out his name. He looked back, but he couldn't see anyone.

Holly stood at the bottom of the stairs and watched the taxi's taillights until they faded out of sight.

"Stupid hillbilly," she murmured under her breath. "He hasn't got the sense God gave a goose. If he thinks I'm going to cry over him, he's got another think coming."

But back upstairs, Holly sobbed as she read the scribbled note Miles had left her on the kitchen table. She got back into bed, pulled the covers up around her shoulders and dozed off.

As dawn broke, Miles was standing on the deck of the Queen Mary with three thousand other brave young men watching the New York skyline as it disappeared into the ocean. When the torch of the Statue of Liberty was no longer in view, a solider began singing the national anthem. As the last notes of the song faded away, Miles thought of Holly who was probably, right now, reading the note he had left for her:

> *Dear Holly,*
> *Please accept my gratitude for your kindness to a young man all alone in the big city. I hope and I pray that your dream of becoming an actress on the Broadway stage comes true. I will never lose my admiration for you, and I do believe someday our paths will cross again.*
> *Love always,*
> *Miles*

THIRTY-TWO

The Queen Mary pushed further out to sea, and Miles felt seasick. Someone said, "God help us all." He turned to look for the speaker, and then realized he was the one who said it.

After that first queasiness, the passage was uneventful. It was 1944 and Miles learned he was one of the nearly 1.6 million American troops headed for the United Kingdom, troops training and waiting for General Eisenhower to give the command to begin the largest invasion the world had ever seen.

Miles and the other soldiers were given space in overcrowded barracks on their first night in the United Kingdom and told they would be moved to other locations the following day. The next morning, the sergeant arrived at the barracks early. Miles had just straightened the bedroll he had slept on. He wished he had been able to get a good night's rest. He stood in line near the water fountain at the end of the barracks, hoping the water here would be cooler and more refreshing than the drinking water on the ship.

"Hubba! Hubba! Hubba! I need ten volunteers. Ten of you step forward," the sergeant yelled. No one came forward.

"Oh, is that how it's going to be, is it?" snapped the sergeant. "Well, that's okay with me. I'll just have to pick and choose. You, you and you. And you three guys over by the water fountain."

Miles raised his head. "Me?"

"Yeah, you, lover boy. That makes six. Now, I need four more."

Four other men raised their hands and stepped forward.

"Okay, now we have ten volunteers. You have one hour to get all your belongings together and line up outside."

Miles took a drink of water and stumbled back toward his bedroll. He wouldn't need more than a few minutes to get his belongings together, his journal, his shave kit, and a few clothes. "Damn!" He grinned at one of the men who had actually volunteered for this assignment. "My recruiting sergeant told me never to volunteer, but it looks like I got volunteered anyway."

The sergeant drove the soldiers to a nearby neighborhood. It was a modest street of single-family homes. A black wrought-iron gate stood in front of each one. The sergeant looked over his list of names and addresses.

"All right, Private Hudson, go and knock on that first door there." He pointed to the first house in the row. "That's Mrs. Brown's door. Let's see if she will be kind enough to take your sorry butt in."

Miles followed orders and Molly Brown, a short, stout lady wearing a snow-white apron, opened the door. She smiled at Miles warmly and waved the sergeant on his way. Then she took a closer look at Miles.

"Land sakes, has our American houseguest finally arrived? I can't wait until Tessie and Mr. Brown get home. They will be beside themselves! Of all things! An American lad staying right here in our own house!" Mrs. Brown grabbed Miles' arm and tugged him into the house. "Well, come on in, and we'll have a slice of cake and spot of tea before we get you settled in."

As they passed through the living room, Miles noticed the cabinet radio and thought of Drucella at home listening to war news on the little Philco. A clock on the mantel chimed nine o'clock. Miles smiled. It would be four o'clock in Jack Lot Hollow. Drucella wouldn't be up yet.

Miles sat in his shirtsleeves scribbling out notes on a small antique desk. The desk stood next to a half-size bed with a blue wool blanket draped over it. The blanket gave the room a cozy look. As Miles had been instructed, he had gotten acquainted with Mrs. Brown, stowed his things in the room she had provided, checked out his surroundings and then reported back to his base to begin training. At the end of the day, he had made his way back to the Brown's home and come up to his room to write in his journal. He had not written much while on the ship, and he had so many stories he wanted to put down on paper. When Mrs. Brown had shown him the room earlier, she had been apologetic about the sparseness of the furniture, but Miles had been delighted. A real bed and a place to write; what more could he want?

A voice echoed up the stairs and into the small room. "I'll be begging your pardon, Mr. Hudson."

"Yes, Mrs. Brown. What is it?" Miles called back.

"Well, sir, the family will be taking our supper in a bit. Won't you pop down and join us?"

Christ, was it suppertime already? Miles picked up the watch Evaline had given him so long ago for Christmas. Where had the time gone to? "I'll be right down, Mrs. Brown."

Miles walked down a narrow staircase to a small, cozy living room with a round braided carpet and a worn sofa and chairs.

"Well, land sakes alive," Mrs. Brown said. "Here is our American lad, Mr. Miles Hudson from the Bluegrass state of Kentucky. Mr. Hudson, I take great pride in introducing you to my husband, Carl Brown, and our daughter, Tessie."

Carl Brown was short, stocky and muscular with a serious look to his face. By contrast, Tessie's face had a mischievous look under her dark pixie cut. She was petite and clad in a blue jumper.

Carl extended his right hand to Miles for a firm handshake. Tessie managed a smile and a, "Pleased to meet you, Doughboy."

"The pleasure is all mine," Miles said, extending his hand to her. Tessie smiled slyly as she took his hand. "What did you call me?" he asked. "Doughboy?"

"My fault, I'm afraid," Mr. Brown answered for his daughter. "I've been telling her stories my father told me about being in the Big One, WWI, you see. He knew some of your doughboys."

Mrs. Brown gestured for everyone to come into the dining room. Miles suddenly felt uncomfortable in his shirt sleeves. The Browns seemed to have dressed for dinner in honor of their guest. Miles stood until the women took their seats at the round oak table.

"He's not only handsome, but he has good manners as well," said Tessie. "Not like most of the blokes I know. Now tell us, Doughboy, is the grass in Kentucky really blue?"

"I can't rightly say, ma'am. You see, I was born in Kentucky hill country, up in the mountains where the grass is green. I don't know much about the flatlands."

"Now, Tessie," said her mother, sharply, "stop all your questions, and stop calling Mr. Hudson 'Doughboy!' He has a good English name. Let the lad enjoy his stew. I made it special for him. Why, I traded Mrs.Wells two carrots for a large onion to get the flavor just right."

"Your stew is very good, Mrs. Brown," Miles said. "In fact, it reminds me of Ma's stew back home." Miles took another big spoonful of the stew, surprised to find a chunk of beef. He had heard there would be no beef once they reached Europe. "And, oh by the way, Tessie, I don't mind you calling me 'Doughboy.'"

"Then it's settled. I'll call you 'Doughboy.' You can be my American Doughboy."

"Well I hope I can live up to that name," said Miles. "The American doughboys were a brave bunch of soldiers."

"You know, mum," Tessie mused studying Miles' face. "He reminds me of the American cowboys you see at the cinema. Talks just like them." She cocked her head to one side, thinking. Then her face brightened and she turned to her mother. "Sorta like Gary Cooper. You know, he played *Sergeant York*, the American who captured all those Germans in that other big war. I just can't wait to show him off to all my friends."

"Now, Tessie, that's enough," Mrs. Brown said, clearing the dishes and motioning for Tessie to help. "You're making our house guest uncomfortable."

Ignoring her mother entirely, Tessie continued to stare at Miles. She tucked a stray lock of hair behind her ear and buttoned her sweater, trying to look more grown up. "Well, Doughboy, how would you like to go out with me tonight? We could go to the Red Heart Pub. That's where all my friends meet to bend an elbow, if you know what I mean."

"I don't think so, Tessie," Miles said. "You see, I had planned to stay in my room tonight and work on my book. I hope you don't mind."

"Your book?" Tessie said with a mock look of horror. "Oh no, not another American writer. These American writers seem to be coming out of the woodwork. You mean you want to stay in that little room and write when you could go to the Red Heart Pub with me?"

"Maybe we could go another night?"

"Then it's settled. This coming Friday night we go to the Red Heart Pub."

On Friday evening after a hard day of training, Miles and Tessie walked down a green English lane, refreshed by the light rain that had fallen that afternoon. Tessie stopped to pick a bright yellow flower growing from the vines that covered a fence row. The flowers and the singing of the birds brought a smile to Miles' face. This was the first time Miles could remember seeing flowers and hearing birds singing since he had left the mountains.

"I feel wonderful. Now I know why most of the great writers come from England. I'm sure it must have been a day like this that inspired Shakespeare to write all those marvelous plays!"

"C'mon, Doughboy," said Tessie. "I think the old gent must have had a bit of talent to help him along."

"Maybe so, but you've got to admit, this is a beautiful evening! On an evening like this, with no sirens, I could almost forget there was a war going on."

They arrived at the pub, a nondescript red-brick building with a varnished wood door. Tess stopped with her hand on the door. "Well, we're here, Doughboy. Ready to go inside?"

"I think so, but I feel a little nervous." Miles straightened his uniform jacket. He could hear the band inside. Was that Glen Miller's "In the Mood" they were playing? Tessie was opening the door. Music and conversation spilled into the street.

"Don't worry. You're with me. Everything will be just peachy." Tessie grabbed his arm and pulled him through the doorway into the Red Heart.

After endless talk about the war and several pints of ale, Tessie was giggling and had almost toppled out of her chair. Her friends, however, continued to urge Miles into conversation. Miles was enjoying most of the talk, but he was a bit wary of Russell, an ambulance driver, and another guy named Paul who had come in with Russell about an hour ago. He had seen Russell elbow Paul and wink several times as Miles talked.

"Now, Miles," Russell said, sliding his glass to the barkeep for another. "Don't you want to tell us how those brave lads from the States came over here during the first World War and pulled old England's chestnuts out of the fire? Hip hip hooray! Three cheers for the lads from the States! And by the way, old boy, why do you talk in that thick brogue accent of yours? We scarcely understand anything you say!"

Miles finished off his pint. There was only one good swallow left. He set the glass on the bar and stared into Russell's eyes. "You know, Russell, if you and Paul don't like the way I talk, we can go outside and settle this matter right now."

"Listen, Russell, love," Tessie said, stepping between Russell and Miles and putting an arm around each of them. The tension between them had sobered her up a bit. She didn't want the night ruined. "I don't care how he talks. He's my American Doughboy, and I'll just be damned if I will sit still and let any one of you blokes say a word against him!"

"Tessie," Russell replied, breaking into a grin, "it looks like your Doughboy can't take a little needling!" Tessie gave Russell a playful poke in the arm and smiled at Miles. She signaled the barkeep for another pint for herself and one for Miles.

"To tell you the truth," Miles said, "I can take some needling, but I won't take it for very long. Where I come from, a little kidding is okay, but you had better know when to stop."

"No hard feelings, old chap," Russell said. "It was all that beer I drank doing most of my talking. You know, old man, we hear all the sayings about American soldiers, now that your country is in this war with us." He looked at Miles, but Miles didn't seem to understand. "You know, like the American soldiers over here are overpaid and oversexed." He saw Miles begin to bristle, so he hurried on. "But, my God, what in Heaven's name would we do without you?" Russell laughed. Only Paul joined in the laughter and it died quickly.

"Sure, Russell," said Miles. "I got no hard feelings about tonight." He stood and took out his billfold.

"Well, Doughboy, all I can say is good luck and good hunting," Russell stood and saluted. "Till we meet again, old chap."

Miles offered a quick flick of the wrist salute in return as he and Tessie headed out the door to stagger down the cobblestones arm in arm.

A few feet down the lane, Tessie started singing, "Show me the way to go home," and Miles joined in, "Cause I'm sleepy and I want to go to bed.

> "Had a little drink 'bout an hour ago,
> And it went straight to my head.
> Wherever I may roam,
> On the land or the sea or the foam,
> You'll always hear me a' singing this song
> Show me the way to go home."

They continued to sing all the way to the Brown's door.

Hurrying downstairs to get to his unit for training the next morning, Miles regretted having so much to drink. He interrupted Carl and Molly Brown's conversation in the living room on his way out. They had been talking about Tessie's behavior the night before. Miles did his best to explain to Carl and Molly that it was not Tessie's fault that they had come home drunk at one o'clock in the morning.

"I'm older than Tessie, and I should have known better," Miles said. He wondered just how old Tessie really was. He had never asked. But his mama had raised him to have manners. He was the man, the gentleman, and he should have taken better care of her. He knew it was his fault.

The Browns would have none of it. They insisted it was Tessie's fault. Miles was their guest, and Tessie should have gotten him home sober before midnight.

By now, the Browns were used to taking things in stride. The family had gone through terrible times since the Germans had declared war on England. They had survived the bombing raids over London and the British Isles. They had seen relatives, neighbors and friends return from the front missing legs or arms and many returned in coffins. They had feared for their home, their country and their lives. In truth, they were exhausted.

When America entered the war, the British people breathed a sigh of relief. These tall, thin Americans with their cowboy accents and overarching confidence were a strange sort to the British. These good old boys from the States swaggered in, smoking their Lucky Strikes, eating Hershey bars and drinking their Coca-Cola. Nothing seemed impossible to these young warriors. When asked who they thought would win the war, there wasn't a doubt in the Americans' minds. They already knew they would do it. They had beaten the Germans in the First World War, and now they couldn't wait to do it again.

The evenings of early spring, when Miles finished his training each day and returned to the Browns' home, were fun times for Miles and Tessie. They explored parts of London that were not bombed out, and sometimes, late at night, they stretched out on blankets in the backyard and talked and dreamed. Knowing what was in store for him on the battlefield, Miles appreciated the beauty of every day: the blue of the sky, the crispness of the morning air,

Tessie's smile. The two grew closer. Miles needed Tessie. He was scared about the war, although he never admitted it. He needed to love someone even if he didn't know if he were truly falling in love.

The summer rains and storms moved in. Miles began having nightmares: battlefields littered with soldiers crying out in agony, the sounds of gunfire. On one particular night, he dreamt of racing Cecil and Wilbur to the flagpole. In the dream he was running hard, exhilarated by the speed, but when he reached out to touch the flagpole, to end the game, Miles was suddenly standing alone in Riverside Cemetery.

The radio news, the build-up of troops, the excitement and fear of the soldiers—everything pointed to the coming, final battle. Miles like everyone, including the Germans, knew the invasion was ready to begin. The entire world was poised and waiting for General Eisenhower to give the command to go.

On the 1st day of June, Miles and Tessie were at the Red Heart Pub, dancing to the music of a local band. The local bands almost always played American music, tonight they played more Glenn Miller. The place was in full swing, when a military policeman stepped up on the stage. The music stopped. "All military personnel report to your units immediately. Repeat. All military personnel report to your units immediately."

The band began to play the popular song of the day, "There'll be bluebirds over the white cliffs of Dover, just you wait and see ..."

Miles and Tessie got up from their table to dance their last dance. He held her close and whispered in her ear, "Well, Tessie girl, it doesn't look like I'll be the one taking you home tonight."

"Oh, that's just like my Doughboy. Always worrying about everyone but himself. I'll get home all right. Don't worry about me."

The song ended and Miles escorted Tessie back to her table. Other soldiers were doing the same with their girls. The calm quiet that had followed the shock of the announcement was beginning to wear-off, replaced by a mixture of fear and excitement. Some of the good-byes around them were quiet and tearful, and others were loud and showy.

Miles and Tessie had known this moment would eventually come. Now, Miles repeated the few simple instructions they had talked about before. "You'll remember to send my journal to my mother in Kentucky. Someone will come by to pick up my other personal belongings." He paused. "And you be sure to tell Carl and Molly I said goodbye, and I'll never forget them."

"Yes, I'll tell them," Tessie said. "And when this bloody war is over, you be sure you come back to me. You hear me, soldier boy? You come back to England, and I'll marry you. You hear what I'm bloody well saying? I want to marry you!"

"How in Heaven's name did I lose my 'Doughboy' name?" Miles was surprised by Tessie's outburst.

"Well, I can't very well call the man I'm going to marry and love, 'Doughboy,' now can I?"

"I guess not," Miles said. He looked at her, admiring her spirit. "I'll come back to you. You can count on that." They stared at each other a moment. They smiled. "Well, we got that settled." Miles turned to go, but Tessie put her hand on his arm.

"But you never said you love me. Do you love me, soldier boy? Do you?"

Miles stopped and turned to her again. "I guess I do. I never felt like this before. Yes, I love you."

They hugged and kissed, and Tessie squeezed Miles' hand.

"You remind me of a little boy with his hair hanging down in his eyes. Like mum says, I guess we're all children after all. Now, go on before I start to cry. I will always love you, Doughboy. Oh, I've forgotten already, soldier boy. I will always love you, soldier boy."

Tessie watched Miles walk out the door and wiped the tears from her eyes.

THIRTY-THREE

F or thousands of Americans stationed in England during the
spring of 1944, France was the distant shore where they were
to meet the Nazis in a struggle to the death. By late May,
German General Rommel had his men in bunkers overlooking the
Normandy beaches, not knowing if the invaders would land there,
or hundreds of miles away. At one of the strong points overlooking
what would be Omaha Beach, German soldiers listened to music
and read letters from home by candlelight. The weather was stormy
on the 5th of June. The following day, the storm moved out, leaving
the sea choppy with large waves. After dawn the next day, a fleet of
Allied ships appeared in the fog off the Normandy Beach and began
to bombard the Germans.

The only prayer Miles could think of was the one Drucella had
taught him when he was a little boy. He prayed it now.

Now, I lay me down to sleep.
I pray the Lord my soul to keep.
If I should die before I wake,
I pray the Lord my soul to take.

All around him other men were praying, too. Some said the Lord's
Prayer. Others asked for forgiveness. Underneath the whispered
prayers, the engines of the landing crafts roared as they moved

toward Omaha Beach. At the front of Miles' craft sat Sergeant Alvin Bowman, poised and ready to lead his men into battle.

One soldier who had just thrown up his last meal looked up to Sergeant Bowman. "Sergeant Bowman, I'm afraid. Are you afraid?"

Sergeant Bowman, a brawny athlete from Connecticut, spit his tobacco juice over the side of the craft. "Hell, yeah, I'm scared," the sergeant replied. "Whoever says they're not scared is either a damned fool, or a liar. Now just do what we have been training to do, and leave the rest to God."

Up until then, Miles had not believed Sergeant Bowman was afraid of anything.

Other landing craft had neared the beach. They bobbed up and down in the chop as the soldiers toppled down into the icy ocean water. Miles got a taste of salt water, as water splashed into his craft. Then, the ramp fell into the water, and Sergeant Bowman stood up and waved his gun forward. "Okay, you fighting sons of bitches. Let's go and earn that paycheck the government gives us! Everyone spread out, and let's get the hell off this beach! Then we'll take care of business."

Somehow, Miles noticed, that speech seemed to calm the men around him. Miles felt a sense of pride to be following Sergeant Bowman into battle.

Miles watched the first soldier, a Coast Guardsman in bathing trunks and a helmet, go down the ramp. It was his job to string a rope for the men to hold on to as they jumped from the craft. Miles, Artie Linder, and Tom Daugherty were the fourth, fifth, and sixth men down the ramp. When Miles was only a few feet away from him, a shell hit the Coast Guardsman, and he disintegrated right in front of Miles' eyes. Then two more German shells smashed into the starboard ramp, killing two other soldiers.

Miles waded through countless bodies drifting in the waves. The shelling continued. Hold on to your gun, Miles told himself. Don't drop this gun. You've got to have this gun. Miles held his gun tightly, using it to push through the debris and bodies floating around him.

Minutes after Bowman's speech, fourteen of the thirty soldiers in Miles' landing craft had made it off the beach alive and joined up with more invading forces who had managed to take higher ground behind an embankment. They were stalled by machine-gun fire.

Miles sat tightening his helmet when the soldier next to him tapped him on the shoulder and began talking. The helmet and a new burst of gunfire kept Miles from hearing him. "What did you say?" he shouted over the gunfire.

"Officers are asking for a volunteer to try and get close enough to take the guns out with a grenade, and it won't be me," the soldier shouted. "Pass it on down the line."

The sound of the machine-gun fire was deafening, but it didn't drown out the cries of dying men. Miles looked out over the hellish scene all around them. He gauged the distance between his position and the German guns. He knew the task would require someone with speed. He made his decision.

Word quickly spread up and down the lines about the young mountain boy from Kentucky who had volunteered to try and take out the machine gun that was taking so many lives, and keeping the platoon pinned down for the best part of the morning. Many of the men wanted to walk up to Miles and just touch him or, at least, shake his hand before he died, but no one dared approach him for fear they might jinx him. They did the only thing they could do. They watched and waited.

Major McNally, accompanied by two soldiers carrying grenades and a vest, crawled up the line to get a look at Miles. Once the major was recognized, the men did their best to salute and come to attention. The major put everyone at ease and spoke softly to Miles. "I hear you're from the mountains of Kentucky, son. Lots of war heroes come from Kentucky. Why, Sergeant Willie Sandlin, he's from down your way. And I heard your dad was one of the famous volunteers from Breathitt County, Kentucky, during our First World War."

"Yes sir, I reckon he was," Miles replied beginning to strip down. He took off his helmet and began unbuttoning his shirt. He didn't want to be carrying any extra weight.

"Only county in the country that didn't draft a single soldier during that war." The major paused and made sure everyone close enough to hear was hanging on his every word. "Breathitt County didn't need a draft board. Why, every man in the county volunteered." He put his hand on Miles' shoulder as Miles started to put on the vest. "Son, you know, in the excitement of the moment, a man can get caught up in a situation and volunteer. You know, it's not too late to back out. No one would blame you if you did."

"I know sir, but I gave my word, and I'm going to go through with it," said Miles firmly. The major removed his hand, and Miles put on the vest that would hold two grenades, only two. Miles buckled the vest and rechecked the buckles. Then he held out his hands for the grenades. He weighed them in his hands, getting a feel for them in the same way he would have for throwing rocks back home.

"They say what you're trying to do can't be done." The major stared into Miles' eyes.

Miles grinned. "Thank you, sir, but you know they could be wrong." Miles put a grenade in each of the vest pockets. They were larger than the rocks he used to select to throw at the knothole in the old hickory tree, but then again, the pillbox window was also bigger than the knothole.

"They had damn well better be, or an entire company could be wiped out."

"I'll do my best, sir." He tightened his belt.

"I know you will, son. I guess you want to get on with it. So, from an old soldier to a young soldier, I salute you."

Miles returned the salute. Artie locked eyes with Miles and said, "Take us home, Speed. Take us home, boy." Miles smiled when he heard Artie use the nickname he earned by breaking the record time for the 100-yard dash during basic training. Then he crawled over the rock embankment on his stomach onto open ground.

He crawled on, taking cover behind anything in his path. He heard machine-gun fire aimed down the hill to his right. He figured medics were probably on the move to help the wounded. He was surprised his luck was still holding. A few more feet, and then the race would begin. The Germans had still not detected him when he rose up from the ground and made a mad dash toward the pillbox and the deadly machine-gun fire.

The other American soldiers in the trenches, seeing Miles' courageous act unfolding in front of them, were bolstered. Now, not fearing for their own lives, they stood up and cheered as Miles zigzagged up the hill, while the machine guns tried to get him in their sights.

"Go Speed! Get those sons of bitches!" they yelled. "Throw those bastards one of those Kentucky mint juleps, Speed!

Miles felt hot lead enter his leg, but he continued on up the hillside. Run like a fox, he thought. Get rid of those grenades. He spotted the small window, like a square knothole, in the pill box. He pulled the pin on the first grenade, aimed and slung it. He knew it was a hit, but as the pillbox exploded, so did Miles' shoulder. Or at least he felt it did. He was knocked off his feet. By the explosion? By machine-gun fire? Had they gotten him in their sights just before he got them with the grenade? His limp body slid back down the hill. His blood—so much of it, everywhere—felt slick and warm.

"Oh God," Miles mumbled, "Oh Lord in heaven, thank you. Now, I can die in peace." He tried not to close his eyes, but he was tired. Running had never made him this tired before. Smoke and fire poured out of the pillbox, and that stung his eyes and throat. But the machine-gun was silent.

The soldiers, still cheering, bolted out of the trench and advanced up the hill. Artie Linder reached Miles first. "You did it, Speed! I knew you would." Artie dropped down to his knees and cradled Miles' head to his chest. "Now you hold on, boy. Don't you go and die on me now. The medics are on the way." Artie looked down the hill. He didn't see any medics rushing to save Miles. "Medics, get your asses up here on the double!" Artie screamed.

"How you doing, Speed? You feel okay?" Artie asked, tears streaming down his face.

With his eyes almost closed, Miles forced a smile. "Artie, I got a letter in my back pocket. Would you see my Ma gets this letter? Would you promise to do that for me, Artie? Would you?'

"Sure, Speed, I promise, but you're going to be okay. Your ticket is already punched. You're going home, Speed. You're going to get a free ride all the way home." His voice was soft and calming. Then he turned downhill, screaming at the top of his lungs. "Medics, if you don't get your asses up here in the next ten seconds, so help me God, I'm going to put a bullet right between your eyes!"

A few other soldiers had reached Artie and Miles now. Artie shrugged off their offers of help. "Hang on, Speed! Hang on? You doing all right, boy?"

"Artie, I feel kinda tired. If you don't mind, Artie, I think I'll go to sleep for a little while."

With his head resting on Artie's chest, Miles closed his eyes and Artie sobbed.

Two medics arrived with a stretcher and set it down on the ground near Miles and Artie.

"Sir, we can take over from here," a medic said, trying to move Artie aside to check the vitals of the wounded man.

"Well, you sure as hell took your goddamn time getting here," shouted Artie. "Now you had better not let him die."

"Sir, I think he may already...."

"Don't say that!" Artie screamed as other soldiers tried to pull Artie away so the medics could do their jobs. "Don't you know you're talking about a war hero? He just saved the lives of over a hundred men. Now, you be careful with him, and if you let him die, I swear to God, I'll track you down when the war is over. So you better not let him die."

The advancing soldiers pulled Artie up the hill and into battle. Artie turned for one last look. He saw the medics carrying Miles on a stretcher. One of Miles' hands had fallen off his lap and was dragging on the ground.

"You idiots!" yelled Artie. "You can't even carry a man on a stretcher!" Artie turned to the other men. "We gotta go back! I can't leave him like this!"

Tom Daugherty grabbed Artie by his shoulders and shook him. "You can't go back, Artie. You did all anyone could do. He's in God's hands now, Artie. We gotta move on."

THIRTY-FOUR

I t was a pleasant afternoon as Evaline walked the gravel road that led to her and Charlie's home. She couldn't understand why she felt such a deep sense of worry and foreboding. When she had left work at Anderson's country store, she had carefully zipped up her shoulder bag which held her thirty-five dollar paycheck. Carrying around that much money always made her a little uneasy, but this was something different. Evaline tried to relax. She kept looking up at the pale blue sky. Soft white clouds continued to float above her. A gentle breeze cooled her face. Why am I so worried? She asked herself again and again. Then, like a bolt of lightning, it hit her. Miles' letter!

In his last letter Miles had used a middle initial E. in the spelling of his name, but Miles didn't have a middle name. Evaline knew how Miles liked to write. He had always said that one day his name would be famous. "Look at how the famous author is signing his name now," she had laughed as she showed the letter to Charlie. But now she was sure that E. meant something much more serious. Since all the servicemen's mail was censored, just what was her brother trying to tell them?

Evaline's thoughts were interrupted when she saw Charlie's pickup truck coming up the road. She was amazed at how well he could drive with one leg in his pick-up, after it had been modified by one of the guys at the sawmill who loved to work on cars and trucks.

He slammed on his brakes, pulled over beside her, and was waving several letters in his hand, and said, "Evaline, guess what?"

"What, Charlie, what?" Evaline rushed to the truck.

"Well, Drucella received two more letters from Miles, and he put a different initial in his name in each letter."

"What do they spell?" Evaline asked.

Charlie spread the letter on the hood of the pickup truck. He pointed to the signatures. "Now all three letters spell out ENG," replied Charlie. "He's in England." He Paused and looked at Evaline. "And everyone knows where the soldiers stationed in England are headed."

"Oh my Lord!" Evaline gasped and quickly covered her mouth with her hand. "Miles will be in the invasion. He's in harm's way. Did you read the letters to Ma?"

"Yes," said Charlie, "but I didn't tell her where he is. I didn't want to worry her."

"We've got to tell her." Evaline climbed into the pickup, and they sped to Drucella's house.

When they told Drucella the news, she sipped her coffee and listened calmly to every word.

"Momma, do you understand what we're telling you?" Evaline said, looking at Drucella. Evaline had been worried about Drucella recently.

"Yes," Drucella smiled. "You see, your Pa was standing by the bed this morning when I woke up, and..."

Evaline and Charlie exchanged looks as Evaline broke in. "Ma, you don't understand. This is serious. Miles is going to be in the invasion."

"I know all about it, child," said Drucella, "and I'm not worried. Your Pa told me not to worry. He said Miles has an angel who is looking after him." She smiled at them again and took another sip of coffee. "Now, Brother Carlson came by this afternoon, and he said the church will have a special service tonight. I want you and Charlie to take me to it. You all go home and get ready, and I'll be ready to go when you get back."

THIRTY-FIVE

World War II had lasted exactly six years, from September 1939, until September 1945, and had involved most all the nations in the world.

But now the War was over, and the train from Cincinnati was only minutes away from its stop in Hazard. Artie Linder gazed out the window through the rain. It was just like Speed had said it would be: the air clean and fresh after the rain, small waterfalls pouring off the sides of the mountain. He saw hillside farms, each with a vegetable garden.

Slowly, the rain faded away, and the sun began to show through the clouds, and Artie now realized why Miles always talked about the beauty of his beloved mountains.

"Well, Artie, we're almost there." Miles sat in the seat opposite Artie. He had been looking out the window, too. Now he turned to Artie. "My family is sure going to be happy to meet you. Why I bet Ma will have fried chicken, mashed potatoes and a big pot of fresh green beans all cooked up for us! I can't wait for you to try her cornbread."

"Sounds good to me, Speed," Artie said.

Miles turned back to the window. He couldn't wait to be home. It had been a long recovery. It had been just over two years since Miles had seen his home and his family, but he didn't expect, or want any fanfare upon his return. No one would meet them in Hazard. He and Artie would take a cab to the little house in Jack Lot Hollow. He smiled thinking of home.

But, the more he thought about home, the more he thought about Cecil and Wilbur, and then he thought about Evaline's letter. He had not intended to memorize the letter, but he had, having relived in his mind each word of it each day.

> *Dear Miles,*
>
> *I have been putting off writing you this letter, but I know it's something I must do.*
>
> *We learned today from Cecil's father that Cecil and Wilbur were in the same unit, and died on the same day.*
>
> *While in intense battle, Cecil stepped on a land mine. Wilbur saw the explosion and ran to Cecil, and picked him up. Wilbur was hit by heavy machine gun fire while dragging Cecil to a safer area.*
>
> *They were both heroes, as you know, as they each made supreme sacrifices for their country.*
>
> *We love you and hope you get back home soon.*
>
> *Evaline*

I really need to think about happy things, thought Miles.

At home, Drucella waited, trembling, by the window. She would see Evaline and Charlie drive up soon, but she was really watching for the cab to deliver Miles. She wouldn't believe her boy was safe and home until he was in her arms.

In what seemed like an eternity, when Drucella saw Miles and Artie walking across the swinging bridge, she ran out the door, with Evaline and Charlie close behind. Drucella wrapped Miles in her arms as Artie stood by awkwardly.

Finally, Drucella released Miles. She composed herself and wiped the tears away with her apron. Evaline and Charlie hugged Miles, too, before Miles had a chance to introduce his guest.

"Everybody," Miles said, "this is Artie Linder from New Jersey."

Artie shook hands all around. When he reached Drucella, she clasped his hand in both of hers. "Artie, you're my boy now, too."

As they walked up the path to the house, Miles stopped every few steps to take everything in—the creek, the house, the barn and the mountain rising up beyond. Yes, it was good to be home, but it didn't feel the same as Miles had imagined it would.

"The government sent your things," Drucella was saying. "And another package came from a girl over there, Tessie. Yes, Tessie. I believe that was her name." She looked at Miles. Miles nodded for her to continue. "Anyway, the note said that you had asked her to send it. I didn't untie it. I just put it on the shelf for you."

Tessie, Miles thought. I wonder how Tessie is getting along. Miles looked again at the beauty all around him and then thought of all the other parts of the world he had seen since he had last stood on this path. He suddenly realized that everyone had gotten quiet. They were waiting for him. "Sorry, I guess I was just thinking how good it is to be home. Come on Ma, everybody, let's go in the house."

The next morning, after breakfast, Miles drummed his hands impatiently on the table. He was restless. He didn't have the calm inside him that he did when he left Hazard for the war. He had nearly died, and now wanted to live every single moment.

"Let's head on out, Artie," Miles said, pushing back from the table and taking his and Artie's dishes to the sink.

"Now, you boys, take it easy." Drucella smiled.

"Oh no, Mrs. Hudson, don't worry about us," said Artie. "I took good care of your boy during the war. I'm sure as hell, excuse me, ma'am, I mean, I'm not going to let anything happen to him now."

A few hours later, Artie and Miles stood under the awning of the Virginia Theatre while their eyes adjusted to the bright sunlight.

"Whoa, Speed, that was one good picture show. That John Wayne is one tough cowboy."

"Yeah, I know. And his horse is smarter than a lot of people I know. Say, Artie, why don't we get something to eat over at the Five and Dime lunch counter?"

"Sure thing, Speed. That sounds good to me, but first let's get a good look at this beautiful babe walking up the street."

An attractive brunette in a pale blue dress approached them. She paid no attention to Artie's admiring stare, but walked right up to Miles and stopped, almost as if she had planned to meet him there.

"Are you Miles Hudson?" she asked.

"Eh?" Miles replied, confused. "Yes, ma'am, I am."

"Yes, ma'am, I am," she repeated in a graceful, light voice. Nancy Ann looked at him from under her dark eyebrows. "Well, one thing's for sure, you haven't lost your mountain accent. And you've gotten taller and lost your baby fat since our high school days."

Miles stared at the girl in front of him. His heart skipped a beat.

"Oh my Lord, my goodness," Miles said, "Nancy Ann all grown up and looking prettier than ever!"

Nancy Ann's lip trembled. "Miles, when the news came over our radio, we didn't know if you were going to live or die," she said. "I went to my room and cried for over an hour. And when we got the news you were going to be okay, why, the whole town went crazy. People were literally dancing on Main Street. I don't know if you know it or not, but you own this town."

"Nancy, this is all blown out of proportion," said Miles. "All I did was toss a hand grenade in the right direction."

Artie broke in. "Ma'am, please excuse Speed's bad manners, and don't believe one word of what he's telling you. I was there, and I saw it all. He is a hero."

Miles turned to Nancy Ann.

"I'm sorry, Nancy Ann, this is Artie Linder from New Jersey, my best friend in the world."

Nancy Ann put out her hand. "I'm honored to meet you, Artie, and I'm glad you're Miles' friend but, Artie, I don't think Miles has any idea just how big this is."

"Come on, Nancy Ann," Miles said. "Don't make this into something it's not."

"Well," Nancy Ann said, "let's all go down to Fouts drugstore, and I'll buy you a copy of the special edition of *Life* magazine that just came out, all about American GIs in decisive battles like D-Day. Your picture is on the cover. I hope they still have a copy or two left. They were selling like hotcakes."

Miles' face paled. He looked at Artie whose eyes had widened when Nancy Ann had mentioned *Life* magazine. Artie grinned and shrugged his shoulders. Miles remembered the war photographers who had been all over the place during their time overseas, even in battle. He supposed that it could be possible, but it wasn't very likely that of all the millions of soldiers in the war, his picture would end up on the cover of *Life* magazine.

"You're kidding, Nancy Ann! Right?"

"No, I'm not kidding. You can believe it or not, but you are a hero."

Miles looked at Nancy Ann standing in front of him, straight and proud, in a simple, tailored dress and peep-toe pumps. As she shifted the package she was holding to her other arm, a lock of her hair fell over one eye, so that she looked just like Veronica Lake in the movie poster behind her. She was more beautiful than he remembered. He forgot about *Life* magazine.

"You know, Nancy Ann, Artie is going home tomorrow. Listen, um… maybe we could get together and talk over old times. Could we do that?" Miles reached for Nancy Ann's hand. She let him take it, but her hand felt lifeless in his.

"It's really too late for that, Miles." Nancy Ann tried not to cry. "You see, I'm engaged to Herman Horn now. We plan to be married next month."

"Herman Horn?" Miles released Nancy's hand and stared at her in disbelief. "Not the Herman Horn I knew in high school? The one always throwing spitballs at everyone? I can't believe you're going to marry Herman Horn." Miles continued to stare at Nancy Ann.

"Well, Herman has changed quite a bit since our school days." Nancy Ann replied sharply. She didn't want to be angry at Miles, but he had no right to be critical. She met Miles' stare and continued in a more even tone. "Herman's a businessman. He owns his own radio shop."

"Does he make any money in it?"

"Oh yes, he not only sells them, he also repairs them, too."

There was an awkward moment of silence between them as they stared at each other. Then Miles looked down and spoke quietly. "Do you love him, Nancy Ann?"

Artie shifted uncomfortably. Nancy Ann and Miles didn't even notice he was there anymore. He turned to look at the movie posters.

"I'm not sure, but he loves me." Nancy Ann shifted the package again and began rummaging in her purse for a tissue. "You know you only sent me two letters, and nothing romantic in either one of them, during the entire time you were away." She cleared her throat. "And I decided I didn't want to wait around and become an old maid schoolteacher."

Miles was silent a moment before he responded. "Nancy Ann, I wish you had waited. I thought you knew I always loved you." He looked at her and attempted a smile. "You're a schoolteacher?"

"No, not yet, but my life-long dream is to try for a scholarship, go to Eastern, get my degree, and come back home and teach English at the high school."

"Nancy, I don't know what to say. I'm at a loss for words."

Miles looked at the sidewalk, Nancy Ann rummaged in her purse and Artie tried to blend into the theatre wall. The silence was lasting too long. Artie needed to rescue Miles. He had to say something; he just didn't know what to say.

"You know," Artie broke in, "I feel like I'm trespassing, like I just watched a dramatic play. I feel like an intruder." He reached into his pocket for a handkerchief and offered it to Nancy Ann.

Nancy Ann accepted the handkerchief, turned her head and dabbed at her eyes. Then she faced him again, smiling weakly. "Artie, I'm sorry you had to listen to all this. I really didn't want to pour out all my feelings in the middle of Main Street."

"That's all right, Nancy Ann," Artie said. He looked at Miles, hoping Miles would join in. But Miles stood silently. "Speed and me have been through some hard times. I guess we can go through another one together."

Nancy Ann took a deep breath. She hugged her purse to her chest.

"Miles, I've got to go home now," she said. "I hope, in time, you'll find a proper way to remember me. I will always remember you and wish only good things for you. Only good things."

Nancy Ann walked away and out of Miles' life.

Artie watched his friend. He knew Miles was hurting. When Nancy Ann turned the corner, he poked Miles playfully on the shoulder and began walking in the opposite direction, the direction Nancy Ann had indicated for Fouts Drugs. "Come on, Speed. We've got to see this picture of you on the cover of *Life* magazine!"

Artie and Miles didn't go to the Five and Dime lunch counter. Miles didn't want the attention. Nancy had been right about Miles' celebrity. People had swarmed around him in Fouts Drugs, shaking his hand or just staring at him. Artie had bought one of the three remaining copies of the magazine, and he and Miles had gotten out of the store as quickly as possible. They went to the Underworld Poolroom. They ate hot dogs and potato chips, and drank beer and played pool for hours. At midnight, the owner, Mr. Woods, began to shut down the lights.

"Sorry, fellas," Mr. Woods said. "It's 12 o'clock. I gotta close down the place for the night."

"How about one more beer for the road?" Artie heard the slur in his voice and laughed at himself.

"Yeah, Mr. Woods, one more for the road?" Miles said.

"Can't do it, fellows."

"Come on, Mr. Woods," Artie begged. "My buddy, Speed here, well, he took an arrow to the heart today. He really needs another beer to ease his pain."

"If I did that, guys, the state could take away my beer license." Mr. Woods stood by the door. "The one thing I can do is to give you guys a ride home."

"We don't want to put you out, Mr. Woods," Miles said sleepily. "We can get a cab to take us home. Can't we do that, Artie?"

"I don't know, Speed. I'm as drunk as a skunk."

"Yeah, me too, Artie, but don't you worry one teeny bit, old pal. You took care of me on the battlefield, so now, old buddy, it's my turn to take care of you."

"How much do we owe you, Mr. Woods?" Miles said as he opened his billfold.

"Miles, your money isn't any good in my pool room. It's all on the house."

"No, Mr. Woods, I can't let you do that. Miles Hudson pays his way wherever he goes. Here's a hundred-dollar bill, will that about do it, Mr. Woods?"

"If it's not enough money, Speed, I got it," said Artie.

"No, Artie, you're my guest," said Miles. "Now put your money back in your pocket. I'm paying our bill."

Mr. Woods came over and put his hands on Miles' shoulders. He remembered him as a boy walking home from school with Evaline. "Son, I'm the only sober one of the three of us," Mr. Woods said. "So, let's lock the door and get the hell out of here before I change my mind and let you guys walk home."

THIRTY-SIX

Drucella rattled her pots and pans, trying to make as much noise as possible while she made breakfast. "The two of them acting like hobos, coming in here after midnight, so drunk they couldn't hit the floor with their hats," Drucella fumed. "I won't have goings-on like that in my house."

"Who are you talking to, Ma?" Miles stumbled into the kitchen and sat at the table. He reached up into the cabinet for a coffee cup. Drucella had turned her back to him. Miles watched her as she placed more wood in the stove.

"I'm talking to myself, but I mean every word of what I'm saying."

"Ma, why didn't you tell me about Nancy Ann being engaged to Herman Horn?"

Drucella was silent for a moment. She lifted the coffee pot from the stove and brought it to the table. "I tried to tell you, but every time I stopped short. I couldn't stand to hurt you anymore after all you've gone through.

"Well," Miles said, remembering Nancy Ann with the hair falling across her eye. "I found out about Nancy Ann yesterday. That's why Artie and me got drunk."

Miles held up his cup and Drucella poured him a cup of coffee. He added half a spoonful of sugar and stirred the coffee before he took a drink. Then he sat watching steam rise from the cup.

Drucella turned away and put the coffee pot back on the stove. "I won't say another word about it," she said as she began wrapping up a row of fried peach pies that sat on the counter. "Will three of these be enough for Artie?" she asked Miles. "I don't want him to go home hungry on the bus."

"Better pack up more than that. He can eat like a horse." Miles stirred his coffee again and looked at Drucella. "But be sure and leave some for me."

Drucella smiled. She finished wrapping up four pies and put them in a brown paper sack.

"You know, Miles," she said, "Artie is like family."

"I know, Ma, he's like the brother I never had." The spoon tinkled against the side of Miles' coffee cup. He hadn't realized he was stirring his coffee again. He thought of Artie still sleeping in the next room and tried not to think of his friend's leaving Hazard. "I'm sure going to miss him."

As they were preparing to leave for the bus station, Miles asked, "Where in the world did the time go, Artie? It seems like we just got here. Are you sure you can't stay a little longer? You know Ma would be tickled pink if you could spend some more time with us."

"Yeah, I know that and so good of her to make fried peach pies to take with me, but to tell you the truth, I am getting a little homesick. Guess I'm getting to miss the big city," said Artie.

Later that day at the bus station, Miles patted Artie on the back just as he was about to board the bus. "Write us when you get home," Mile's shouted.

"You all can write too, can't you?" shouted Artie over his shoulder.

Finding a seat by the window, Artie waved at Miles, and Miles waved back. Neither were aware that the other noticed, but each brushed away a tear, and then the bus was gone.

THIRTY-SEVEN

T he *Life* magazine with Miles' picture on the cover made Miles famous, but it was something he disliked intensely. He began to stay away from town, and spent most of his time walking mountain trails and taking pictures with his Sure Shot camera. He spent hours in his room with his oil paints, trying to paint one of the many pictures he had taken. Other days, he'd try to write about his war experiences. His seclusion, however, did not stop the curious and the hero-worshippers.

The sightseers could turn up any day of the week, but mostly, they descended on Sundays. Miles refused to answer the door, retreating to his room or to the kitchen. From either location, he would hear Drucella greeting these strangers, some traveling to Jack Lot Hollow from as far away as Ohio and Florida. "I'm sorry, but Miles is not feeling very good today. Maybe you all could come back another day."

Few of the strangers left willingly. Most seemed to want something for their efforts in coming all the way to Jack Lot Hollow, even if they had come uninvited. Miles remembered Drucella's encounter with one of the first strangers. "Well, ma'am, I brought you a copy of *Life* magazine," said the man, craning his neck to get a look past Drucella and into the living room. "Your boy is on the front cover. I didn't know if you had a copy or not." When Drucella had ushered him out onto the porch and shut the door so he couldn't see inside, he had switched tactics. "By the way, ma'am, would it be okay if I took a pebble from your yard, or maybe an ear of corn from your garden? Just a little something to remind me of my trip to your home here in the mountains."

One morning at breakfast, Miles and Drucella sipped coffee at the kitchen table while they discussed plans to discourage the souvenir hunters.

"Ma, there's only one thing for me to do," Miles said that morning.

"What on earth is that, son?"

"I think it's time for me to leave Hazard, at least for a while."

"Where would you go, son?" Drucella didn't stop the mending she was doing, but Miles knew she was listening.

"I've always wanted to go out west, you know, go to California or maybe New Mexico, see some of the country I fought for."

"I wish you would stay in Hazard at least a little while," Drucella sighed. "And, besides that, I talked with Landon just the other day when he said he wanted you to stay."

Drucella put the mending in her lap, happy to be talking about Landon with Miles. "He told me he was real proud of you, proud of all those medals you won in the war. You know he loves you very much."

Miles got up from the chair and placed his journal on the mantle. He crossed to Drucella, putting his arm around her. "You know Ma, Pa's gone, but I really do believe he's looking down on us. And I'm sure one day we'll all see him again." Drucella nodded. They smiled at each other.

Miles walked to the mantle, intending to pick up his journal again, but he changed his mind. "Ma, I got to talk to Charlie and Evaline about leaving Hazard. I'm not going to write today. I'm going to go back to bed and rest. I just can't cope with everything going on in Hazard."

Drucella watched him walk toward his room. She stopped him as he reached the hallway. "Son, I know you got a lot of things on your mind," And I hope you don't mind, but I got to know something."

"What's that, Ma?" Miles turned to her.

"Well, son, I got to know that you're all right, that you're not all crazy inside. Did all the things you had to do in the war make you mean and mad at everything? Did it, son?"

"No, Ma, I'm not feeling mean and mad at anyone," Miles said gently. He was aware that Drucella was watching him carefully. "I did hurt real bad for a while, Ma, but I had to let go of all the bad things. If I hadn't, I don't think I could have made it back home."

Drucella breathed a sigh of relief.

"Well I'm glad you're okay, son. You know we heard all sorts of tales about soldiers coming home and their kin thinking they were all right. Then just one little thing made them go crazy, and without any warning they go out into the woods and put a gun to their head and pull the trigger. I don't think I could go on if that happened to you."

"Aw, Ma, don't think things like that. I'm all right. I'll get back to my old self. But I sure miss Cecil and Wilbur."

Miles turned and walked to his bedroom. He was surprised by his Ma's question, and he wondered if other people could see in his eyes all the pain he felt from the war.

The following morning, Miles was awake and dressed ten minutes before his Roy Rogers alarm clock went off. He slipped out the door without awakening Drucella.

Outside, the early-morning fog was thick. Miles turned and looked back toward the house. The fog and dampness settled around him, and voices of long ago filled his mind. "Hey, Miles, you run faster than a fox! Come on, Miles, play fair. It's not fair that you win all the time. Hey, Miles!" Then the three of them were running right beside him, Wilbur, Cecil, and Miles as children, jumping over the bushes, hiding behind outhouses and throwing rocks at knotholes in trees. When they reached the flagpole, they bent over laughing and breathing hard in the mountain air. He wanted to run with them, but he didn't try, because he knew they were not really there. He walked on through the dampness. He had places to go and things to do.

Miles walked into the Five and Dime and ordered breakfast at the counter. A few weeks earlier, he had been surprised and saddened to learn that Nell, the pretty waitress who had stood up for him against the gambler, Black Hart, no longer worked there. Al, the short-order cook, said she had come to work one morning and given her notice. She was moving to Columbus, Ohio. She had promised to write, but she hadn't so far.

After a breakfast of pancakes and sausage, Miles placed a five-dollar bill on the counter. The waitress pushed it back toward him. He glared at the waitress who looked embarrassed and confused. She'd been told not to charge Miles. But she rang up the sale and gave Miles his change. A young mother holding a small boy's hand approached him. "Are you Miles Hudson?" she asked.

"I guess I am," he said.

"Mr. Hudson, would you mind shaking Tommy's hand and signing your name on this napkin for us?"

"Yes ma'am, I can do that."

After he signed the napkin, several customers stood up and clapped. Miles' face turned red. He touched the top of his head in a half salute and hurried out the door. It was now eight o'clock, and the businesses on East Main Street were closed except for Melvin's Used Car lot.

Melvin Jones, a sharp trader, was greedier than most of the other businessmen in Hazard. If he couldn't make a hundred percent profit on a used car, then it would never leave his lot.

A young man with a water hose was spraying the dust off a 1936 grey Chevrolet on the front row, the showpiece of the lot. Miles spotted a 1939 Ford station wagon in the center of the lot among the various Fords, Buicks, and DeSotos. He opened the Ford's door and sat down on the soft leather seat. When he slid out of the car, he patted the Ford's hood. "How have you been overlooked so long?" he said to the car quietly.

A tall, thin man wearing a cowboy hat walked up to the car. He had a big smile. "Well partner, how do you like this little jewel?" Melvin asked.

Miles didn't waste any time. "It's nice, real nice. Now how much can you come down on that sticker price in the window? Five hundred and ninety-nine dollars seems really high for a used car."

"Well partner," Melvin said easily, "it doesn't matter what kind of a price I put on the window. You would still want me to come down on my price. You see partner, I got three people working for me. I got to pay rent on this lot, plus I got to make a living. You see where I'm coming from, partner?"

"Yeah, I see where you're coming from," Miles said, mimicking Melvin's easy tone, "but let's get one thing straight. I'm not your partner. I'm here to buy a car, and if you want to sell me one, you better get the price right."

Melvin peered at Miles more closely. "Now just hold your horses." He wagged his finger at Miles. "Just one minute. Now, I know who you are. You're the guy who took the machine guns out on Omaha Beach. Well, Mr. Hudson, thank you for what you did, but I still have a business to run. I can let you have it for five hundred and eighty dollars, and I'll still be losing money on the deal."

Miles found it hard to keep from smiling. He didn't want Melvin to know how much he was enjoying haggling over the price. Miles was thrilled that so many of the people in Hazard had offered to give things to him, but what he really wanted was to be treated like any other of their customers.

"I'll tell you what I'll do, partner," Miles said. "If you clean it up real good, and fill it up with gas, I'll take it."

Melvin adjusted his cowboy hat. "Since you called me partner, partner, I'm going to give you a free tank of gas and put a spit-and-polish shine on that wagon for you."

Miles stuck his hand out for Melvin to shake. "You got a deal."

Melvin turned toward his office. "Jodie," he yelled, "get that '39 Wagon shined up and ready to go. Mr. Hudson just bought it."

It was a good deal. Miles circled Hazard three times before turning into Jack Lot Hollow and driving the mile and a half to Charlie and Evaline's house.

THIRTY-EIGHT

When Miles drove into Evaline and Charlie's yard, he cut the engine and sat silently for a moment, enjoying the feeling of owning the car, and remembering how Mr. Herd had taught him to drive a farm tractor, and how much the tractor and a car were alike - a steering wheel, a gear shift, a clutch, a gas pedal, and a brake. Driving an Army Jeep was easy for Miles, and a car even easier.

Evaline and Charlie came out to meet him. Evaline leaned into the car window, and said, "Well, look at you driving your own car and looking like a Philadelphia lawyer." She moved aside so Miles could open the car door. He stepped out of the car, and she gave him a big hug. "So you're really going to do it, all the way to California?" Miles nodded. "I wish I could go with you," she said.

"Evaline, I would have left Hazard three months ago, but I'm still worried about Ma being by herself."

"Miles, don't worry about Ma," Evaline said, "she can take care of herself. She always has. She has a double-barrel shotgun, and she's not afraid to use it."

"And, besides that, Miles," said Charlie, who walked over and put his arm around Miles' shoulder, "I will personally make sure she never needs anything."

"You've got to stop worrying about Ma," Evaline said, running her hand over the hood of the car, "and load up this little Ford and point its nose toward the West Coast."

The following morning, Miles was awakened by Drucella's singing. He wished he could spend another hour in bed, but Drucella continued to sing one of her favorite hymns.

Rock of Ages, cleft for me,
Let me hide myself in Thee;
Let the water and the blood,
From Thy wounded side which flowed,
Be of sin the double cure;
Save from wrath and made me pure.

"Well, good morning, Rip Van Winkle," Drucella said as Miles came into the kitchen. "Were you going to sleep all day? The coffee is hot, now how do you want your bacon and eggs?"

"Over-light is fine as long as you got plenty of them. I'm as hungry as a bitch wolf."

"As hungry as what?" Drucella raised her eyebrows. "I've never heard that saying before. I don't like that kind of talk in my kitchen."

"Sorry, Ma. Could you pour me some coffee?"

"I can if you stop all that talk about a wolf." Drucella picked up the coffee pot and filled Miles' cup.

"Ah, Ma, we had a soldier in our outfit from West Virginia always saying stuff like that. He kept everyone laughing. Didn't mean anything by it."

"Now eat your bacon and eggs before they get cold," Drucella said, smiling. She set a plate of food before him.

"You know, Ma, I really miss all those crazy guys."

"I know you do, son." Drucella Paused. Miles could tell Drucella had something else on her mind. He kept eating, waiting for her to continue. "But I got to know: When are you going to California? Are you going today?"

"Yes, Ma." Miles looked at Drucella. He wasn't telling her anything she hadn't already known. He looked away and took another bite of his breakfast.

"Then I guess your Pa was right." Drucella picked up her coffee cup from the counter and sat down at the table with Miles. "He said you would be leaving today."

Miles took a good look at Drucella. Her hair was pinned up on top of her head, and she was wearing her favorite gray dress. She looked strong enough, but she worried Miles when she talked about having conversations with Landon.

A tear welled up in the corner of Drucella's eye. "I know no one believes me, but your Pa comes down from the mountain every day and talks to me."

"I believe you, Ma," Miles said. "If Pa talks to you, then I think it's a good thing. You tell him when I get to California I'm going to make something of myself. Maybe I'll write war stories for the movies. Why, when I get on my feet, I'm going to buy you a plane ticket to California. Would you like that Ma?"

"I think you're getting ahead of yourself," Drucella said, bracing herself up and refusing to let the tears come. "The next time your Pa comes down from the mountain, we'll talk about all this."

"Sure, Ma," said Miles, "that's the thing to do."

"Why I've never been outside Hazard, and here we are talking about me going to California." Drucella shook her head. She got up and looked out the window toward the barn and the mountain beyond. "Lord have mercy, I guess people can dream, can't they? You know, I could take care of the house and cook for you. Maybe you could get a house with an orange tree in the back yard. Wouldn't it be nice to go out in your yard and pick an orange? When I was growing up the only time we got an orange was on Christmas morning." She turned to Miles and smiled.

"Sure, Ma," said Miles, "you could pick all the oranges you want."

When Miles had eaten his breakfast, and finished packing his station wagon, he took a walk by the creek. When he returned, Drucella was in the living room, just getting up from the sewing machine. "I guess you're excited to get started. You cut your walk short today."

"Yeah, Ma. I'm going to take a nap, and then I'll go."

"I don't want to see you leave," Drucella replied. "I'm going to go down to my garden. I still have six rows of beans to hoe. When you leave, lightly toot your horn, and I'll know you're on your way."

Drucella walked down to her garden and sank her knees into the earth. A few minutes later she got up and began the hoeing. She didn't know how long she had been working when she heard the horn toot, but it didn't matter. She still had another row to hoe.

THIRTY-NINE

iles wheeled his Ford wagon into Eugene's Gas Station. Before he could come to a complete stop, the bell over the office window rang and the door swung open. Eugene's two attendants made a mad dash to the car.

"Need a fill-up?" Chester asked.

"Sure." Miles got out of the car and headed to the Coke machine. "Go ahead. And be sure and check my oil."

While Chester filled the tank, the other attendant wiped the windshield and checked the tires.

Near the Coke machine, Miles spotted Eugene working on a truck. Miles put his hand in his pocket and found two nickels.

"Can I buy you a Coke?" he called out to Eugene.

Eugene looked up from the engine he was working on. "Sure, thanks," he replied. Miles put the two nickels in the machine, got the Cokes and handed one to Eugene.

"By the way, Miles," Eugene said, "any truth to the rumor that you're leaving town today?"

"I'm on my way out of town right now." Miles looked over to the gas pump to see if the boys had finished.

"Aren't you getting a late start?"

"Not really," Miles said, "I plan to drive through the night and be out of Kentucky before the sun comes up."

Eugene drank his Coke thoughtfully. "Miles--" Eugene began. Then he paused and set the bottle down on the pavement. He began again. "Miles, I hate to be the one to break this to you, but Nancy Ann and Herman are getting married this afternoon."

Miles frowned and looked down.

"Sorry I told you," Eugene said, "but I thought you might want to know. I guess I should have kept my big mouth shut."

"It's all right, Eugene." Miles took his last swallow of Coke. "I got to face up to it sooner or later. I won't pretend I'm not bothered by the wedding. Nancy Ann is still an okay girl as far as I'm concerned. It's just something that didn't work out. It's no one's fault. I hope they'll be happy."

Eugene put his arm on Miles' shoulder. "I'm glad you're taking this as well as you are. I've been really worried about you."

"I'm going to be okay," Miles said. "I survived World War II. I can survive this, too."

Miles shook Eugene's hand. Then he paid for the gas, got in his car and pulled away from the station, turning right onto Main Street.

"Hey!" Eugene yelled from the station, "You're going the wrong way!"

Miles stopped and leaned out the window. "Yeah, I know. I wanted a last look at Hazard."

Miles drove down Main Street and then turned left onto High Street. He parked his car across from the Methodist Church. He slumped down in his seat. He could hear the music coming from inside the church. All at once, the doors of the church opened and people poured out, smiling and shaking each other's hands. As Nancy Ann and Herman emerged, everyone applauded.

Then a man in the crowd spotted Miles' station wagon and pointed. The crowd grew silent. Miles sat up and raced his engine. Why had he stopped here? He needed to leave now, but when he saw Nancy Ann let go of Herman's hand and walk toward the street, he didn't move. She stopped at the edge of the sidewalk, no longer smiling. She looked confused and slowly waved her hand at Miles. Miles waved back and quickly drove away.

Miles' next stop was Riverside Cemetery. He parked his car and walked through the gate. He turned left and followed the road as Drucella had told him to. He continued on past the tombstones on both sides of the road. Then he saw the maple tree on the hill. Drucella had said to look for it. He saw the two white crosses side by side. Cecil and Wilbur, his two best friends, were now hurling through Eternity. Tears streamed down Miles' face as he picked up twigs and scraps of trash that the wind had blown around the grave sites.

"Hey guys, why did you have to go and get yourselves killed?" Miles said as he wept. "Do you think it was fair to leave me here all by myself? At least you guys went off together and served in the same unit."

Two lots down from Cecil's and Wilbur's tombstones, three gravediggers were taking a rest, drinking a few beers. When they saw Miles looking at them, one of the gravediggers picked up his coat and placed it over the empty beer bottles lying on the ground beside them. Miles wiped his face with his sleeve and walked over to them. They became quiet as they watched him approach.

The one who had covered the empty beer bottles with his coat stood up. "Say fella," he said to Miles. "I know you're grieving real bad, but…" He broke off studying Miles face thoughtfully. "Seems like I know you from somewhere, but I don't know where." Then comprehension crossed his face. He turned to his buddies. "Oh! My Lord! Joe, you know who this is?" He reached out to shake Miles' hand. "I read about you in the newspapers. I can't wait to tell my wife I met a war hero."

"If you don't mind," Miles said gently, "could we forget about all that? Maybe we could just talk, and if it's okay with all of you, I wouldn't mind sharing a beer with you. Maybe we could drink a toast to my two best friends?"

"We can do that," the man said. "Joe, open us four fresh beers, and everyone stand up straight and dust off your clothes. This is something you'll be able to tell your grandchildren about."

The men made toasts to Cecil and Wilbur, and Miles told them funny stories of the things the three of them had done growing up. When they finished their beers, Miles shook hands with all of them once more and went on his way.

Miles drove past the Goose House and continued down Kentucky 15. He settled back into his seat and took a deep breath of the fresh mountain air coming through the open window.

The Ford climbed one mountain after another. The road dipped up and down as it followed the river. Miles settled back into his seat and felt the car easily navigate the terrain.

In the distance ahead, he saw a pickup truck with a homemade sign: *Apples for Sale: 10¢ each.*

Miles wasn't going to stop, but then decided it wouldn't hurt to have a few apples to eat later. He pulled over, got out and walked up to the stand.

Two little girls who were holding hands stood next to their grandfather behind the stand. They had light-brown hair; one looked to be about six years old, the other maybe two years younger. The older girl said, "My name's Laney, and this is my younger sister, Natalie. Would you like to buy some apples from us, Mister?"

"Well, I guess so." Miles winked at the grandfather. "Let's see, they're a dime apiece so I could buy three for 30 cents."

"You could, Mister," Laney replied, "but if you buy four, we'll give you one free." Natalie was already getting out a paper sack for the sale.

"That's not a bad deal," said Miles. "What kind of apples are they?"

"They're Winesap apples, Mister, a good eatin' apple." She said it with such enthusiasm that Miles struggled not to laugh. Her grandfather must have taught her that.

"It's a deal," he said, digging into his pocket and pulling out two coins. "Here's two quarters, and you can keep the change."

Laney took the money, and her grandfather began putting the apples in the paper sack Natalie had handed him. The grandfather handed the sack to Miles. "Thank you, Sir, my name is Henry," he said. "I'm trying to teach my granddaughters, Laney and Natalie, the importance of money."

"Nothing wrong with that," Miles replied. He looked at the little girls and smiled. "Thanks for selling me the apples and have a good evening."

As he walked away, Natalie called after him. "Mister, are you going a long way?"

Miles turned. The sun glinted off the apple stand and off the little girl's hair. "Yeah, honey," he said, "I'm going a long, long way."

Miles got back in his car and drove off. The breeze was light, and the Ford drove smoothly up and down each mountain. The car's engine hummed like a sewing machine.

As Miles looked out the window, he said out loud, "God's in His House, and all's right with the world."

Back in Jack Lot Hollow, Drucella was on the porch, resting from her work and watching the sun dropping between the mountains.

"There you are," she said. She was talking, but no one was there. "Miles has gone to California. Guess what? Our boy wants me to come to California. Come on in the house and I'll tell you all about it."

She got up and held the door open. "I'll fix us a fresh pot of coffee."

MESSAGE FROM THE AUTHOR

I hope you have enjoyed traveling back in time with me through the pages of *Under the Flagpole*. It was very special for me to write about my people's inherited courage and pioneer spirit.

I am now well into writing another novel, *In Search of Papa*. This one is not about a person I knew, but about a person I wish I had known. In some respects he and I are "connected" through numerous mutual friends who not only knew him, but who drank and fished with him.

The new novel is about the "friend" I never met, Ernest "Papa" Hemingway. Our mutual friends referred to him then, and now as "Papa," a nickname he gave himself, because he didn't want to be called Ernest.

I hope you'll join me later this year as we go *In Search of Papa*.

Henry